Amelia o
her smug
into her own book unapologetically.

It gave Bennett the rare opportunity to study her properly. Or more important, an opportunity to try to understand his own unexpected reaction to her. Arguably, this room was filled with the most desirable young ladies of the *ton*. His five remaining Potentials were too polite to risk reading while others were speaking. All of them were very pretty. Any one of them would make him a perfect wife. Why was it, then, that his thoughts, as well as his gaze, kept creeping back to Miss Mansfield?

It was plainly obvious that she had thoroughly enjoyed besting him. The other young ladies would be mortified to have intentionally caused him offense. Miss Mansfield reveled in it. Maybe that was why she fascinated him? She was so different from every other woman of his acquaintance and she certainly did not behave like them. Despite the fact that she was raised in Cheapside and worked for a living, she was heartily unimpressed by his title. Yet he wanted her to be impressed.

That was an interesting thought. He *wanted* to impress her. How very...unusual.

Author Note

It's funny how inspiration strikes. The historian in me is always learning. I saw a documentary about the Peterloo Massacre, which prompted me to read up on the turbulent political situation during the Regency. At that time, there was a genuine fear of revolution in England. The aristocracy were terrified that the masses would all rise up against them, so parliament did everything in its power to suppress them. It was a time of public demonstrations, clandestine meetings and riots well before Peterloo.

Then, by chance, I came across a nineteenth-century book on etiquette written by a vicar's daughter. Not only was it an interesting window onto a different side to that time period but, when read with modern eyes, some of the instructions within the book were hilarious. After that, I decided it might be fun to write one of my own, which is exactly what I did in this book. My hero, Bennett Montague, the sixteenth Duke of Aveley, has written a book entitled *The Discerning Gentleman's Guide to Selecting the Perfect Bride*. Obviously, what Bennett thinks his perfect bride might be like and what my heroine, Amelia Mansfield, is actually like are on completely opposite ends of the spectrum. When you have a pompous duke, it stands to reason that the very last person he would ever consider marrying is an outspoken political radical—yet it was tremendously entertaining to throw them together and see what happened...

Virginia Heath

—

The Discerning Gentleman's Guide

HARLEQUIN®HISTORICAL

**Recycling programs
for this product may
not exist in your area.**

ISBN-13: 978-0-373-30750-0

The Discerning Gentleman's Guide

Copyright © 2016 by Susan Merritt

Printed in U.S.A.

When **Virginia Heath** was a little girl, it took her ages to fall asleep, so she made up stories in her head to help pass the time while she was staring at the ceiling. As she got older, the stories became more complicated, sometimes taking weeks to get to the happy ending. One day, she decided to embrace the insomnia and start writing them down. Virginia lives in Essex, England, with her wonderful husband and two teenagers. It still takes her forever to fall asleep.

Books by Virginia Heath

Harlequin Historical

That Despicable Rogue
Her Enemy at the Altar
The Discerning Gentleman's Guide

Visit the Author Profile page at Harlequin.com.

For Alex
Who always tries to do the right thing for other people.

Chapter One

On the road to London, November 1816

Choosing a wife is not a task that should be undertaken lightly. Too many young gentlemen allow their hearts to rule their heads and rush into marriage without any forethought whatsoever—but remember! So many who marry in haste repent at leisure.

You must take time to select the perfect bride because a wife is a reflection of who you are. What if she is not a good hostess? Or is too forthright in her opinions? Or prone to temper tantrums or bouts of excessive melancholy?

Such a wife will ultimately turn out to be a hindrance to you and you will rue the day you entered into the Blessed Union.

This collection of advice, gathered from the wisdom of my esteemed late father and the follies of my peers, is intended to warn you of the pitfalls that might lure you into making a regret-

table choice and to guide you through the process of selecting the perfect wife.

'What drivel!' Amelia Mansfield tossed the book on the carriage seat and stared at it as if it had just bitten her. 'Your nephew must be a very pompous man indeed to have written that rubbish. After reading just one paragraph, I am already dreading the prospect of spending a month trapped in his company.'

Lady Worsted smiled, clearly amused by her reaction. 'Bennett is not so bad, Amelia. He is prone to be a little imperious at times, but then again he is a politician and politicians are rather inclined to tell us what to do. And, of course, he is a duke. Therefore, he is expected to be a little pompous. All dukes are bred that way.'

The title, as far as Amelia was concerned, was yet another strike against the man. In all of her twenty-two years she had never met a single man in possession of one who was not completely obnoxious, her own father included. In fact, her father, or Viscount Venomous as she preferred to call him, was probably the most obnoxious and disagreeable of the bunch. Just thinking about him made her mood sour.

'It is a shame that we are not going to your nephew's castle. I should have enjoyed that. I have never stayed in a castle before. Do you think he might take us there during your visit?'

'I believe that we may go there for a few days, if Bennett can be spared. Aveley Castle is just an hour or so away from London and my sister loves it there.' Lady Worsted's sister was the priggish Duke's mother. 'But any visit will be fleeting. In these challenging times Bennett needs to be close to Parliament—he is one of the Regent's most trusted advisers, after all.' Another strike against him. 'I am sure that we can find plenty of entertainments in town. The season is in full swing. I do believe that you will enjoy it.'

Having been denied a season because of her father's treachery, Amelia had long consoled herself that she was completely disinterested in such puerile pursuits. Balls and parties were for silly girls who had no other ambition than to marry well, embroider and live a life of subservience to their well-born husbands. When she had been younger she might have enjoyed the spectacle and the dancing that the season offered, but she had been a viscount's daughter then and would have been able to dance. Now she was a mere companion, she would be doomed to watch the festivities from the wings while the older ladies gossiped. That was not how she wanted to spend her first visit back to Town in almost a year.

Amelia already had a long list of things that she wanted to do whilst visiting the capital. She had missed the place and, more importantly, she had missed the many political associations and reform groups that represented all of the many causes she held so dear. Unfortunately, a goodly few of those wonderful organisations and the people who ran them had been unfairly labelled as Radical by aristocrats who felt threatened by their common-sense opinions. For too long she had only been able to read about their work second-hand. This winter she would once again attend and contribute to the proceedings and help to campaign for all of the changes that needed to be made in society if poverty was ever going to be alleviated. More importantly, she

would be able to help out at the soup kitchen run by
the Church of St Giles. It was a place she owed a great
deal to and it would always occupy a special place in
her heart. Although she had religiously sent them half
of her wages since she had left London last year, she
had missed getting her hands dirty. The sense of ful-
filment that she got from helping other unfortunates
was its own reward. It mattered; therefore as a consequence she mattered too.

Unfortunately, Lady Worsted would find all of these
totally worthy causes totally unsuitable while they were
guests of the Duke and would doubtless forbid Amelia
from going if she knew about them. The older woman
had been most insistent that, as a member of His Majesty's government, he had to be spared the taint of any
scandal and, as so much about Amelia was scandalous
already, it would probably be best if she avoided all of
her dubious good deeds while they were his guests. It
would also be prudent, her employer had cautioned,
to avoid mentioning her unfortunate past for exactly
the same reason.

Fortunately, life as Lady Worsted's companion
meant that Amelia always had a considerable amount
of free time as her employer made so few demands
on it. It was a mystery why she even bothered with a
companion in the first place. It was not as if she was
lonely. Lady Worsted had a great many friends and acquaintances who liked to visit her and, better still, the
old lady was rather fond of her afternoon naps. Which
meant that Amelia hoped to be going on a great many
'long walks' while she was a guest at the Duke of Aveley's conveniently located London town house. She
was not prepared to miss the opportunity to become

fully involved in her good causes rather than dreaming about them from a distance. Political groups were not that well organised in Bath, nor were the people, and even the poor muddled along without needing a great deal of her help. But London was the heart of it all, the beating, pulsing, putrid centre of everything, and she was determined to make up for lost time. For the next month she would be useful again and her voice would be heard. Amelia could not wait.

Noticing that Lady Worsted had already nodded off in the seat opposite, Amelia reluctantly picked up her host's book again and glared at the cover. *The Discerning Gentleman's Guide to Selecting the Perfect Bride.* The Duke probably thought himself to be quite the wit in making the title rhyme too. The man sounded like the most crushing of bores, full of his own paternalistic self-importance and too bothered with social etiquette and appearances to be able to see further than his protruding aristocratic nose. Men like that were all the same. With nothing else to do to pass the time, Amelia selected a random page and began to read.

Bennett Montague, Sixteenth Duke of Aveley and member of His Majesty's Privy Council, glanced at his pocket watch in annoyance before slotting it back into his waistcoat pocket. It was already six o'clock and his aunt should have arrived by now. Whilst he did not blame her personally for the inconvenience—even this late in the day travelling in London could be horrendous—dinner was always promptly served at seven. At this rate, it would have to be put back.

His butler, Lovett, appeared at the door to his study. 'The carriage is arriving, Your Grace.'

'Thank goodness!' He would not have to adjust his tightly organised schedule after all. All was well in the world again. As was expected, Bennett went out to the hallway to greet his aunt, conscious that he still had several letters and one speech to write before the night was done. He found his mother and Uncle George already there. As they waited, he noticed something odd about his usually ramrod-straight butler. He was listing slightly to the left.

'Lovett,' he hissed, 'have you been availing yourself of my port again?' Bennett wouldn't have minded, but they had guests after all—an uncommon event in recent months due to his enormous workload.

Still listing, Lovett had the good manners to look sheepish. 'I am sorry, Your Grace. I had a moment of weakness.'

One of many. If the man had not been such a loyal and resourceful servant with a keen sense of timing when it came to helping him to escape, Bennett would have dismissed the man on the spot years ago. However, he was rather fond of him despite his wayward tendencies. Without Lovett, he would have had to have spent hundreds of pointless hours socialising with people he had no interest in. 'Is it Mrs Lovett again?' If his butler was to be believed, that woman was apparently the reason why her husband turned to drink on a regular basis, although Bennett was confident this was just a convenient excuse.

'Indeed it is, Your Grace. I have just found out that she is expecting again.'

'Again! Clearly I do not give you enough to do, Lovett. How many children are we up to now?' He knew the answer full well and all of their names, but this was the game they played when Bennett could not muster the enthusiasm to properly tell his impertinent, invaluable servant off and spared his butler from admitting that he just had a penchant for good port.

'This will be the tenth, Your Grace, providing Mrs Lovett does not have another set of twins.'

Fortunately, the front door opened, relieving Bennett from any further pretence of admonishing his servant, and he stepped forth to welcome them. His aunt looked as robust as usual and would expect him to see that. Another social game that served no purpose. 'Aunt Augusta, you look well. Clearly the air in Bath suits you.'

She accepted his compliment and presented him with her powdered cheek. 'You look as though you could do with a little restorative air yourself, Bennett. You are altogether too serious for a young man. I have scarcely been here a minute and already I can see that you wish to be elsewhere.' He did not correct her assumption because he did have a great many more important things to be doing right at this very moment than standing in his hallway and making small talk, and it would not hurt if she knew that. His aunt smiled at his bland expression. 'Allow me to introduce you to my new companion, Miss Amelia Mansfield.'

A petite woman with the darkest eyes he had ever seen stepped forward. Usually, Bennett took no real interest in his aunt's companions. There had been so many of them over the years that their plain faces had all begun to merge into one interchangeable and banal façade and he barely bothered flicking them a glance. But Miss Mansfield was quite different, so his eyes lingered. For a start, and even though she was wear-

ing a very large, very dull bonnet, there was nothing
plain about her. The dark, catlike eyes were framed
with ridiculously thick sooty lashes. Two bold black
slashes formed her eyebrows and her full mouth was
quite the most impertinent shade of red. If it had been
appropriate, which it wasn't, and if he had the talent for
it, which he most definitely did not, it was exactly the
sort of face that might have inspired him to flirt with
the lovely owner of it. Therefore, Bennett inclined his
head politely because that was the correct thing to do.

'Miss Mansfield.'

And she just about inclined hers in return.

'Your Grace.'

Then, as an afterthought, she bobbed him a lacklustre curtsey. It was customary when curtseying that
the woman also dipped her eyes in deference to the illustrious person she was curtseying to. That was the
correct form, after all, and everybody understood it.
Everyone, apparently, except Miss Mansfield. She held
his gaze in the most disconcerting way before turning
towards the others. There was certainly no attempt
at deference in that pointed stare. In fact, if he was
not mistaken, he was almost certain he saw a flash of
some other emotion hiding in those chocolate depths,
although he could not quite put his finger on what it
was. Despite her blatant disregard for etiquette, Bennett could not stop watching her as she was introduced
to his mother and Uncle George.

'Do you read, Miss Mansfield?' his mother asked.

'Amelia reads everything she can get her hands on,'
Aunt Augusta answered in her stead. 'And she reads
aloud with tremendous skill. It is most entertaining.

She has a talent for bringing the words and characters on the page to life.'

'Then you will be an asset to my reading salon. I do hope that you will join us. Every Wednesday evening a select group of us gather to read and discuss writings that have had a profound effect on us. It makes no difference whether you like fiction, poetry or academia—we are an eclectic bunch and it is a lively way to spend the evening. And it is my only chance to properly entertain at the moment while my son is so busy in Parliament.'

When Miss Mansfield smiled he noticed that it made her unusual eyes prettier.

'I should like that very much.'

Perhaps Bennett was imagining it, but she definitely greeted them with more enthusiasm than she had him—although why he was put out by that he could not quite fathom. Uncle George was instantly smitten with her and had no problem in showing it. 'I am positively charmed already, Miss Mansfield, and would be thrilled if you sit with me at dinner. It has been far too long since I have enjoyed the company of such a delightful creature over a meal.'

'Be wary, Miss Mansfield,' his mother cautioned, smiling affectionately at the man who had been a surrogate father to Bennett for so many years. 'I am afraid George still thinks that he is in his prime. He will spend the entire meal flirting with you outrageously or telling you scandalous stories that are completely unsuitable for your delicate young ears.'

'You wound me, Octavia!' His uncle pretended to be affronted by this suggestion, which made all of the ladies laugh instantly. Bennett had always envied his uncle's easy way with the female sex, but this time he found that talent irritating. Unfortunately, judging by the charmed expression on her pretty face, Miss Mansfield was similarly smitten with Uncle George.

'I shall look forward to it.' She positively grinned at the old rogue in return. It was like being blindsided by a sunbeam; everything about her lit up. Her rosebud mouth curved mischievously, transforming her face into a thing of complete beauty, two adorable dimples appeared on her perfect cheeks and those big brown eyes grew warm and inviting. 'It has been far too long since I heard a genuinely scandalous story over dinner.'

A dinner that would be severely delayed at this rate unless Bennett intervened and put an immediate stop to all of this nonsense. He snapped open his pocket watch again and frowned to make the point. 'I will get Lovett to show you straight to your rooms as dinner is in less than an hour.' Which gave him enough time to conquer the small mountain of paperwork lying unattended on his desk. 'If you will all excuse me.'

To his own ears his voice sounded a bit clipped, yet for some reason he was decidedly out of sorts. Bennett forced a polite smile before turning on his heel and heading purposefully back to his study. He felt the oddest tickle of awareness, which instantly raised his hackles and made him glance around. He caught Miss Mansfield openly staring at him again and not in a good way.

Bennett was not prone to vanity—he did not have the time required to dedicate to such an endeavour—but he knew that he was considered quite handsome by most women. He was used to female admiration and, on occasion, even blatant flirting. He was a duke, after all, and a very eligible one at that. However, Miss Mansfield was regarding him as if he was some sort of scientific specimen that she did not fully understand. People just did not do that. Not to him. If they did, basic good manners dictated that it was done covertly and he was blissfully unaware of their scrutiny. It was most disconcerting. Bennett scowled as he marched onward towards his study, for the first time in as long as he could remember feeling very uncomfortable in his own skin and ever so slightly offended.

Amelia had two good frocks that were passable to wear to dinner. Neither filled her with enthusiasm. Out of sheer defiance she picked the one with the lowest neckline, grabbed her finest shawl and pinched some colour into her cheeks and lips to give herself some confidence. The Aveley residence on Berkeley Square was the grandest house she had ever set foot in and she hated the fact that she found it more than a little bit intimidating. From the moment she had walked up the marble steps towards the imposing black double front doors, the sheer opulence of the place had taken her breath away. But inside? Well, that was a completely different level of exquisite altogether.

The floor in the hallway was a striking chessboard of black and white marble. An ornate and sweeping staircase drew the eye upwards to a painted ceiling that had literally left her awed by its beauty. The artist had turned it into a window to Heaven. Cherubs floated amongst clouds, gazing down at the viewer below in angelic serenity. Amelia had really never seen anything like it. If the shock of her new surroundings was not enough, she had blinked in surprise when she had first glimpsed the owner of all of that splendour. The Duke of Aveley looked nothing like the haughty, beady-eyed and paunchy aristocrat she had imagined him to be.

Like the angels suspended above her, this man appeared to have been created from the brush of the most talented of artists. He was broad-shouldered and golden. That was the only word for him…*golden*. Over six feet of manly magnificence had stood in front of her, completely at odds with the arrogant pomposity that had apparently spewed from his pen. Aveley had thick, slightly wayward blond hair, weaved with threads of wheat and bronze, intelligent cobalt eyes and a tempting mouth that drew her eye just as effectively as his wonderful ceiling did. The female part of her, which she always tried to ignore, had reacted in the most peculiar way. Her pulse began to race, nervous butterflies began to flap in her stomach and her knees felt decidedly weak. If she did not know better, Amelia would have said that she was *all aquiver*, which was a ludicrous but apt description for the way she'd suddenly felt. He was a square-jawed, straight-nosed delight to behold. Exactly the sort of fairy-tale man she had once dreamed she would live with happily ever after before the harsh realities of life had taught her that there were no such things as fairy tales.

And then he had looked at her as if she was exactly what she was—little more than a servant and nothing of any consequence—bringing her crashing soundly back to earth with a thud. For the briefest of moments Amelia had felt a rush of pure, unadulterated disappointment before she'd shaken herself and reminded herself that she was a fool to have expected anything less. She knew better than to judge a book by its cover, no matter how splendid that cover might first seem, and she was not usually prone to silly fluttering or even sillier ideas that involved a titled man in her future.

At the time, her uncharacteristic reaction to him had bothered her immensely but, after a small period of reflection in her luxurious new bedchamber, she now understood that she had simply been completely overwhelmed. Not just by the handsome, pompous Duke, but by her surroundings and the prospect of being amongst proper society again for such a prolonged period of time. It *had* been a long journey and she *was* quite tired. It was hardly surprising that she was a little out of sorts and she had been surprised that the pompous Duke had not looked anything like she had imagined. It was rare that a title did not immediately disappoint. She had not been expecting someone who resembled Adonis, therefore she could forgive herself for her brief moment of disbelief and the understandable nervous reaction that followed. Equilibrium restored, she stiffened her spine and walked with purpose.

A footman directed her down a long corridor to a formal dining room at the end, where she was seated in the middle of a grand table set for five. Sir George was the first to arrive and plonked himself down in the chair opposite her and instructed a servant to fill up both of their wine glasses with a flick of his hand.

'How splendid, Miss Mansfield, that I have you all to myself. I dare say you are burning with curiosity and have a hundred questions about this house and its family that you want to have answered. Unfortunately for you—' he took a healthy glug of his wine and grinned conspiratorially '—I have a very loose tongue when under the influence of even the merest drop of alcohol; therefore I suggest you grasp the opportunity to take advantage of that fact before the others arrive and I have to behave myself.'

Already he was her favourite person here and she had known him less than a few minutes in total. 'The house is very impressive. Has it always been in the family?'

Sir George rolled his eyes in irritation at the apparent banality of her question. 'It was designed for the fourteenth Duke by none other than Robert Adam himself. It is also the biggest house on Berkeley Square. Surely that is not the best thing you could think to ask me about—I, who have an intimate knowledge of this illustrious family and all of their goings-on? Bennett's father was my elder brother, after all.'

There was a look of challenge in his face that encouraged her to be bolder. 'Is the Duke a close friend of the Regent?' If he was, it would confirm all of her worst suspicions about the man.

Sir George took a thoughtful sip of his wine before answering. 'Bennett is one of his advisers—however, the King's son is not particularly good at taking his advice.'

'That does not answer my question, Sir George.' If the pompous Duke was a great friend of Prinny's, she would find every second in his company loathsome.

To his credit, he laughed at his attempt at evasiveness. 'If the point of your question was to find out whether or not the Duke of Aveley holds the Regent in high regard, then I have to tell you that to say that he does not would be tantamount to treason and would place his position in the Cabinet in jeopardy. However, to answer you in a roundabout way, I can say that my nephew, like his father before him, is a statesman and to be an effective statesman you have to be a diplomat. As such, I believe he uses that diplomacy to his advantage in order to get things done for the good of the country. He does not socialise with the Regent very often, if you get my meaning, and when he does it is only at events that are important to the state.'

The fact that her host did not gamble or carouse with Prinny made him only slightly less offensive. It was no secret that Lord Liverpool, the Prime Minister, put a great deal of stock in Bennett Montague's opinions—which made him her natural adversary. Liverpool was unsympathetic to the plight of the poor and preferred to repress dissenters rather than negotiate with them. 'The newspapers claim that the Duke will be Prime Minister before he is forty.'

'Oh, dear!' Sir George chuckled as he swirled his wine around in his glass. 'Please do not say that in front of Bennett. He has every intention of taking that office before he is thirty-five and even that is too long a wait for his ambitions for the nation.'

Further prying was prevented by the arrival of the Dowager and Lady Worsted. The Duke's mother took her seat at one end of the table and Amelia's employer sat down next to her. 'Where is Bennett? I am famished.'

Sir George glanced pointedly at the clock on the sideboard. 'It is still two minutes before seven. He will arrive exactly on time, as always.' He gave Amelia another amused conspiratorial glance. 'I set my watch by him. He is far more reliable than all of the other timepieces in the house.'

As they made polite conversation, Amelia could not help tuning into the gentle rhythmic ticking of the clock and counting the seconds going past. Surely the man was not such a dull stickler that he would be so precise? But he was.

Chapter Two

*It is essential that a good wife has a basic knowl-
edge of politics. As your hostess, she will need
to ask pertinent questions designed to stimulate
worthy discussion between your male guests...*
—*The Discerning Gentleman's Guide to
Selecting the Perfect Bride* by Bennett Montague,
Sixteenth Duke of Aveley

As the big hand finally touched the hour, the Duke
of Aveley strode into the dining room as if he owned
the place, which she supposed, in all fairness, he did.
Amelia flicked a glance at Sir George and could see
her own amusement reflected in her new friend's eyes.

'Good evening, everyone.' The Duke sat himself
down and snapped open his napkin with almost military precision. 'Lovett—we are ready.'

At his command, the servants began to swarm
around the table with the first course, a delicious thin
soup. However, and no doubt just to vex her, Amelia's
heartbeat became more rapid at the sight of him again.
He really was quite splendid to behold. It was such a

shame that the interior was not as wonderful as the exterior. A bit like a beautifully iced cake that was old and dry beneath its fancy casing.

The Duke did not bother with unnecessary social chit-chat. 'Mother, I have looked at the list of invitations that you gave me. Whilst I believe that I can manage the Renshaw ball and the Earl of Bainbridge's soirée in December, I am afraid I cannot spare the time for any others in the coming month.'

'That is a great shame, dear,' his mother said with obvious disappointment. 'Are you sure that you cannot squeeze in a fleeting appearance at Lady Bulphan's? Your presence would be quite a coup for her and I did promise her that you would. Priscilla was so looking forward to seeing you.'

'I am afraid not. It is a particularly taxing week at Parliament. Besides, I will still see Priscilla at the reading salon. I am sorry.' Amelia noticed that he did not look particularly sorry at all. He was more interested in his soup than the invitation.

'Who is Priscilla?' Lady Worsted asked her sister.

'She is Lady Bulphan's eldest granddaughter and one of the young ladies on Bennett's Potential list.'

As everybody else around the table apparently knew what this was, Amelia felt obliged to ask her employer for clarification, although she was well aware that, as a companion, she really had no right to ask. 'The Potential list?'

Lady Worsted smiled innocently, but there was definitely a spark of something mischievous in her wily old eyes. 'It is Bennett's list of prospective candidates for the future Duchess of Aveley. He has been work-

ing his way through it these past two years. The last I
heard, there were ten in the running.'

'We are down to five now,' his mother explained
helpfully as she tilted her bowl to one side to spoon up
more soup. 'He hopes to have narrowed it down to the
final choice by late spring—but you know how these
things are.' Clearly she did not think that such a thing
was a tad odd—but then again her son was a duke.

'Is there a particular front runner?' Lady Worsted
glanced at Sir George and smiled. The pair were clearly
sharing an ongoing joke that the Duke's mother was
not included in.

'We had high hopes of Lady Elizabeth Pearce but,
alas, she did not pass muster,' said the Dowager on a
sigh. 'It turned out that she was prone to temper tantrums and not nearly as level-headed as she had led
us to believe.'

Good gracious. He even conducted his own affairs
in line with the edicts outlined in his silly book. Amelia had never heard anything so ridiculous. 'Are the
five front runners aware of their rivals for the *coveted*
position?'

Both Lady Worsted's and Sir George's eyes widened
at her subtle use of sarcasm, but the pompous Duke's
focus remained on his food.

'Of course,' his mother replied, looking amused that
Amelia would think otherwise. 'Bennett is very careful not to pay particular regard to any one of them.
They are all treated equally and will be until he has
made his decision.'

'He is scrupulously fair.' Sir George nodded in
agreement although the hint of a smile hovered on the
corners of his mouth. 'He always dances one dance

with each of them at every ball, never the waltz, of course, lest it give them ideas.'

'Heaven forbid.'

'And every Thursday each girl receives an identical bouquet of flowers.'

Amelia nearly choked on the soup. 'Identical? How very…romantic.' Lady Worsted gave her a light kick under the table. 'I am sure that they are delighted to be singled out for such special attention.'

Not that Amelia had any suitors, but if she did she would expect the man to be wooing her and her alone. If she ever got wind that her imaginary beau was sending identical bouquets to another four ladies, she would use the stems to give him a sound thrashing before showing him the door. 'Are all five passing muster?' She wanted to giggle so much that she had to bite down hard on the inside of her mouth to stop a giggle escaping.

Sir George was also definitely on the verge of laughing. He dipped his head and slurped a big spoonful of soup into his mouth clumsily just to give himself an excuse to choke on something. His splutter caused the man in question to gaze up and stare, perplexed, at the slight commotion, giving Amelia the distinct impression that he had not been listening to their conversation at all. Probably because he was so important.

In his own mind.

The Duke cast a critical eye down the table and, satisfied that everyone was finished, signalled to the butler to clear the soup bowls away.

'Bennett is very particular,' Lady Worsted said, patting her nephew's arm affectionately. 'Isn't that right,

Bennett? You wouldn't want to be saddled with the wrong sort of wife?'

It took a few seconds for Bennett to respond to the question because he really hadn't been following the conversation. The final paragraph of his speech to the House of Lords tomorrow lacked something and he had been mulling over different sentences that would finish it off with a flourish. That was probably poor form, he realised. While Uncle George and his mother were used to his complete immersion in government matters, he had not seen his aunt since last Christmas and she deserved his full attention for one brief family dinner.

'I do apologise, Aunt Augusta; I was a little preoccupied. Would you repeat the question?'

'We were discussing your Potential list and I commented on the fact that you wouldn't want to be saddled with the wrong sort of wife.'

Bennett was so bored with that chore. In many ways he wished it all over with so that he could get on with his work without having to bother with all of the silly social engagements that wasted his evenings and ate up his valuable time. However, as his father had repeatedly instilled in him, the Dukedom needed a strong bloodline if it was to continue to serve the nation properly. And if he was going to be Prime Minister, he needed to be married. A bachelor, his father had often lamented, did not instil the great confidence in people that such an illustrious office required. He needed to find a good wife, of sound aristocratic stock, who would be an asset to his political ambitions. Someone above reproach, who knew how to behave accordingly and who had family connections that would provide him with more allies in the house so that he could finish what his father had started. Bennett tried to appear interested for the sake of good manners, so trotted out one of his tried-and-tested sayings. 'Indeed. Marry in haste and repent at leisure.'

As the servants swiftly reset the table for the next course, Bennett sensed Miss Mansfield's eyes on him again. He turned to her politely and then instantly forgot the art of making polite dinner conversation the moment he took his first proper look at her.

Why he had not noticed her the moment he'd stepped into the room was a complete mystery to him now. Without the barricade of the enormous bonnet, he could see that she had gloriously dark, shiny hair. So dark that it was reminiscent of the polished ebony keys on his mother's pianoforte. The sort of hair he would like to unpin from its tight chignon and run his fingers through to see if it actually did feel like silk—as he imagined it would. She certainly resembled nothing like an old woman's companion. Companions usually blended into the background. Miss Mansfield rendered the background and foreground completely inconsequential. Her choice of gown for dinner was merely the icing on the cake. It was too boldly coloured for a start. The forest-green silk stood out in stark relief against the subtly striped cream wallpaper, emphasising her pale skin and graceful neck. Bennett tried not to notice the barest hint of cleavage that the square neckline suggested, forcing his eyes to remain resolutely on her face. Unfortunately, that meant that he had no choice other than to stare into those dark, mesmerising eyes and at that lush red mouth.

'I have been reading your book,' the enticing red

lips suddenly said, startling him out of his unexpectedly errant and out of character musings.

'Indeed?'

When he had first put pen to paper, out of complete boredom after being snowed in at Aveley Castle one Christmas, he had had no concept of how desperately society craved sensible guidance on the art of courting. Now, almost a year since his scribblings had first been published, he was quite used to receiving the effusive praise of his many readers. To begin with he had been quite dismissive of the book's success. It was just a collection of advice that he had received from his father. The book had been a memorial, of sorts, and he had certainly not thought anybody would care about it overmuch. It was merely a way for Bennett to ensure that his father's wise words were saved for perpetuity and it served to maintain the correct focus while he searched for his own bride—an aide-memoire, as it were. Then, as time passed and more and more copies of the thing were printed and sold, he had realised that his many readers often had genuine questions, so he tried to be accommodating. As a politician, he owed it to them. It was his civic duty to educate people—another of his father's edicts that he had taken to heart. Besides, at least it would give him something to talk to this alluring creature about without appearing to be a completely mute fool. 'Have you found it helpful in any way?'

Her brown eyes widened in what he assumed was surprise while she stared at him for several seconds. She had tiny flecks of copper in her irises that burned like fire, he noticed, then chided himself for his peculiarly poetic mood.

'I have certainly found it *insightful*,' she finally said, her face devoid of any emotion that would give him a clue as to whether *insightful* was a compliment or a criticism.

'Miss Mansfield is not currently looking for a husband,' his aunt interjected, looking decidedly amused. 'So I dare say your advice is wasted on her.'

'It is a very long journey from Bath to London and I had finished the book I had brought with me. Lady Worsted gave me her copy because she *thought* that it might help to pass the time.'

'I see.'

Although he really didn't. Bennett had the distinct impression that he was missing something. There was the merest hint of censure in the word *thought*, as if it contained some hidden message that he was not receiving and nor was he meant to. Was she suggesting that she found his writing boring? And who was she to judge him, anyway?

Perhaps sensing his unease, Uncle George changed the topic to a more comfortable subject. 'Have you made any progress with the House of Commons on taxation?'

Bennett shook his head, instantly frustrated. 'They are still resolutely against extending income tax to pay for the war debts and are far more interested in shouting at each other to make any progress on anything. Those fools cannot see further than their noses. It is preposterous to think that the nation can continue to borrow vast sums of money when we are not making enough to effectively pay it back.'

'It is grossly unfair to expect honest working men to pay even more money into the government's coffers when many struggle so hard to make ends meet as it is. Already they are taxed to the hilt. To add to their burden is unjust. The Members of Parliament are right to oppose it.'

To Bennett's complete surprise, those words were uttered by Miss Mansfield. And quite vociferously too. Typically, like most people, she was completely missing the point. 'The bulk of taxation should not come from the poorest, Miss Mansfield, and under my proposals nor should it. It should come from land and from the profit from trade. The Members of Parliament are voted into office by the wealthy landowners and merchants who would pay the most under the scheme, and so are naturally resistant to it. Therefore, the MPs continue to oppose it merely to secure their own political futures.'

She blinked at him and then her dark eyebrows drew together as she contemplated his words. 'Whilst I do agree that those who have more should pay more, you have to understand that the costs of taxation are unfairly passed down to the poor by their unscrupulous masters regardless. Wages are cut, workers are forced to work longer hours and the prices of essential commodities, like flour or sugar, are raised as the merchants try to recoup their lost profits. Without proper legislation to protect the most vulnerable in our society, all that income tax did was make the rich want to stay richer whilst it forced the poor to become poorer. We cannot repeat that experiment.'

Bennett tried to moderate his irritation at her emotional grasp of politics. 'They might do those things in the short-term, Miss Mansfield, but things will level out eventually, you will see. Income tax is a necessary evil, I'm afraid.'

'And in the meantime would you doom thousands of people to suffer unimaginable poverty? That is indeed evil.'

Chapter Three

*Marry a woman who thinks before she speaks.
It will save you a great deal of time having to
correct her...*

Amelia had been too forthright. She was prepared
to concede that at least. She had clearly insulted the
pompous Duke over dinner, although his politeness
was too ingrained for him to have chastised her for it.
Instead, Lady Worsted had stepped in and changed the
topic to the Renshaw ball and both Amelia and their
host had remained seething and silent for the rest of
the meal, their difference of opinion hanging like a
dirty sheet between them for all to see. Afterwards,
Lady Worsted had given her a lecture on keeping her
thoughts to herself and had insisted that Amelia apologise for her outburst once his aunt had smoothed the
way. That was just as well because Amelia really could
not bring herself to do so quite yet, especially when
she was not even slightly sorry for challenging the man
on his narrow-minded views. How typical of an aristocrat like him to have no concept of how his decisions

would affect the masses! Just like her father, the Duke expected everyone to blithely accept his laws and decisions, no matter how bad the effect.

However, calling him *evil* was a step too far. Even for her. If he wanted to, he could send her packing immediately and she would not be able to do any of the things in Town that she'd planned. Worse, if Lady Worsted had dismissed her for her impudence, she would not even be able to scrape enough money together to survive for a week. Most of her wages went straight to the soup kitchen because Amelia did not need them. As Lady Worsted's companion, she was amply fed, had a roof over her head, fresh sheets on a comfortable bed and enough hand-me-downs to clothe herself more than adequately. Why would she need the money?

However, her lack of it and what that might mean should her current circumstances be brought to an abrupt end was certainly food for thought. The very last thing Amelia ever wanted was to be homeless again. Or dirt poor. She really needed to learn to hold her tongue, no matter how hard that might actually be in practice. She might not like her employer's nephew, but she thought the world of Lady Worsted. Lady Worsted had taken a chance on her when nobody else would, plucking her from a life of poverty and giving her a home. Lady Worsted found her pithy comments and sarcasm entertaining and was gracious enough to gloss over the unfortunate stains in her past. If her employer wanted her to hold her wayward tongue in front of her nephew and apologise to him for her perceived insult, then Amelia was duty-bound…no—honour-bound… to do that.

It made no difference that the pompous Duke clearly had limited, if any, experience of what life was like for the majority of the nation's subjects. It was not Amelia's place to educate him. Even if she tried, she doubted he would listen. His hereditary beliefs were too ingrained and he clearly felt, like all aristocrats, that they had a divine right to govern the rest of the country simply because they had been born. This evening he had given her *that look* when she had dared to question him. *That look* that men always gave women when they wanted to put them back in their place. *That look* that said that she was incapable of understanding his line of argument, based solely on the circumstances of her sex. As if being in possession of a womb rendered her somehow more stupid than all humans who were born without one.

Ha! Amelia was better informed than most men and probably cleverer than them too. Not only had she read every learned treatise she could get her hands on, she had also experienced life from both sides of the same coin. She had been rich and cosseted and she had been poor and insignificant. Both states had shaped her personality and had given her more insight into the human condition than anyone else she could think of. His Royal Highness the Duke of Pomposity could not compete with that hard-won knowledge. If she had been born a man, she would run for Parliament herself. If ever an institution needed more wisdom, more empathy and more vision, it was that one. Just thinking about all of the injustice they perpetrated in the name of governance made her livid.

Too agitated to even think of going to bed, Amelia decided to head for the kitchen for some warm milk to help her sleep. Then she carried the steaming mug back out towards the deserted palatial hallway and allowed herself a few minutes to simply take it all in.

Although she had not set foot in her father's London residence in a decade, she had a clear, indelible memory of the place. She only had to close her eyes to see the highly polished wooden banisters that she had surreptitiously slid down when nobody was watching, the sparkling chandelier in the entrance hall, the comforting smells of beeswax and polish that always reminded her of happier times when they had lived as a family. Back when she was little and her father still adored her mother—before he had found a way to annul their marriage in order to get a son—she had thought their house in Mayfair the loveliest house in all of England, but it paled in comparison to this. This was a level of luxury that Viscount Venomous would truly envy.

Amelia looked up at the wonderful ceiling and spun in a slow circle. She loved to draw and, although her attempts at art were pathetic in comparison, she could not help but appreciate this clever artist's work. Every single cherub was different, flowers and leaves were dripping out of their chubby hands, but from this angle it was difficult to comprehend the total effect of the painting. A quick check of the hallway confirmed that she was still alone, so she quickly deposited her cooling milk on an ornamental table and lay down in the middle of the floor. Only then did she fully understand what the picture was trying to show.

The four corners of the high ceiling were filled with the flowers and fruits produced in the four seasons. Vibrant green holly, winter berries and bare twigs represented winter in one. Copper leaves, golden corn, horse chestnuts and acorns for autumn, spring daffodils and cherry blossom bloomed in another corner, then finally fat roses of every colour depicted summer. The cherubs were joyfully grabbing handfuls of nature's bounty to sprinkle on the world below. It was whimsical and delightful, the tiny details sublime, and she could have stared at it for hours. It was exactly what she needed to alleviate her sour mood.

Bennett read through his speech one last time before he cast it aside in irritation. It was good, of course, because he had a way with words, but he was still not completely happy with it. Or perhaps it was not his speech that was vexing him? He was still smarting from Miss Mansfield's scathing rant from earlier.

He had never been called *evil* before. He had been criticised in Parliament for being too moderate or too reforming, but he had never taken offence because that was politics. His father had been absolutely right. Change was a gradual process and it could not be rushed; it was normal for people to be resistant to it. Bennett's first and foremost role in Parliament was to gradually whittle down opposition to change so that society, as a whole, could make progress.

Miss Mansfield had no understanding of such things. Her suggestion that he was personally responsible for making the lives of the poor more wretched than they already were was not only grossly unfair, it was downright insulting. He was very aware of their plight. In fact, he had always taken a particular interest in it. If something was not done to alleviate their suffering, then he feared that the very foundation of English government was in jeopardy. The last thing

anybody wanted was a revolution like there had been
in France or in the American colonies.

Why else would he be so insistent that the wealthy
had to take on more of the responsibility for taxation? If
the government could raise more from taxes, then that
money could be used to improve society. One of his
own aspirations was to see the compulsory education
of all poor children in government-built schools. Many
of his contemporaries were against making the masses
literate, claiming that it would merely encourage more
revolutionary tendencies, but Bennett firmly believed
that reading was a skill that could only serve to improve their prospects in adulthood whilst making the
nation greater. That certainly did not make him evil.

His aunt had spoken to him about Miss Mansfield,
claiming that she had been dealt a bad hand by life and
that she was a truly wonderful young lady when you
got to know her. Bennett was yet to see any evidence
of that, but it was obvious that Aunt Augusta was very
fond of the chit, so for that reason alone he would be
benevolent towards her. However, he was not going to
be quite so polite the next time she offered her unso-
licited and tart opinions.

No, indeed! Next time he would give the woman
the sound dressing-down she deserved, no matter how
devilishly pretty she looked.

A quick glance at the clock on the mantel told him it
was past midnight, again. He had to be back in Westminster by eight. If he was not going to fall asleep in
the middle of the afternoon debate, he really needed to
get some sleep. All of these late nights spent working
until the small hours were beginning to take their toll.
Unfortunately, these were trying times for the govern-

ment and his workload was immense. Something had to be sacrificed in order to get it all done and at the moment that something was sleep.

Wearily, he unfolded his stiff body from his chair and stared at his discarded hessians next to his desk. Despite the fact that he knew that propriety dictated that he should put them back on, he could not bring himself to. They were new boots and they hurt. The polished leather was still so stiff that they pinched and rubbed in all manner of places. Besides, it was late and none of the servants would comment on his lack of footwear. Lovett had them all far too well-trained for that. In fact, if he chose to walk around the house completely naked except for a strategically placed fig leaf, none of them would dare to bat an eyelid. That thought made him smile, and smiling made his face ache. Clearly his smiling muscles were protesting at being used. It felt unnatural—which probably meant that Aunt Augusta had been quite correct when she had said that he was looking far too serious for a young man. He made a mental note to smile more. Perhaps it was vanity, but his esteemed father had not smiled a great deal, so by the time he was forty he'd appeared very dour indeed—even when he wasn't.

But serious politics was not exactly a cheerful endeavour. And it was completely absorbing. His father had groomed him to serve in government. *We are Montagues, boy*, he would say, *and we were born to shape this country*. Later, when his father had realised that he was ill, Bennett's training for the highest office had begun early. By the tender age of fifteen, he was ready and eager to step into his father's footsteps. His final conversation with his father had been a solemn promise to continue his family's political legacy. Bennett had taken the oath seriously and had worked tirelessly since to do the right thing. So tirelessly that he was always tired.

Perhaps his mother was also right and he needed to get out more. Bennett could not remember the last time he went out for a ride or walked in the park or even visited Aveley Castle, the place he loved more than any other. He made another mental note to take a weekend off soon. He deserved a little time to relax. He was also tired of being cooped up in his carriage. Tomorrow he would ride to Westminster. The exercise would do him good. He glanced at the stiff hessians again and decided to be rebellious for once. Tonight, propriety could go to hell. Picking them up and tucking them underneath his arm, he headed off to bed.

He was so tired that he did not see the woman lying spread-eagled at the foot of the staircase until he almost stepped on her. The sight gave him quite a fright.

'Miss Mansfield! Are you injured?'

Convinced that she had had an accident, Bennett dropped to his knees at the exact same moment that his aunt's companion sat bolt upright in alarm. Their foreheads bashed together with such force that Bennett actually thought that he saw stars. He fell back onto his bottom, clutching his sore head and glaring at her as she clutched hers.

'Did you fall?' he snapped harshly.

Still rubbing her own forehead, she shook her head. 'I was just admiring your ceiling.'

'And to do that you needed to prostrate yourself on the floor?'

'The floor offered the best perspective. I did not hear

you coming, else I would have immediately alerted you to my presence.' She glanced furtively at his abandoned boots, lying haphazardly at his side where he had dropped them in his panic. 'I am *so* sorry, Your Grace! I did not mean to alarm you.' She did look suitability mortified, he supposed. 'For a big man you walk with unusual stealth.'

'My boots pinch,' he found himself explaining and then stopped himself. The fact that he was not correctly dressed was by the by. She was the one who had been in a position that was improper. People just did not sprawl over the floor to look at a picture. Under any circumstances.

Beneath his fingers he could feel a bump beginning to form under his skin. An unstatesmanlike bump that would, no doubt, look quite ridiculous tomorrow when he delivered his speech. Without warning she moved closer, looking concerned, and began to gently pat around the swelling on his head herself. The close proximity was unnerving. Bennett could not remember the last time that somebody had touched him without his consent. Every morning his valet shaved him and he briefly touched the gloved hands of the ladies he danced with. That was about as much human contact as he could manage. He usually preferred to keep a good foot or more of distance between himself and another person, just in case they accidentally brushed against him…

Except, as the faintest whiff of something deliciously feminine and floral wafted up his nose and she smoothed her soft hands over his skin, he found that he was quite enjoying her ministrations. Her face was inches from his and her brown eyes were regarding him with gratifying distress. It made him feel almost special.

'You should probably put something cold on this or you will have a terrible bruise. I did not realise that I had such a hard head.'

Her own forehead was not undamaged. Without thinking and against his own better judgement, Bennett felt compelled to trace his fingers lightly over her matching bump. 'So should you. Clearly we both have hard heads.' Her skin was warm and smooth like velvet. He had the sudden urge to explore every bit of it and a peculiar yearning in the pit of his stomach that was most unlike him. Self-consciously, he dropped his hand.

She sat back then and smiled at him, obviously not feeling anywhere near as awkward by the intimacy as he did. 'Instruct your valet to rub some soap or butter into your boots. It softens the leather. Failing that, I have heard that if you fill your shoes with potato peelings that helps to stretch them a bit.'

'I will.'

'And witch hazel is particularly soothing on a bruise. I am sure that the servants will be able to fetch some.'

'Indeed.'

Bennett had a reputation for being a great orator. His speeches were the stuff of legend, but suddenly he could not string a full sentence together or think of another sensible thing to say. To cover his discomfort, he rose to his feet, wishing that he was not standing in front of her without his boots on, then offered her his hand to help her up. When she took it he felt an odd tingle shoot from his fingers, up his arm, ricochet off his ribs and head straight for his groin. Her hand felt so small in his and when she was upright again he noticed that her dark head barely reached his shoulders.

Odd.

At dinner she had appeared so formidable, yet she was in fact so petite. And he was still clasping her hand like an idiot. A monosyllabic idiot. Stiffly he released it and promptly stuffed his own wayward hands behind his back, where they could do no more mischief, and stood racking his brain for something—anything—to say.

Miss Mansfield mirrored his pose and stared briefly at the floor, drawing her plump bottom lip through her teeth as she did so. It made him wonder what she would taste like. When she did look up it was through her lovely long lashes and he could have sworn he saw the faintest tinge of a blush on her cheeks. Alarmingly, he wanted to touch it.

'I would like to apologise for my tone earlier—at dinner. I can be a little passionate about certain causes, and the plight of the poor is one of them. I did not mean any personal offence.'

Those soulful eyes of hers robbed him of any coherent response. Bennett wanted to accept her apology gracefully. In his head he could see the words that would be perfect for the task and clear the air between them.

I accept your apology, Miss Mansfield. No offence was taken. It is admirable that you take an interest in worthy causes.

Except he was having trouble getting his lips to form the words because they appeared to be strangely preoccupied with latching themselves on to hers.

He really did not quite know what had come over

him to be contemplating such an obvious breach of propriety with his aunt's latest companion. Dukes could
not go about kissing young women willy-nilly in their
own hallway, or anywhere else for that matter. It simply wasn't done. So he nodded. Just the once. Stiffly.
Like the most uptight and pompous prig and cringed
inwardly at his over-starched formality.

'I have an important speech tomorrow.' He barked
this out with such force that he saw her blink repeatedly
as she stared back at him, a little alarmed. He could
hardly blame her for that. At certain times in his life
he had really wished he had Uncle George's easy way
with people. This was one of those times. She had just
tenderly checked his injury, given him tips on how to
stop his boots hurting his feet and apologised for her
outburst at dinner and all he could manage was almost
granite stiffness.

In a last valiant attempt to make amends, Bennett
attempted a smile. Once again, his facial muscles did
not want to comply and he feared that it appeared to
poor Miss Mansfield to be more of a grimace. Then,
to his complete horror, Bennett found himself turning
briskly on his ridiculously large stockinged feet, his
hands still gripped firmly behind him like an admiral
inspecting the fleet, before marching up the stairs as
fast as he could without breaking into a run. All the
while he could feel the discarded hessians mocking him
from the hallway below—*Perhaps you really should
have put us back on?*

Chapter Four

The perfect young lady never, ever leaves her chaperon...

Amelia's bedchamber faced strategically outwards onto Berkeley Square, so it was easy to judge when the coast was clear. Lady Worsted and the Dowager were safely in their carriage bound for Bond Street and would not be home until late afternoon. She had seen Sir George leave a good hour earlier, cutting quite a dash as he walked out of the square, bound for his club. She had not seen *him* at all today, but she had heard his carriage leave at an ungodly hour, so she presumed that she now had the entire place to herself—give or take about forty servants.

Feeling a bubble of excitement, she hauled her old clothes out of the bottom of her trunk. Finally, she was able to go and visit her old friends at the soup kitchen.

A few minutes later and her transformation was complete. The presentable Miss Amelia Mansfield, gentlewoman's companion, was gone and plain old Amelia stared back at her from the looking glass. The familiar outfit brought back a whole host of unwelcome memories—hunger, cold, tiredness, hopelessness—but it also gave her strength. She was more than these old clothes, always had been and always would be, but at least now she could use them to help others suffering from the dreadful disease known as poverty.

Judging the back door to be the best exit for a woman who looked like she did, Amelia hurried down the ornate staircase and darted back towards the kitchen. With any luck, nobody would see her.

'Miss Mansfield?'

Lovett, the butler, appeared out of nowhere and regarded her with open curiosity. There was nothing for it; Amelia had to explain her appearance. Sort of.

'I am off to do some charitable work with the poor.'

The butler looked her up and down, taking in the shabby grey dress that had been washed once too often, the ratty woollen shawl and the old and scuffed boots. 'Are you sure? If you go to help them looking like that, they might take pity on you and offer you charity instead.'

His face might be deadpan, but his tone was definitely sarcastic. Even so, for some reason Amelia was certain that she had found herself an ally. 'Where I am going, people are suspicious of fine clothes.'

'Then I am not altogether sure that I approve of you going there. Where is this place you can only go dressed like a vagabond?'

She seriously considered lying but already knew that the wily butler would immediately become suspicious and might well send a footman to follow her. 'Covent Garden.' It was almost the truth.

One of Lovett's eyebrows quirked upwards. 'Who

would require your charitable efforts there? The market traders perhaps? Or one of the theatre owners? I doubt the brothels or gaming hells need the help of a gently bred young lady.' He tapped one foot impatiently and Amelia found herself squirming in the intensity of his gaze.

'If you must know, I am going to help out in a soup kitchen in the Church of St Giles.'

The butler's reaction was instantaneous and quite explosive. 'Seven Dials! The most degenerate slum in the entire city? Are you quite mad, Miss Mansfield? His Grace will hit the roof if he finds out that I allowed you to head to the Rookery!'

'Please don't tell the Duke, I beg you. I can assure you that I shall be perfectly safe, Lovett. I know the people there and they know me.'

Unsurprisingly, he did not look convinced. 'Seven Dials is filled with criminals. Thieves and crooks the lot of them.'

'Which is exactly why I shall be perfectly safe there, dressed like this,' she said reasonably. 'Nobody has anything worth stealing and all of the thieves and crooks go to Mayfair or Bond Street to practise their trade.'

Lovett's mouth opened to correct her and then closed as he regarded her quietly. 'I have never thought of it like that. I suppose you might be right—but that doesn't mean that I'm going to let you go there alone. Soup or no soup. His Grace will have a fit. You are not to leave the house.'

'I am a grown woman and it is my afternoon off to spend exactly where I so choose. Like you, I am a servant. I doubt anyone tries to tell you what you can and cannot do in your free time. At least I am using mine for a good cause. It will be much easier for both of us if you keep it to yourself.'

The butler watched her for several seconds and, to her complete surprise, acquiesced immediately. 'Very well. Just this once I shall keep it between us. But I shall expect you home well before it gets dark or I will tell His Grace and then there will be hell to pay.'

Relieved that he had relented so easily, Amelia beamed at him. 'Thank you, Lovett. I shall be back by four. I promise.'

'Will you be coming in through the back door, Miss Mansfield?' When she nodded he smiled and gestured her to the passageway behind the kitchen. 'This is the door to the servants' stairs. Go up two flights and veer left. The third door brings you right out near your bed-chamber.' That confirmed it. He was her ally. Amelia stood on tiptoe and kissed the man on the cheek.

Seven Dials looked exactly like it had when she had left it a year before. The narrow streets were still filthy, the doss houses and dwellings were still barely fit for the rats to live in and the dank smell of despair perme-ated everything. As she had predicted, nobody gave her a second glance in her ragged clothes, although one or two did stare at her boots covetously. Boots, even bat-tered ones, were a rarity here.

The only decently built brick edifice was the parish workhouse that dominated Norfolk Street and the sight of it sent an involuntary shiver down Amelia's spine. Only the truly desperate ventured through those doors and her poor mother had been one of them.

Clutching the small bunch of violets that she had just

bought from a street vendor, Amelia marched past the workhouse and turned into the tiny overgrown cemetery lying next to its walls. There were very few headstones here. These were paupers' graves and all of them were unmarked. Somewhere under the grass were her mother's remains. She did not know where. There had been no formal burial ceremony for her to attend. Her mother had gone into the ground with all of the other wretched souls who had died in the same week. It had been a cruel and insignificant ending to a lovely young woman who had once been toasted as the most beautiful heiress in Philadelphia.

Amelia placed her tiny posy on the ground and stood for a few moments, allowing all of the memories, both happy and sad, to wash over her. Just once a year she allowed herself to remember the pain. Any more than that and the anger it created threatened to consume her. It was far better to channel that anger constructively, doing good deeds, giving something back, to forget about all of the cruelty and malice that had sent her here in the first place.

She had been just eighteen when her mother had died. Despite her best efforts, Amelia had been unable to save her. By then they'd been penniless and destitute. Once her father had secured an annulment, as far as he was concerned they were both dead to him. The seventeen-year marriage might never have happened and he had had no contact with either of them for years. That had destroyed her mother and plunged her into a pit of self-pity and self-recrimination that she was never inclined to claw out of. She had been raised to be a rich man's wife and had blamed herself for the end of the marriage. 'If only I could have given him a son, Amelia, then he would still love me.' From the age of twelve, Amelia had heard those words at least once a day. By the time she'd turned sixteen she had completely lost patience with them.

By then, her mother's physical health had been deteriorating rapidly too. Amelia had done her best to earn enough to keep a roof over their heads, but as her mother needed more care even that proved to be impossible. The only place that they could turn to for help had been this workhouse, and Amelia had been determined not to go there.

In a last-ditch attempt to get her father to do the right thing, she had trudged through the dark streets to Mayfair in biting rain and sleet to beg for his help. As usual, he'd refused to see her. He no longer had a daughter. How could he have a daughter when he had never been married? When she had kicked up a fuss and refused to leave, two burly footmen were sent to forcibly drag her down the street and threw her face down in an alleyway, warning her never to darken His Lordship's door again.

One dank, wet February morning a few days later, her desperately ill mother had walked into the building behind her and had never walked out. Consumption had made her poor lungs so weak that pneumonia killed her. Apparently, her last words were words of love for her former husband because, even when things were at their worst, her mother still clung to the hope that he would want her back.

For a while Amelia had drowned in bitterness. Her American grandparents had died shortly before their daughter had married, she had no money, no home and no one to turn to. After a series of low-paid and menial jobs, she had learned how dangerous life for a woman alone truly could be. At least in the workhouse all they had required of her was her work. Out on the streets, her youth, beauty and petite size made her the target of every lecher in London. On numerous occasions she'd barely escaped with her virtue intact.

Those had been the darkest days, until she had realised that being bitter was not going to change anything about her unfortunate situation. These were the cards that life had dealt her; she might not like them, but it was up to her to play her hand as best she could. Rather than simply lament the injustice and remain a victim of it, as her mother had, it would be much more cathartic, and far more useful, to fight against it. Besides, her father did not deserve that sort of power over her. Amelia would forge herself a good life just to spite him.

From that point on, things had improved. Because she was well spoken and able to read, Amelia had managed to get a job in a draper's shop and earned enough to pay for a room. Then she'd searched for better employment and eventually secured a position at the Minerva Press circulating library in Leadenhall Street. That had been the making of her. The library was not only a place where she could read and learn about all of the causes that interested her, it had proved to be a wonderful place to meet like-minded people. Soon she was attending meetings, supporting worthy causes and following a new path that would help to bring about change for all of the other victims of injustice.

She had loved that job and would still be there to this day had it not been for the unfortunate events of the sixth of March last year. On that fateful day, she had been spotted marching towards Westminster in protest of the Corn Bill, a shocking piece of legislation that increased the price of bread for the poor. What had started as a peaceful rally had quickly deteriorated into a riot. Amelia had barely escaped the mob intact—but once word of her involvement reached her employer he dismissed her on the spot without giving her the right of reply. He did not want a Radical and an agitator sullying the reputation of his establishment and dismissed her without references. When her savings had started to dwindle, and determined not to sink back into the life she had once endured, Amelia had rashly applied for the position of a lady's companion out of utter desperation.

Maybe it was cowardice, but she never wanted to be that lonely girl in Seven Dials again. The girl who relied on charity and who had lived on her wits. The letter she had written had told the truth, mostly, explaining that she had once been from a good family and did not wish to end up in the gutter. She had not expected to get an interview, and it had taken the last of her money to travel to Bath. Why she had gone, Amelia could not say because she'd been certain that she would not even be allowed past the front door. But Lady Worsted had not only seen her; miraculously, she had given her the job. Now, in an enormous twist of irony, she was right back where she had started her life—in a fancy house in Mayfair. Almost full circle.

Except this time she was not related to the aristocrat who owned the magnificent house. The Duke of Aveley had exceeded her expectations, though. He was every inch the arrogant stuffed shirt she had imagined him to be. Yes, he was unbelievably handsome, there was no denying that, and her pulse did flutter each and every time he regarded her with his intense cobalt stare. Unfortunately, any attraction she had for him had died the moment he'd opened his mouth. Yesterday he had proved himself to be both condescending and emotionless when she had tried to tend to the injury to his head. Despite that, her silly pulse had fluttered out of control the moment she had laid her hands on his perfect golden skin.

Well, perhaps he was not completely devoid of all emotion—he did *irritation* very well. He had not been even slightly grateful that she had tried to help him and had been highly critical of the fact that he had almost tripped over her. And then, even after she had swallowed a great deal of her pride, at Lady Worsted's insistence, and apologised to him for her forthrightness, he had looked at her as if she were nothing but a great inconvenience to him. Then he had stomped off without so much as a by-your-leave. She had never met a man so full of his own importance in her entire life!

Bennett had not had a good day. The debate had been a farce. The majority of those who had taken part had been more determined to shout louder than the next person than to listen to reason. There had been no time for his speech, which was probably a blessed relief because the House had deteriorated into more of a mob than a gathering of educated gentlemen. On days like this, it was a wonder that they ever got any laws passed at all. His head still hurt from all of the noise.

And his feet still hurt because of his unfortunate choice of footwear yesterday. Worse, he was also sporting an impressive swollen bump on his head, which had inspired Lord Liverpool to stare at it and laugh. It was difficult to be taken seriously as a politician when your forehead was protruding and purple. To add insult to injury, a drover's cart had lost a wheel in the middle of Piccadilly, plunging the early-evening travellers into chaos. It had taken him over an hour already to navigate the mess, and it was getting colder by the second, but at least on horseback he was moving. If he had taken the carriage today as he usually did, he would still be sitting stationary somewhere much further back.

He steered his mount towards the side of the road so that he could pick his way past all of the spilled wooden barrels blocking the road. Out of the corner of his eye he saw a young woman who was the spitting image of Miss Mansfield walking briskly along the pavement. He shook his head in annoyance. That woman really had dominated enough of his thoughts since last night, and his dreams too, if he was imagining her to be here.

The problem was, he was still smarting from his incredibly stupid behaviour last night. He really did not know what had come over him. Well, he did, he supposed, if he was being honest with himself. His suppressed anger at her acidic comments over dinner combined with an unexpected dose of raw lust had churned his emotions up and rendered him incapable of normal conversation. Bennett really did not approve of emotions at the best of times and usually kept them all neatly contained inside himself as he had been taught. However, Miss Mansfield was uncommonly pretty. He would even go as far as to say she was the most attractive woman he had collided with in a long time. That, combined with her irritatingly forthright

opinions, gentle, caring hands and kissable mouth had
scrambled his senses and frazzled his normally sensible mind. Obviously, he had gone far too long without
a woman. When was the last time?

Months and months ago, he realised with a jolt. Perhaps just over a year. *Good grief!* It *had* been over a
year. Since he'd started seriously searching for a wife.
He had not expected it to take quite this long to select
the right one. No wonder he had such vivid ideas about
Miss Mansfield! That could be the only explanation
to it all. Such errant thoughts were the very last thing
he needed at the moment. There was far too much to
do. He made a mental note to redouble his efforts and
whittle down the Potential list to just one. Someone his
father would have approved of. And he would begin at
the Renshaw ball on Saturday night.

Feeling intensely relieved to have sorted the problem
out in his head, Bennett finally manoeuvred around
the last of the barrels and was able to nudge his horse
into a slow trot. Miss Mansfield's scurrying twin was
just ahead of him, hunched into her shawl against the
bitter cold. As he came alongside, the woman turned
her head towards him and he realised that he was not
going mad at all.

Chapter Five

*A woman is like a delicate flower. It is your duty
to protect her...*

'Miss Mansfield?'

With no other option available to her, Amelia
stopped dead and gave him a weak smile. It would
have been innocent-looking if her face had not been
frozen solid by the wind. 'Oh, hello.'

Stupid, stupid girl! She had promised Lovett faith-
fully that she would be back at Aveley House by four
o'clock. Of course, then, she had only intended to help
out at the soup kitchen. But Seven Dials had been positively buzzing with political rumour and outrage.
Clearly, the plight of the poor had worsened in her
absence.

When she had found out that there was going to be a
clandestine meeting of factory workers in Ludgate, to
discuss the dangers of working with the new machines,
she had thought that she would be able to attend, hail a
hackney and be back in plenty of time. Unfortunately,
the awful crush of people travelling had forced her to

walk. Now she was horrifically late and completely chilled to the bone. She had been certain that the butler was going to kill her; now, it seemed, he would have no need. She was already doomed.

'What are you doing here, all alone?' he snapped, peering down at her from atop his horse. The animal's hot breath formed puffy clouds in the frigid air and Amelia was sorely tempted to huddle beneath the beast's nostrils in the hope that it might warm her a bit. 'The London streets are dangerous for a woman alone once it gets dark!'

'I l-l-lost track of t-t-time.' Now her teeth were chattering as well. How splendid.

'You are cold,' he said, stating the obvious, and then he looked up and down the street as if he was searching for something. After a few seconds his face hardened and he glared at her imperiously. 'There are no cabs.'

'I am aware of that fact. H-h-hence I am walking home.'

'My aunt will never forgive me if you catch a chill.'

'Never mind, I am made of stern stuff. If I walk briskly, then I will soon warm up.' Amelia began to walk, keen to be away from him and having to explain where she had been.

'You cannot walk home alone.'

His horse was trotting alongside her at a snail's pace and appeared to be quite irritated about it. It glared at her accusingly as throngs of people began to swarm around them. 'I shall be quite all right, I assure you. B-B-Berkeley Square is less than a m-m-mile away.'

'Then I shall walk alongside you.' To her horror he made to slide off his horse. Amelia held up her hand to stop him.

'Really, there is no need. Your poor horse is already becoming agitated in this crowd. Take him home; I will not be far behind.'

It took her a moment to realise that one of his gloved hands was outstretched. Surely His Royal Highness, the Duke of Pomposity, was not suggesting that she should ride on the horse with him? Just the two of them? On one saddle? In the middle of Piccadilly? Her disbelief must have been evident in her expression.

'Come on,' he said impatiently. 'This is hardly the moment for you to become all missish. You are the one who decided it was perfectly acceptable to be out here alone. In the dark. Unchaperoned. If I stick to the back alleys, nobody will see us and we will be home in half the time. Besides, I can hardly leave you to fend for yourself, and I have no desire to walk when I have a perfectly good horse.'

Words truly failed her. She would never have expected him to show such kindness to a lowly being like her. For a moment she considered how improper it would be for her to sit on the same horse as a man, then quickly decided that she did not care. Amelia was too cold to refuse him. If he was prepared to risk the impropriety, so was she.

She grabbed his hand and found herself hoisted from the ground in one smooth motion, as if her weight was of no consequence, before she was deposited across the saddle and, by default, his lap. At a loss as to what else to do and feeling quite precarious, Amelia was forced to slide one hand about his waist just to balance herself while he guided the horse around the many pedestrians. Within minutes, they had left Piccadilly and entered a dark alleyway, away from the jammed main thoroughfare.

Wordlessly, he adjusted his position on the saddle to give her more room, then arranged his arms so that they still held the reins but formed a safe cage around her. Another thoughtful gesture for her comfort, she noticed begrudgingly. He felt so warm and so solid it was difficult not to want to snuggle against him. Instead, Amelia tried to make polite conversation, in the hope that it might somehow serve to warm her or make her feel less awkward.

'Thank you. It is very kind. I was not looking forward to walking the last mile home. It has got cold quickly, hasn't it?'

'It's winter and it's dark. What else did you expect?' He sounded peeved again. Or perhaps that was just his natural tone of voice. Either way, there was no answer to his clipped question, so she huddled into her shawl and decided to remain mute.

After several uncomfortable minutes he spoke again. 'You are still shivering.'

'It will stop.'

'What possessed you to come out without a proper winter coat? My aunt will kill me if I let you freeze to death.' One of his hands let go of the reins and reached around to undo the buttons on his greatcoat. Then, to her complete shock and mortification, he pulled her backwards so that she was closer to his big, solid body and wrapped the ends of his coat around her protectively. Amelia was instantly, and gratefully, surrounded in his warmth. Instinctively, she turned her chilled body towards his chest and burrowed nearer to the heat, then regretted it instantly when he stiffened.

'I'm sorry,' she muttered as she pulled away. 'I forgot myself. I am just so very cold.'

She heard his breath come out in a ragged sigh. 'It's all right. Warm yourself. Nobody can see.'

He pulled her back under the heavy folds of his coat again and held her close with one arm. Beneath her fingers she felt the muscles on his flat abdomen tense briefly before he forced them to relax, although she was certain she heard his heart quicken. Or perhaps that was just her own heart she could hear? Her pulse had certainly stepped up since he had pulled her closer. But he made no further attempt at conversation.

Silently, he wound his way skilfully through the quiet streets, clearly intent on ignoring Amelia completely. It was difficult not to enjoy the feeling of being held so close to him. Not only did the position ward off the biting cold, but he felt good under her palms. This was not the body of a pampered aristocrat. It was firm and strong. There was muscle beneath the fine clothes that she had not expected to be there. He also smelled deliciously of something male and spicy; the subtle aroma seemed to come directly from beneath his fitted waistcoat and shirt, teasing her nose and making her forget all of the reasons why she disliked him.

'Why were you in Piccadilly?'

His curt voice rumbled against her ear and broke the sensory spell that had apparently bewitched her. She knew where she stood when he was being pompous; it made him easier to deal with, so the lie came smoothly.

'It has been such a long time since I have been back in London, I went on a long walk to see what has changed. I lost track of time.'

He was silent for a moment, then she felt his chest

rise and fall on a deep sigh. 'Whilst you are a guest in my house, Miss Mansfield, I must insist that you do not go out alone again. You have my express permission to take a footman with you whenever or wherever you go. These streets can be dangerous for a woman alone.'

The delivery might have been a bit brusque, but the sentiment was sweet. 'Thank you. I shall do that going forward.' No, she wouldn't. A footman would tell him where she had been.

Another awkward silence prevailed.

'How was your speech?'

'Irritatingly postponed for another week. Apparently, Parliament needed to have a tantrum today, so all important business has had to be delayed. Again.'

His tone, for once, sounded conversational. If he could be friendly, Amelia supposed she could too—in the spirit of their enforced truce.

'A tantrum? That is an interesting turn of phrase.'

He sighed again and the last remnants of his tension seemed to disappear. 'From time to time, or, to be more precise, at least once a week at the moment, the members of both houses feel the need to noisily vent all of their frustrations with the world. When they do, it descends into chaos because so many throw their hat into the ring to shout their opinions loudly.'

'You sound as if you disapprove.'

'I heartily disapprove. It is a waste of everyone's time. Such exchanges never achieve anything. However, it is exactly that sort of nonsense that the newspapers report, so many members play to the gallery in order to get the publicity. That defeats the object of Parliament, in my opinion. It should be a place for educated debate, compromise and purpose—not a circus. It makes it impossible to get anything meaningful done.'

'What got their dander up today?'

'The King's spending habits, or, more specifically, the cost of his extravagant folly in Brighton.'

The papers were filled with outrageous claims about Prinny's Pavilion, detailing the vast cost entailed in building each part and questioning the need for it in the first place. Yet here was one of his cabinet calling it a folly. 'Do you disapprove of that too?'

'The country is drowning in war debts and international trade has virtually collapsed, therefore I can find no justifiable reason why His Royal Highness needs another building for his pleasure.'

His words shocked her. Had he really just criticised the monarch?

'I can see that I have rendered you speechless, Miss Mansfield.' He sounded quite pleased with himself at the feat. She peeked up at him from the cocoon of his coat and saw that he was almost smiling.

'I must confess I am surprised. You are part of his government.'

'I am part of Lord Liverpool's government and, as such, our first and foremost duty is to serve the nation—not the monarch. We had a civil war about it a few hundred years ago now, you might recall. I believe we executed the King as a result.'

That was definitely sarcasm, something else about him that surprised her, but a language that Amelia was happily fluent in. 'But do you serve the nation, sir? Many accuse Parliament of merely feathering its own nest and those of the wealthy gentlemen you represent.'

'Firstly, I sit in the House of Lords, Miss Mansfield,

so nobody has elected me. The only master I loyally serve is my own conscience. I do what I believe is best for the nation, so that England might prosper and its subjects will be happy.'

'However, as a member of the aristocracy, your personal sympathies will be influenced by the plight of your peers because you have no understanding of any other sort of life. You have never experienced poverty or degradation, for example, so I doubt you have as much sympathy for the plight of those less fortunate as you do for your own people.'

'My own people? I believe that I serve the people of Britain, madam—those are *my* people. And it might surprise you to learn that I have eyes and ears, Miss Mansfield. I do see what goes on around me and I am not immune to the poverty and degradation I believe that you are alluding to. My proposal for income tax, for example, which you took particular offence to last night, is a direct response to the plight of the poor.'

As his tone was conciliatory rather than combative, Amelia decided to give him the benefit of the doubt before she ripped his silly proposals to pieces again. 'How so?'

'The main problem of taxation in this country is that it is so piecemeal and indirect. Successive governments have taxed everything from windows to sugar and you are quite right; those taxes have had an awful effect on the poor. What I am proposing is a complete overhaul of the *entire* system. Unfair and indirect taxes would be scrapped and the manner of collecting them, which has been so abused by corrupt officials, would also change. Taxation would be centralised, collected by salaried government tax inspectors and based solely on an individual's personal wealth. Those who have more should pay significantly more.'

When he put it like that it sounded reasonable, but she was not prepared to let him know that just yet. 'Is that what your postponed speech was about?'

'No. That is about the declining state of public health, another cause that the Commons prefer to ignore. I want Parliament to invest some money to clean up the slums.'

'Does their foul stench offend your aristocratic nose?'

'Actually, madam, the unnecessarily high death rate offends my aristocratic sensibilities. If the streets were cleaned, and the unfortunate residents were not forced to live in such squalor, I believe that fewer of them would tragically die so young.'

Amelia was shamed by her own uncharitable assumptions. 'Then I am sorry for what I said about your aristocratic nose.'

A deep chuckle reverberated through him and then her, sending little tingles to the furthest corners of her body in a very pleasant way, and she found herself unconsciously leaning a little closer to him before she stopped herself. Amelia could not remember ever feeling quite so comfortable in such close proximity to another person, let alone a male person—a titled male person with big strong arms. Had she ever been so intimately held by a man? If she had, it clearly had not had such an intoxicating effect on her, else she would have remembered it. Yet it felt strangely comforting and strangely right.

They rode in silence while he manoeuvred the horse around a crowd into a completely deserted street be-

yond. Frozen mist had begun to fall, giving the alleyway an eerie, otherworldly air that made everything
else apart from them seem fuzzy. Even the noisy hus-
tle and bustle of the rest of the city was muted. It felt
as if it were suddenly just the two of them. All alone.

'I did not know that you were familiar with our capital. How long has it been since you were last here?'
His soft, deep voice encouraged her to draw closer still,
perhaps because they were in such close proximity that
he barely had to speak above a whisper.

'Just over a year ago now. I grew up here.' Amelia
winced at her candour. She probably should not have
told him that. Lady Worsted had been quite specific
in her insistence that Amelia should not make things
awkward by mentioning her past to anyone. It made
his next question inevitable.

'Where?'

*Two streets away from you, in a grand house with
servants.* 'From the age of twelve I lived in Cheapside
with my mother.' They had, for a very short while,
while her father plotted and schemed to get his marriage to her mother annulled.

'Does she still live there?'

'She died a few years ago.'

'Ah—I am sorry to hear that. I know how painful it
is to lose a parent. My father died when I was fifteen. I
still miss his guidance.' That was a surprising admission from a man who was so stiff and reserved. He had
feelings, then? She had wondered. 'So that is why you
became a companion? You were alone in the world?'

How did one explain her odd situation? *Technically,
no. I still have a father, although he is determined to
forget that he has a daughter, especially now that the*

law says that he hasn't. The lie he had offered her was
easier than the truth. The truth was so awful it made
her angry just to think about it and Amelia had long
ago promised herself that she would not give Viscount
Venomous the satisfaction of rousing her emotions.
'Yes. I went to work for your aunt. She has been very
good to me.'

Another intimate chuckle rumbled behind his ribcage, which played havoc with her pulse. 'Aunt Augusta is a wonderful woman—although she can be
a bit of a challenge. I think she has frightened off at
least six companions since she was widowed. There
has been a new one every few months. Apparently,
you have proved yourself to be most resilient to have
weathered almost a year. How have you managed it?'

Amelia found herself relaxing again as this topic
was easier to talk about. The rhythmic motion of the
horse's trot, the warmth seeping back into her bones
and the gentle timbre of his soothing, deep voice was
becoming hypnotic. So hypnotic that at some point she
had rested the full weight of her back against his chest
so that his body could form a protective heated cocoon
about her. It might be a tad improper, but it felt far too
good to move just yet. 'Lady Worsted finds me amusing. She says that I am a breath of fresh air.'

'You are certainly nothing like any of her previous
companions. They were all very straitlaced and sensible—which is probably why Aunt Augusta frightened
them off. Much as I adore her, she can be difficult,
outspoken, and has a tendency to be naughty whenever she gets the chance. I never quite know what she
is going to do or say next.'

'I think that is why we get on so well. I also have

a tendency to be a bit unpredictable. I act first and think about it later. I am not particularly straitlaced and sometimes I am not very sensible either.'

'Hence you were out alone, in the dark, without a chaperon. I am sure if my aunt heard about this she would be angry that you had put yourself at risk.' There was no irritation in his voice this time; it had been replaced by a gentler chastisement that was designed to appeal to her conscience rather than a direct order.

'I will try not to do it again,' she said, hoping he would believe her. She had another meeting to attend tomorrow with the factory workers, if she could get away, and they were always desperately short-handed at the soup kitchen.

'That is not the answer I was hoping for. I want to hear the words *I will not do it again.*'

'Now you are splitting hairs. That is exactly what I just said.'

He laughed at her cheekiness. 'I am a politician, Miss Mansfield. I know full well the power of words. The way something is phrased tells me a great deal about a person's intent. Just now, for example, you specifically used the words *I will try.* There is a vast chasm of difference in the meaning of *try* and *will*; therefore that leads me to believe that you have no intention of listening to me at all on the matter.'

'Perhaps...'

'Another response that confirms your lack of commitment. Now I see why you and Aunt Augusta get along so well.'

His easy sarcasm made her giggle. 'Are you suggesting that I am...how did you put it? Difficult, outspoken and naughty?'

Yes, he was and he quite liked those traits, bizarrely.
Perhaps because she was a lady's companion who'd
grown up in Cheapside and was, therefore, completely
off-limits. 'You are certainly unconventional, Miss
Mansfield; I will give you that.'

She was also playing havoc with his nerve endings,
cuddled against his chest, compliant for once and nes-
tled in his lap; those nerve endings were getting lustful ideas again. The temperature might be close to
freezing, the fog creating glistening ice crystals on the
brickwork they passed, but Bennett was hot.

Very hot.

All over.

'I shall take that as a compliment. I would hate to
be considered conventional.'

Her body trembled slightly with her laughter and it
made him wonder if she would tremble with passion
too. It had been a reckless and ill-considered decision
to put her on his horse whilst he still sat on it. As a
gentleman, Bennett probably should have offered the
horse to her and walked home. He certainly should
not have dragged her against him and shared his coat
with her. What he had originally intended as an act of
polite chivalry was now almost torture. Whatever had
possessed him to do so when such things were simply
not done, he could not fathom, aside from the fact that
he had felt the most overwhelming urge to protect her.
Leaving her alone with his horse had been as unacceptable as ignoring her and letting her walk.

Of course, then she had been shivering with such
violence that it had caused him genuine concern. Now
that she was all soft, friendly and warm from the heat
of his body, he knew he would be doomed to think-

ing about how well her rounded bottom fitted between his thighs and how her hair smelled of spring flowers for the rest of the evening—and probably most of the night too. Each time she spoke, her soft breath warmed his chest through his clothing and he wished that there were not quite so many layers of fabric between her lips and his bare skin. Or so many layers between his bare skin and hers.

He definitely needed a wife!

Bennett had never been so grateful to see Berkeley Square as he was when he rounded the corner. Even the mist cleared beneath the glow of the streetlights.

'I should probably walk the rest of the way,' she said, straightening and making them both suddenly self-conscious of their brief impropriety. 'I don't want to cause you a scandal.'

'Indeed,' he said, more stiffly than he intended. Whatever spell they had been under was now broken. The familiar awkwardness swamped him until he could not think of anything else to say, so he steadied her with his arm as she lowered herself to the ground. Her body was trim and small beneath his hand. But rounded and soft and achingly womanly in all of the right places. Bennett wanted to run his big, clumsy hands all over her.

'I shall see you at dinner, *Your Grace.*'

And the way she said that made him want to kiss her smart, impertinent mouth.

Chapter Six

*The perfect young lady never snorts or guffaws—
or, heaven forbid, draws attention to herself when
amused. If she finds something particularly humorous, she will always have the good grace to
cover any unbecoming outburst with her fan...*

The reading salon was an experience. That was the
only way Amelia could think to describe it. The spa-
cious drawing room was positively teeming with ladies,
aside from the brave few gentlemen who had graced
them with their presence. The Duke was not yet one of
them. The Dowager and Lady Worsted held court in the
centre of the room and the other ladies clamoured to
be seated as close to them as they could, like chickens
frantically pecking at freshly thrown corn and twice as
noisy. There must be close to twenty people crammed
into the room, which led Amelia to believe that it was
not quite the 'intimate and cosy meeting of like minds'
she had been promised.

Several extra chairs had to be brought in to accommodate everyone and, sensing that it was likely to be

a very long night, Amelia commandeered one of them and positioned it in the far corner of the room, where she judged few would notice that she intended to while away her time reading something worthwhile. She had tucked a pamphlet on the horrors of child labour inside a copy of Lord Byron's poetry, but Sir George had pulled his chair close to hers, so the factory children would have to wait.

'Is it always this crowded?'

Sir George scanned the eager faces and then smiled. 'To begin with no, but then Bennett began hunting for a wife and all at once we were overrun with eligible young girls who declared an overwhelming interest in the written word. This, my dear Miss Mansfield, is a gathering of a few genuine literary stalwarts, the diehard hopefuls and what is left of the Potential list.'

Now the rush to sit closest to the Duke's mother made perfect sense. 'Who are the lucky five still in contention?'

Sir George crossed one leg over the other and made himself comfortable. 'Why don't we have a bit of fun? You strike me as a very clever girl. See if you can work out who the remaining five are, and if you guess them correctly I shall tell you a bit about each lady.'

'I do love a challenge. But if I guess them correctly I would like to be rewarded with some interesting gossip about the young lady rather than a dull biography.'

'Agreed.'

'All right, then, let me see...'

After reading his silly book, Amelia had a wealth of information about what the Duke would find acceptable when selecting a bride. If any one of these ladies was still on the list, then her demeanour and manners would be perfect. Good posture and a subtle sense of fashion were a prerequisite. The perfect bride would never draw unnecessary attention to herself in bold colours or showy confections. That meant that the young lady wearing the unfortunate frothy dress in a vile shade of orange was definitely just hopeful. Next to her sat a regal blonde in an understated gown that was slightly deeper than powder blue. The colour must have been specifically chosen to complement her fine eyes. Aside from the clothing, the girl also kept subtly glancing towards the doorway. She was looking out for him. 'That one is a Potential. Two chairs left of Her Grace.'

Sir George chuckled, clearly enjoying their game. 'Indeed she is,' he whispered out of the corner of his mouth. 'That is Lady Bulphan's granddaughter Priscilla. Good breeding there, or so I am led to believe. Flawless reputation. Even-tempered.'

'That is hardly interesting gossip. She sounds dull.'

'Oh, she is, my dear. Dreadfully dull. There really is nothing else to say about her.' Sir George was clearly unimpressed with Priscilla. 'Except that her father is also a member of Liverpool's cabinet and a valuable political ally.'

'The lady with the reddish blonde hair next to Lady Worsted is also one from the list.'

Sir George shot her an impressed glance. 'What gave her away?'

'She is hanging on the Dowager's every word like a loyal puppy, yet Her Grace is merely requesting that the footman needs to bring in more chairs.'

'That is Lady Eugenie. She is the daughter of a marquis and very eager to please. Now that you come to mention it, with all those ringlets she does resemble a spaniel. I had never noticed it before. You are very astute, Miss Mansfield. Rumour has it that Lady Eugenie's grandmother was a simple farmer's daughter, although, as yet, there is no proof of such a scandalous association.'

'Good gracious—a farmer's daughter! I am surprised the Duke even speaks to her.'

'Ah, but her father is the ambassador to Holland and England does a lot of trade with the Dutch East India Company.'

It was easy to spot the next two. Both were blonde, politically well connected, dressed in pastels, and both were clutching well-thumbed copies of *The Discerning Gentleman's Guide to Selecting the Perfect Bride.* Amelia took an instant dislike to both ladies for grovelling. 'Please tell me that we are not going to be subjected to passages from your nephew's book?'

'I dare say one or two pertinent chapters might be dissected. They usually are if Bennett makes an appearance.' Amelia's face must have given her away. 'Is your disapproval for Bennett or his admirers?'

'His admirers. Obviously.' How on earth could a man write such narrow-minded, nearsighted drivel? Now that she knew him a little better, some of those words felt a little at odds with the author. It seemed implausible that a man who dealt in important affairs of state, and spoke so passionately about cleaning up the slums, would seek a wife who parroted his own book back at him in order to catch his eye. Surely he would prefer a clever girl? 'It strikes me as desperate to lower oneself by grovelling for attention in such an obvious way. I dislike sycophants.'

'Ah.' Sir George was watching her in blatant disbelief, his eyes dancing with mischief. 'And pompous
dukes who write etiquette manuals, perhaps?'

Amelia ignored him and went back to studying the
women in the room to cover her unease. Why was she
so bothered that those silly girls were intent on fawn-
ing over him so pathetically? If he enjoyed that kind of
attention, then it confirmed all of her worst fears about
the man. Then he would be shallow and self-absorbed,
even though she had seen the tiniest glimpse that he
might not be, and that bothered her.

Conscious of Sir George's scrutiny, Amelia redou-
bled her efforts to unmask the remaining Potential.
After several minutes of surreptitious study, she was
forced to admit defeat. 'I have no idea who the fifth is.'

'Lady Cecily is not here yet. She likes to make an
entrance. She won't arrive until the readings have
started or until she has judged that Bennett might be
here.'

'That way, he will have to turn to look at her.'

'Precisely.' He looked very impressed. 'It also means
that she can position herself closest to him. I quite admire her industry. In fact, *industry* is quite a pertinent
word for her. Her father is a powerful industrialist and
as rich as Croesus too. Owns ships, factories, deals in
stocks and bonds. He is a great supporter of Bennett's
political aspirations.'

'Is she blonde too?' The Duke clearly had a penchant for them. Even Lady Eugenie erred more on the
side of reddish blonde than ginger. Sir George regarded
Amelia thoughtfully for a moment.

'She is.' Of course she was. He would marry someone golden like him, and they would go about making

perfect, angelic, aristocratic, golden children to match. 'Does that bother you?'

Amelia stiffened at the suggestion. 'Why on earth should his choice of bride bother me? I have no interest in the outcome.' Sir George began to smirk knowingly, but fortunately further conversation was prevented by the Dowager calling the gathering to order.

'Good evening, everyone! We have a feast of entertainment this evening and so many of us that I doubt that we shall have time to get through it all. Our first reading is from Lady Eugenie.'

The slightly ginger blonde stood up and began to read a passage about unrequited love from a novel. It was clearly intended to be a declaration of her affections to the absent duke. Once the dramatic reading ended, one or two observers asked a few polite questions and they moved on to the next. Several dreary but heartfelt presentations followed that soon bored Amelia to tears. Certain that nobody was paying any attention to her, she quietly opened the book in her lap and began to read her pamphlet.

It was some time later when she felt a distinct shift in the atmosphere. A quick glance upwards confirmed her suspicions. The Duke of Aveley had arrived. He might well have meant to slip in quietly, but there was no mistaking the sound of rustling petticoats and creaking corsets as the unattached ladies suddenly sat up a little straighter, their eyes widened falsely to show them off to their best advantage and small secret smiles were pasted on their apparently rapt faces as they listened to the poem being read to them. One by one, they stole a glance at him, hoping to catch his eye, yet all to no avail. The only person he deigned to look at was his mother as he quietly ensconced himself against the wall closest to the door, looking every bit like a man ready to bolt at the first opportunity that presented itself. A position, Amelia noted, that was perfect for observing the Potentials, as if they were prime horse-flesh and he was a buyer at Tattersalls. Dispassionate. Objective. Removed.

In case he caught her eye and assumed that she was also competing for his attention, Amelia quickly focused again on her pamphlet, risking only the occasional peek beneath her lashes at the golden Duke assessing his harem. He paid no woman particular attention, she noticed, watching them all with polite indifference. The Duke of Aveley clearly did not feel the need to woo anyone. The Potentials, on the other hand, fell over themselves to out-simper and out-primp their rivals. There was so much batting of eyes that Amelia was surprised that she did not feel a breeze from all of the exertion. Yet he took it all arrogantly in his stride as if this attention was nothing less than he was due.

A few minutes later, a blonde goddess burst through the door, dressed in seashell-pink silk and clutching a slim leather volume to her chest. This must be Lady Cecily, then. Her attempt at looking flustered did not fool Amelia one bit. There was a cold, hard look of calculation in the young woman's eyes as she glanced at His Royal Pomposity. 'I hope I have not interrupted anything?'

Oh, no, you don't, thought Amelia uncharitably. *You would enjoy nothing more than distracting any attention away from another young lady.* She shared a meaningful glance with Sir George, who must have thought much the same because his usually smiling mouth was a little pursed.

'Not at all,' said the Dowager. 'We had just finished discussing a poem, my dear.'

'Perhaps I should read next, then? As I am already standing?' Lady Cecily bestowed her sweetest smile towards their hostess. 'Unless you had already selected someone to go next?' When nobody else spoke up, she opened her book at the page that she had marked with a ribbon. Although not before she had placed her perfectly proportioned figure in the Duke's direct line of vision.

'Here we go again,' muttered Sir George quietly into Amelia's ear. It was only then that she noticed Lady Cecily's choice of literature and inwardly groaned. She was going to shamelessly read from *The Discerning Gentleman's Drivel.*

It started innocuously enough, but the moment the other Potentials began to listen to Lady Cecily's rendition of the Almighty's words, with expressions of awe and wonder on their pretty faces, Amelia decided to go back to her pamphlet. They might wish to worship at the altar of Aveley, but she had no intention of humouring them while they did so. Valiantly, she tried to shut out the sounds, but snippets kept permeating into her brain and curdling her stomach until she thought she might burst from the effort of it all.

All accomplished young ladies should read. However, their choice of literature is telling. Most novels are acceptable, so too are books filled with illustrations of flora and fauna. A young

*lady's mind should not be filled with anything too
scientific or academic to comprehend...*

Amelia rolled her eyes. Unfortunately, in her irritation she had also snorted. Quite loudly, it seemed. All
eyes in the room suddenly swivelled towards hers in-
credulously. Lady Worsted tried, and failed, to stifle a
grin. Lady Cecily-With-Potential paused and positively
glared at her, and even the Duke himself honoured her
with a glance. One of his eyebrows lifted in question
but, to his credit, he appeared more amused than insulted by her unintentional outburst.

'Did you have something to add, Miss Mansfield?'

The wretch asked this with a completely straight
face. Demurely shaking her head and then pretending
to cough made a knot of unpleasantness form in Amelia's gullet, but she did it for the sake of Lady Worsted. 'I apologise for the interruption—I had a frog in
my throat. Please *do* continue.' For good measure she
smiled sweetly at Lady Cecily even though her stomach tightened in protest.

The Potential smiled politely back at her, but there
were daggers shooting from her blue eyes.

*It is essential that a good wife has a basic knowl-
edge of politics. As your hostess, she will need
to ask pertinent questions designed to stimulate
worthy discussion between your male guests...*

'Pah!'

Amelia truly had intended to keep quiet, but the
sound came out of its own accord, fuelled by her growing annoyance at the man's imperiousness and the pa-

thetic adoration of his women. Next to her, she heard Sir George muffle a giggle and would have nudged him firmly in the ribs were it not for the fact that she was the centre of attention again.

'Come now, Miss Mansfield. You obviously have something to say. We all insist that you say it.'

The Duke's expression was still bland, but there was something swirling in his silvery blue eyes. Challenge? Humour? Sarcasm? Well, if he was going to have unreadable eyes, then she would have no option but to meet the challenge.

'As you have asked, Your Grace, I would like some clarification of your intent in that passage. I am curious to know which topics you feel the female sex would have trouble comprehending.'

Chapter Seven

A wife's first duty is to obey her husband. There-
fore it is the husband's first duty to enlighten her
as to what he wants her to do...

The minx had neatly put him on the spot and Bennett
was damned if some tiny part of him didn't admire her
for it. Every head in the room, the majority of them female, was now turned towards him expectantly. Only
a few of them were waiting for his wisdom. The rest,
Uncle George and Aunt Augusta included, were waiting for him to fall flat on his arse. His aunt was suck-
ing in her cheeks to prevent herself from grinning; it
made her look as if she had just swallowed a lemon.

Why had Lady Cecily read from his book? Although
he hated it, it happened, he was forced to admit, far
too frequently because the Potentials believed that
he would be pleased to hear his, or in actual fact his
father's, words spewing from their pretty lips. Bennett would have preferred they read something—anything—else in the hope that it would give him a clue
as to whether or not they were in any way compatible

with him. Did any of them share his taste in literature? Did they prefer poems to essays? Marlowe to Shakespeare? Novels or newspapers? Hearing his own words read back to him with such reverence always made him want to cringe with embarrassment and told him nothing about the lady spouting them, other than the fact that she was keen to be his wife. But how could *he* be keen to marry any of them if they remained virtual strangers to him? And Lady Cecily had inadvertently given the outspoken Miss Mansfield the perfect opportunity to hoist him with his own petard. He would need to formulate his answer carefully.

'I think, perhaps, my choice of phrasing was unfortunate in that instance, Miss Mansfield. It is not so much that a woman would have difficulty comprehending a specific topic, rather that there are certain *unsavoury* topics that I would protect them from. Politics, for example, can be quite cut-throat. Tempers are often high, which makes it a challenging environment for most ladies. They might become upset or feel threatened by the forceful masculine way of discussing such matters.'

The Potentials nodded back at him in agreement, their limpid eyes grateful for his thoughtfulness on their behalf, like a quintet of marionettes all controlled by one puppeteer. It was most disconcerting. Now he was thinking of them as puppets? *Good grief!*

Miss Mansfield did not look so delighted with his response.

'I see. That is interesting because in another chapter you also say that *"the perfect wife supports worthy good causes with her charity. She needs to fully*

*understand which causes are the worthiest so that she
can guide her fellow women in the right direction".*

She paused for effect, like the greatest of orators.

'How can the perfect wife achieve such a feat if you
are to shield her from the harsh realities of life, and
politics in particular? Surely a solid understanding of
politics is essential in such an endeavour?'

Had she just quoted his words back to him verba-
tim, and without the benefit of his book in front of
her? He really had not expected that, but he recognised
the words because his father had repeated them often
enough. Clearly Miss Mansfield had a memory that an
elephant would envy. She also, Devil take her, made
a valid point. When Bennett had written the book he
had merely been recording snippets of advice handed
down by his father. He had not considered that different pieces of advice might contradict one another.

While Bennett struggled to formulate a suitable answer to save himself from looking stupid, his uncle
had given up trying to hide his delight at the turn the
evening had taken. He was openly grinning, his eyes
crinkled with amusement. The traitor even went as far
as patting Miss Mansfield on the back for her insight.

'You are quite right, Miss Mansfield,' he admitted reluctantly. 'When compared side by side, those
two chapters would seem to give a confused message.'
Bennett was a renowned diplomat. He could save this.
'However, many books might seem to offer conflicting
advice if passages are taken out of context. The Bible,
for instance, in Exodus tells us that it is wrong to kill.
Thou shalt not kill. That is the sixth commandment.
Yet Exodus also tells us that it is permissible, under

God's holy law, to take a life for a life, eye for an eye and a tooth for a tooth.'

Miss Mansfield blinked at his logic and he thought, for a moment, he had won this battle of wits. But, like a cobra, when she struck it came out of the blue and her bite was deadly.

'How interesting. Are you now comparing your own words, Your Grace, with the words of God?'

Bennett's jaw dropped and for several painful moments he simply stood there, frozen, except for his mouth, which was opening and closing of its own volition, much like that of a reeled fish. 'Well…well…of course not!' he finally stuttered. 'I was simply making the point that isolated passages of text, when taken out of their proper context, might appear to contradict each other.' He felt like a fool—yet he also enjoyed the challenge she presented. What a magnificent politician he would be if he could effectively spar with her and win! Unfortunately, tonight she had bested him because he could not think of a single response that would put her firmly back in her place. Given half a chance, it was now quite apparent she would eat him alive. 'But your point is well made, Miss Mansfield. And thank you, Lady Cecily, you honour me by selecting a passage of mine to read here tonight although, I must confess, I would rather hear a passage from a great writer than my amateurish scribblings. Lady Priscilla, what have you chosen to read?'

Lady Priscilla obediently jumped to attention and began reciting some awful poem that served to take the focus away from him. For several minutes he pretended she held his complete attention until everyone in the room was similarly engaged. Only then did he risk a glance at Miss Mansfield. He caught her shamelessly staring at him. Despite the fact that she had just made him look a fool, his breeches started to become a trifle snug. His pride had just taken a serious dent, so what his groin had to be happy about he could not fathom. He had been outmanoeuvred by a common woman.

In public.

Because of his own arrogant stupidity.

Up until that moment, he had not even considered that his father's advice was contradictory. He had never had cause to question it before, and as much of it had been given in the weeks leading up to his father's death it seemed disloyal to do so now. But how could he expect a wife to lead the charge in supporting the worthiest causes if she was kept in the dark about politics? On that matter, as much as it pained him to consider it, clearly his father had been wrong and Bennett should have spotted the error before he consigned it to perpetuity in print. *Touché*, he mouthed silently across the room.

Miss Mansfield offered him a saucy shrug alongside her smug smile, then buried her nose back into her own book unapologetically. It gave Bennett the rare opportunity to study her properly. Or, more importantly, an opportunity to try to understand his own unexpected reaction to her. Arguably, this room was filled with the most desirable young ladies of the ton. His five remaining Potentials were too polite to risk reading while others were speaking. All of them were very pretty, very accomplished and perfectly bred young women. Any one of them would make him a perfect wife. Why was it then that his thoughts, as well as his gaze, kept creeping back to Miss Mansfield?

For a start, he reasoned, she looked nothing like them. Her dark hair and soulful dark eyes were not exactly fashionable, yet her beauty made the other women in the room pale in comparison. She also did not appear to pay him any particular regard, which was not merely unusual, it was unheard of. Worse, the woman went out of her way to bait him. It was plainly obvious that she had thoroughly enjoyed besting him. The other young ladies would be mortified to have intentionally caused him offence. Miss Mansfield revelled in it. Maybe that was why she fascinated him? She was so different to every other woman of his acquaintance and she certainly did not behave like them. Despite the fact that she'd been raised in Cheapside and worked for a living, she was heartily unimpressed by his title or his position in the government. Yet he wanted her to be impressed.

That was an interesting thought. He *wanted* to impress her. How very…unusual.

Bennett could not remember ever having felt the need to impress a woman before. He could also never remember engaging in an intellectual argument with a woman before. Yet just now, just as she had that first evening at dinner, and when he'd foolishly ridden home with her, Miss Mansfield had asked him genuinely challenging questions that made him think. Perhaps his attraction to her was not a purely physical thing, as he had hoped? There was a distinct possibility that he admired her quick, clever mind as well as the alternative perspective she put on things. She certainly would be a match for some of the braying idiots who sat with him in Parliament. Just thinking about her

giving one of those pompous fools a proper set-down
made him smile.

Inadvertently, he found his gaze repeatedly wandering back to the maddening Miss Mansfield. When
he realised that his uncle was staring back at him
with great interest, Bennett let the silly smile slide
off his face and pretended to concentrate on the reading. Keeping his eyes trained forward proved to be
quite a challenge and when Lovett finally interrupted
him with their prearranged urgent message he almost
hugged his servant with gratitude for providing him
with an escape.

Chapter Eight

It is important that a lady knows how to behave in every social situation. Chaos will ensue if rank and social etiquette are not strictly adhered to...

The Renshaw ball was every bit the crush Lady Worsted had promised. From her position with the matrons and wallflowers, Amelia happily watched all of the dancers twirling about the floor in all of their finery. She had never seen so many different shades of silk in one place, nor so many feathers. Lady Worsted was sporting a vivid custard-coloured ostrich concoction that added at least ten inches to her height. And it was not the most impressive headdress in the room. That feat went to the hostess herself. Lady Renshaw sprouted so many plumes that it might have been easier just to sit a peacock on her head and be done with it. Every time she turned, the woman inadvertently tickled someone else's nose with it.

And the dancing! The tiny, shallow part of her that was still aristocratic envied all of the beautiful gowns and the way that they drew attention to the young ladies

wearing them. She marvelled at the way they moved
in unison as they gracefully performed all manner of
intricate steps. As a child, her mother had taught her
some of them, so Amelia recognised the cotillion and
a few of the country dances, but she had no idea what
was currently being performed on the floor. Her eye
kept wandering to the Duke and his most recent partner, Lady Priscilla. He performed the steps excep-
tionally well, managing to look graceful yet entirely
masculine. Each time he and Priscilla came together
they exchanged pleasantries. Priscilla hung on his
every word. The Duke looked bored.

Amelia supposed that being so adored must become
wearing. From the moment they had all arrived in the
ballroom, a veritable swarm of brightly coloured young
ladies had gravitated towards him, eyelashes fluttering
and fans flapping, and he had politely, if a little indif-
ferently, greeted them all in the same way. Even the
Potentials. Except he had made a point of adding his
name to each of their dance cards. Not that she wanted
him to, nor was she jealous, but it had not occurred to
him to scratch his name on Amelia's empty card, even
for the sake of politeness. But then again, why would
he? She was little better than a servant and, as far as he
knew, there was nothing aristocratic about her. He was
also probably still sulking over her comments at the
reading salon earlier in the week, and they had scarcely
exchanged more than two words since that night.

The orchestra struck up the highly anticipated first
chords of the waltz and the dancers hurried to reach
their new partners. His Royal Highness the Duke of
Pomposity bowed to Lady Priscilla and escorted her

to her mother and then began to make his way towards their group slowly.

'Miss Mansfield, would you do this old man a favour and take him for a spin around the dance floor?' Sir George had already taken her hand as if it were a foregone conclusion that she would accept him.

'I can't waltz,' she admitted quietly. 'I have never been taught it.'

'If you can count to three, then you can waltz. I taught Bennett to waltz in five minutes flat. It is not a complicated dance. Besides, it is the gentleman's duty to lead. Any mistakes will be immediately attributed to me and every girl should waltz at her first ball.' As they were already at the edge of the dance floor, further argument was futile and Amelia was secretly delighted to have been asked to dance at least once, even if her partner was old enough to be her father and only asking her to be kind.

Sir George surreptitiously positioned her arms correctly and began to count the rhythm as he swayed her from side to side. 'One-two-three, one-two-three, one-two-three. That's it, my dear; now we shall attempt a slow turn.' He continued his helpful whispered count while Amelia picked up the steps and, before she knew it, she was gliding around the floor almost as skilfully as the others.

'This is easy!' She could not prevent herself from beaming at him. 'You are an excellent teacher, Sir George. I almost feel graceful.'

'And you make me the envy of all of the other gentlemen here. Already I can see that a few young men have stolen a sneaky glance at you, all wondering who you are and if you are taken.'

She rolled her eyes at his silly comments. 'I am a lady's companion, Sir George, and not in the league of all of these beautiful young ladies. But your compliment is very well received regardless.'

'Nonsense. Once we have finished, I predict that all the young bucks will be queuing up to dance with you and then I shall be left to watch with Her Grace and Augusta.' He pretended to find that prospect dire, but he had not left the ladies' sides all evening, save this one dance.

'Do you mind if I ask a personal question?'

He grinned wolfishly in response and Amelia realised he must have been quite irresistible in his prime. 'Ask away, my dear.'

'Why did you never marry? As the brother of a duke, you must have been quite eligible.'

'Ah—' he sighed as he twirled her '—I came close once, but I was enjoying the bachelor lifestyle too much. I was quite a rake in my day.' Amelia could well believe that. Even now, with his hair grey and a slight paunch, he was still a very distinguished-looking gentleman. A lot like his nephew in many ways—tall, blue-eyed, square-jawed—although nowhere near as irritating. 'When my brother died, while dear Bennett was still so young, I stepped into the breach as a male guardian of sorts and I have stayed that way ever since. They are my family now. Bennett is like my own son.' His eyes briefly flicked warmly towards the Dowager and Amelia realised that it was perhaps not only *dear* Bennett who made him stay. 'It is an odd arrangement, but one that suits us well enough.'

with vitriol. It made no difference that each successive pregnancy and subsequent miscarriage had made her weaker, nor did he notice the vibrant light go out of her eyes as she had withdrawn further into herself in her desperate attempt to please the man she still loved. By then, he had wanted shot of his barren wife and had stopped at nothing to ensure that he got his way.

In the end, he had happily sacrificed his only daughter to do it and then washed his hands of the pair of them. The hastily, but conveniently, procured annulment not only erased the marriage, it erased Amelia's legitimacy. Of course, because the law was a complete ass, that also meant her father cheerfully kept the tiny fortune that his former wife had brought to the marriage without even considering that immoral. Amelia's American grandparents were dead and their beautiful daughter had long been forgotten by Philadelphia society. What difference did it make if he kept the money? It had become his money the very moment that they'd married and he had done his best to be a good husband. It was hardly his fault that Amelia's mother had let him down. Viscounts needed heirs, after all—any gentleman would understand that. Perhaps this new wife would be better at doing her duty?

The young Viscountess was obviously keen to make a good impression on the Dowager Duchess of Aveley. 'Your son is a truly great statesman, Your Grace. I know that my husband is a great admirer of his work. He has supported him in the House on numerous occasions.'

Her father only supported causes that feathered his own nest, but he was no fool. Viscount Venomous knew the importance of keeping on the right side of those who wielded power. It made her feel a little queasy to think of the Duke exchanging polite conversation or, worse, camaraderie with her awful father. That really would be unforgivable—but not beyond the realms of possibility. They were both lords and her father also had very definite opinions on what did and did not make a good wife. And choosing the wrong one or, as her father had, a barren one was unthinkable. How had the Duke put it in his stupid book?

Such a wife will ultimately turn out to be a hindrance to you and you will rue the day you entered into the Blessed Union.

The Duke of Aveley, like all titled men, would probably feel sympathetic towards her father and condone the despicable course of action he'd taken to remedy the situation. She felt a stab of pity for the future Duchess of Aveley. That unfortunate woman would have a great deal to live up to.

'I am sure Bennett is grateful for the support. These are taxing times for the government. He spends a great deal of time trying to convince his fellow lords to support his policies. If only a few more of them were as reasonable and supportive as your husband.' The Dowager was smiling warmly at the interloper and Amelia desperately wanted to contradict the good opinion she held of her father—but to do so would be churlish and impertinent and against Lady Worsted's express instructions.

'It is such a shame that they have not had the opportunity to discuss your son's ideas in greater depth. Conversation in Parliament or at a ball is always so brief. Would you think me too forward if I extended an invitation for you all to dine one evening at Bray House? I know my husband would be grateful to hear more of His Grace's plans.'

Amelia knew a great deal about Viscount Venomous's politics and was quite certain that it did not extend to philanthropic ideas such as cleaning up the slums. However, her father would see it as a great coup to have the influential Duke of Aveley sitting at his table, and obviously his young wife knew it.

'I should like that. However, I will have to check with Bennett. His commitments to Parliament are quite excessive at the moment and he struggles to find the time to attend too many social engagements. If you forward an invitation to the House, then I am sure that he will consider it.'

Her mother's replacement was not prepared to give up the prize that easily. 'Better still, why don't we wait until the man in question returns and I will ask him when it would be convenient?' The Dowager's eyes widened slightly at the young woman's presumptuousness, but she nodded her agreement nevertheless. 'If I go and fetch my husband now, I am certain we can agree on a suitably convenient date.'

Amelia felt sick. Throughout the entire exchange she had not considered the fact that her father was here. The very last person she ever wanted to see again was that man. Despite that, she had carefully planned what she would say to him if their paths ever crossed again. There had been many years to perfect the exact words that she wanted to say to him. The speech was short and to the point.

You robbed my mother of her soul and her fortune

and then you cast her out with nothing. Her blood is on your hands.

But here, in a room full of people and in the company of the Dowager and Sir George, she was not entirely sure that she was strong enough to face him. Not without being adequately prepared and with her heart hardened. She did not want to allow sadness or anger to cause her words to falter. She would not give him that satisfaction. At this precise moment, tears were already prickling the corners of her eyes and she would never cry in front of him.

Worse still, he would not take her presence well. There would very probably be a horrendous scene, furious words would be exchanged and it would be Amelia who would ultimately suffer. To protect a fellow aristocrat, she would be unceremoniously removed from the ballroom and might even end up losing her job. Whilst Lady Worsted knew who her father was and was accepting of that fact, the scandal that surrounded the end of his marriage to her mother would likely be enough to encourage the Duke to insist that his aunt sever all ties with her. That was why Lady Worsted had insisted on secrecy, after all—to protect her precious nephew from the taint of any scandal. Amelia would be left with nothing, again, and be forced to pick up the shattered pieces of her life for a third time. If she had to confront her father, it must be on her terms and at a time of her choosing. This was not it.

As soon as the Viscountess hurried away, Amelia excused herself from the Dowager and Sir George and rushed from the ballroom with her face cast down. There was no question that her father might not recognise her if he happened to see her. Even after four years, he would know her instantly. Amelia was the mirror image of her mother. It was one of the reasons he had grown to dislike her so very much. And that feeling was mutual.

Only when she was certain there was nobody watching did she dart down a dark corridor. She needed a few minutes alone to calm herself, then she would find Lady Worsted and tell her why she had to leave. Her employer, she knew, would help her to escape.

She soon found herself in a darkened parlour. Realising that she was far too agitated to simply sit, Amelia grabbed a folded woollen lap blanket from one of the chairs, draped it tightly around her shoulders and let herself out of the French windows that overlooked the garden. A walk might soothe her frayed nerves and give her time to think about her unexpected predicament. Fortunately, she still had the presence of mind to leave the door slightly ajar before she stalked briskly into the cold winter night, but even at that brisk pace the unpleasant memories still chased her into the garden.

Chapter Nine

*The sensible gentleman does not select his bride
with haste. Take your time, compare the lady with
many others, and the superior attributes of the
most suitable candidate will quickly make themselves apparent...*

Bennett stared up at the stars and sighed. This was
not how he had expected things to be. For over a year
he had stalwartly taken his father's advice and done
his best to find himself the perfect wife—and he was
apparently no closer to finding her than he had been
at the start. Only then he had been hopeful. He had
followed every sensible edict to the letter, so keen to
honour the memory of his father by marrying a woman
whom he would have chosen to be his daughter-in-
law, yet now it was his own lack of enthusiasm that
appeared likely to sabotage all of that hard work. A
lack of enthusiasm for the seemingly perfect women
he had found and, if he was completely honest with
himself, a selfish refusal to settle for something that
did not feel intrinsically right for him. Priscilla, Cecily

and the other Potentials met every one of his father's criteria—but he did not feel a single drop of passion for any one of them. If he never saw any of them ever again, he doubted he would even notice their absence. Surely that was not right?

Yet Miss Mansfield, with her sharp tongue and common connections, already occupied his thoughts far more than those other women had collectively managed in over a year. She also reminded him that he was just a man. So often nowadays he was so busy trying to be the perfect politician that he had forgotten that he was a man first and, as such, prone to the basic urges that all of God's creatures had in common. The most obvious manifestation of this realisation was lust. He experienced it every single time he saw her and almost every time he thought of her. Which, he conceded, was rather a lot. Bennett could not recall any other woman who ever had that effect on him. But lust was only part of his problem.

For some inexplicable reason, the arrival of Miss Mansfield in his life made him feel somehow dissatisfied with it. He felt lonely. An odd emotion that he had never, ever considered before, yet he recognised it for what it was. It was so overpowering that it threatened to swamp him. Worse, Bennett had realised that he had been achingly lonely for years. Suddenly, he desperately wished that he had somebody to share his life with—not just an adjunct that he called his wife. The future Duchess of Aveley had to be more than that. He wanted someone whom he could share the daily trials and tribulations with, someone to laugh with and argue with. Wake up with. Talk to. He could not imagine that person ever being one of the women he had thus far considered as his potential bride.

It might well have been foolhardy and ill-considered, but the thing he had enjoyed most about the ride home with his aunt's companion had been the enforced intimacy. If he ignored the surge of desire he had experienced, the conversation had been a revelation. Already he knew that Miss Mansfield had a keen sense of right and wrong, had made the best of her life after the tragic death of her mother and was fiercely independent. The woman had strong opinions and was not afraid to voice them. It was so refreshing *not* to be agreed with all of the time. Miss Mansfield certainly made no attempts to court his good opinion and he quite admired her for that too. He found sparring with her hugely entertaining—which meant that already she was far more intriguing and interesting than any of the Potentials. Totally unsuitable, of course, because there were just too many things about Miss Mansfield that clashed with everything he fundamentally needed his future wife to be. But definitely intriguing.

However, his reaction to her had provided him with food for thought. His perfect wife needed attributes he had not previously considered and his father had not foreseen. Her own opinions, within reason, some sort of uniquely defining aspect of personality that set her apart from all other women and a fondness for sarcasm. And he wanted to desire her. That attribute now had to be top of his list because his hunger for Miss Mansfield would not go away unless he could find another woman that he wanted in his bed as much as he did her.

Which left him, frustratingly, right back where he'd started and no closer to finding a suitable wife now than he was when he had foolishly written that blasted book. Miss Mansfield had even managed to sully his father's sensible advice. From the moment he had been born, Bennett had relied on those knowledgeable words to steer him. Once she had pointed out that single contradiction, he had found more. The book was most descriptive on the importance of manners, good breeding and the role of a dutiful wife but made no mention of qualities that he now personally wished for in his marriage. Like mutual interests, a shared sense of humour and desire. If he did not find any of the Potentials even remotely interesting, what would they spend a lifetime talking about? Or would they coexist under the same roof in polite indifference? In which case, was he doomed to feel lonely for ever? Surely a marriage should be more than that? Surely his parents' marriage had been more than that?

But his father had always stated that emotions were a woman's indulgence and that Bennett should not waste any time on them. But, no matter how hard he had tried to suppress that aspect of his character, to his eternal shame he experienced them nevertheless.

He always had.

Unlike his father, Bennett had always felt things keenly. Anger, injustice, compassion, frustration, happiness, lust and now loneliness. Feelings that bubbled under the surface despite his very best efforts not to acknowledge them. At times the effort of holding them back was almost too much and Bennett feared that, like a volcano, those silly emotions might one day all erupt simultaneously, leaving him looking foolish, completely exposed and vulnerable. What would his pragmatic, sensible father have made of that? He would have been horrified. Ashamed. Disappointed. And his legacy would crumble like dust.

Yet the more he considered it all, how exactly were those feelings wrong? They were basic, essential human emotions that shaped the character of the nation. Life would be dull and bland indeed if everybody ruthlessly masked them and did everything quietly and politely. In which case, his father had either neglected to tell his son how to best deal with his own emotional responses—or, worse, might *not* have considered that such things were, in fact, very important. Surely a good politician, a good servant of the people, should feel deeply about things that mattered—or else why bother?

And if his father's advice was not entirely trustworthy, what else had the man got wrong? Had he sent Bennett down the wrong path? All of these doubts and questions about his own personality and fundamental beliefs left him feeling guilty. What sort of a son was he to question a man so respected by his peers that his words were still quoted by the great and the good in Parliament almost fifteen years after his death?

Not a worthy one.

Frustrated, he sat heavily on a bench; the marble was freezing and instantly chilled him. Bennett welcomed the uncomfortable sensation. At least it gave him something physical to take his mind off his emotional turmoil. A refreshing chill might be just what he needed to help clear his mind.

Amelia reached the end of the ornamental garden and decided that she was being ridiculous. Not only was it freezing, but she was delaying the practical. The quicker she found Lady Worsted, the quicker she could escape this ball and ensure that she continued to avoid her father and the misery that thinking about him created. Meeting him again would serve no purpose. It was too late for revenge—not that she would not wish to see the man suffer, but because it would not change the past. And it was in the past.

Her father was consigned to her past; he had no part in her future. Amelia had a new life, one she had built for herself and that she enjoyed. So what if she had missed out on balls and finery? She had filled that gap with education and good deeds. Her life was filled with purpose, unlike her mother's had been. Her mother had gone to the grave hoping that her husband would want her back. Amelia would never allow herself to appear pathetically desperate for a man's affection or be a victim of his scorn.

If she had been sensible, she should have realised that there was bound to be the possibility of colliding with the Viscount now that she was mixing with the ton again. Her father rarely left London and he did like to socialise. The prospect had not really occurred to her because Amelia had seen the hateful man only a handful of times since her twelfth birthday, and had not actually set eyes on him in four years. Or heard from him. Even after her mother had died in the workhouse, he had not made any attempt to check on his daughter. As far as he knew, she might also be dead and buried in that sorry excuse for a graveyard in Seven Dials. He probably wished that she was. All of those nasty loose ends from his regrettable marriage to an unsuitable woman would be neatly tied up. All chance of scandal and gossip would be gone. The fact that she had thwarted him in something cheered her.

Amelia wound her way around some ruthlessly clipped bushes and stopped dead. Sitting on a bench on the path back to the house was the Duke. After a moment of dithering, she darted back behind the cover of the shrubbery. She could hardly go breezing past him as if it were perfectly normal to go strolling around a strange garden wrapped in a blanket. He would want to know why she was out here and Amelia had no desire to tell him another lie.

Except there was something about his posture that bothered her. Those gloriously broad shoulders were definitely slumped and he had a faraway look on his handsome face that appeared, from this distance, to be sad. Much as she wanted to avoid him, his lost expression called to the Good Samaritan inside her. She had always hated seeing anyone upset; it was in her nature to try to make things better. He had come to her aid in Piccadilly; her conscience reminded her that it was only right that she returned the kindness.

'I see that you are hiding too.'

Her voice startled him and his head snapped up sharply.

'I was merely taking some air. The ballroom is unnecessarily stuffy.' He appeared to be embarrassed to have been caught and stood up. His military posture returned instantly. Those impressive shoulders were pulled back and he clasped his hands stiffly behind his back. The man was so wooden and formal sometimes that it made him quite difficult to talk to. Had she not seen another side of him in Piccadilly, she might have simply bid him a good evening and continued towards the house. But she now knew him to be occasionally kind and quite thoughtful underneath all of that stiffness, and she had definitely just caught him hiding. She would persevere and extend the hand of friendship, and in doing so would avoid going back into that awful ballroom just a little while longer.

'Well, I am hiding. I feel a little out of my depth in that grand ballroom.'

That admission appeared to confuse him. Amelia could tell that his human side felt compelled to sympathise, while the duke in him wanted to ignore it. He was still standing ramrod-straight, but his feet shifted from side to side indecisively while the two halves of his personality went to war. After a few moments the human won.

'I needed to get some air.' He unclasped his hands and exhaled deeply, then stared out into the darkness. 'It seemed to me that you were enjoying yourself. Especially when you were waltzing with Uncle George.'

'It was very kind of him to dance with me. But I do not belong in a ballroom and I am certain everybody in there knows that. Companions are not meant to dance.' Perhaps telling him that would spare her from attending any other grand social functions while she remained in London, thereby eliminating any possible chance of colliding with her father.

'You hid your discomfort well. I never would have guessed you felt out of place.' His eyes turned to hers briefly before fixing back on whatever it was he was looking at so intently in the distance. Clearly, basic conversation was not something he felt particularly comfortable with, but perhaps it was simply that he was uncomfortable to be conversing with someone so

socially inferior. Companions were not meant to be-
friend dukes—that he might also think so rankled.

'Would it be impertinent for a mere companion to
ask an illustrious duke why he has also escaped to the
garden, or should we continue to pretend that it was
the stuffiness that brought you so far from the house?'
Amelia stared at his profile and watched the ghost of
a smile curve his lips at her bold question.

'You are impertinent, Miss Mansfield, but I suspect
you do not care that I might think that. If you want to
know the truth, I find occasions like this tiresome.'

'I would have thought you would find some entertainment in them. Surely you must call some of those
people friends? You spend a great deal of time standing on your own.'

He was silent for such a long time that Amelia was
certain that he had decided their brief conversation was
at an end and that he was waiting for her to realise it
and move along. But he surprised her.

'I am afraid that it is no longer that simple, Miss
Mansfield, and I find myself in an unusual predicament. It is common knowledge that I am part of the
government, and thus almost everyone wants to ask me
about some aspect of state business—I have to be very
careful how I answer them. My discretion is essential,
but I would rather not cause offence by telling people
to mind their own business. Therefore, it is prudent to
avoid extended conversation with anyone.'

He was still resolutely not looking at her and for
some reason she knew that he was admitting to only
part of the truth. 'That does indeed sound tiresome.
However, it must be even more tiresome to be the most
eligible man in the ballroom.' That had been obvious

and quite something to witness. 'I did notice how some of the mothers swarmed around you the very moment we arrived. Much like the young ladies did.'

He turned to her then and smiled properly, clearly amused at her observation, and Amelia realised that his real smiles were deadly. Not only did his eyes dance, he appeared boyish and charming. And so much younger than he seemed when he was all stern and pompous.

'Is this another one of your conversational traps, Miss Mansfield? If I agree with you, I will sound conceited and you will have another reason to give me a set-down. Or should I pretend that I have no idea what you are talking about, when we are both painfully aware that your observations were correct. Either way, you will be condescending, and I am well aware of the fact that I do not deserve anyone's pity.'

Perhaps she had been a smidgen hard on him since her arrival in his fine house, especially as he had shown her some kindness? And his smile was doing peculiar things to her; she felt a little guilty for making him feel like that. 'I was merely making an observation about your unique situation. All of that blatant admiration, *all of the time*, must become cloying. I imagine that it also feels quite disingenuous. They have come to be *seen* to socialise with a duke—not you personally.' Amelia was starting to believe that the Duke and Bennett Montague were sometimes very different people, and for some reason that realisation worried her.

He watched her for a long moment before he nodded reluctantly. 'You are very astute, Miss Mansfield. After a while I feel as if the walls are closing in on me and I have to escape. Just for a little while. And I…'

He closed his eyes and sighed, and she knew that he was feeling awkward at confessing so much.

'And you can breathe in the garden.'

'Exactly.' His eyes drifted upwards to contemplate the night sky. Despite the cold, it was perfectly clear and he seemed content to lapse into silence again.

'I do understand. I also like to look at the stars when I am not feeling myself. They remind me how insignificant I am. It puts all of my woes and worries into perspective. When I look at all of those lights in the sky and realise that they are probably millions of miles away from me, I realise that, like them, I am just one speck in the entire universe and there is probably somebody out there who has worse problems than I have.' Amelia had never told anybody that before and she was not sure why she had just told him. It had been hard to see the stars in Seven Dials. It was too built-up, too overcrowded and too polluted to see much beyond the rooftops, but occasionally she had caught glimpses and those glimpses had always soothed her.

He regarded her thoughtfully. 'Do you have a love of astronomy?'

'I know nothing about it really. I can identify the moon and the North Star, but I do wish that I knew more.'

Chapter Ten

Do not allow your passions to control your decisions. Passion soon dies, attraction fades, but a pragmatic union to an obedient wife will stand the test of time...

'Can you point out the North Star?' Bennett asked with a hint of challenge. He watched her scan the night sky until she found the one that burned the brightest and pointed at it triumphantly.

'There it is! Just to the left.'

'If you move your eyes slightly above that, do you see the constellation that resembles the letter *W* turned upside down?' She nodded slowly, her eyes fixed on the heavens. 'That is Cassiopeia. In the winter we get the best view of this constellation as it is directly above us.' As a boy, he had enjoyed staring at the sky through the telescope Uncle George had bought for him. How long had it been since he had done something like that, just for the pleasure of it? At least ten years. That was a sobering thought.

'Do the skies change with the seasons?'

'Indeed they do.' She grinned then and he felt a ridiculous sense of pride at having told her something that pleased her. 'If you look back at Cassiopeia and then move your gaze slightly to your left, there is a larger constellation called Andromeda. She was Cassiopeia's beautiful daughter. Many of the constellations were named after the characters from Ancient Greek mythology. The brightest star is her head.' Bennett traced the shape of the constellation with his hand in the air. He was probably boring the poor girl but couldn't seem to stop. 'Her arms are outstretched.'

She frowned delightfully. 'If those are her legs below, she is not in a very ladylike position.'

'The poor girl had been chained to a rock and was about to be eaten by a monster. I doubt she cared overmuch about correct posture.'

A little bubble of laughter escaped and she might have just given him the moon. 'Didn't Perseus save her?'

'He did.' Bennett began to trace the shape of the other constellation in the sky to help her to find it. 'There he is. He is flying towards her with his sword outstretched.'

'I can't see it.'

Without thinking, he moved closer and took her hand. The effect it had on him was instantaneous. Just one touch and all at once it wasn't enough. He wanted to pull her into his arms and trace the sensitive skin on the undersides of her wrists, place a kiss directly where her pulse beat, but such a thing was simply not done and, if it was, not with a companion. So instead he helped her to trace the constellation in the sky and then swiftly dropped her hand in case he acted on his urges.

'I think it is lovely that those old legends are used to such great effect. Are there others?'

She was staring intently up at the stars, a position that exposed the pale column of her neck. Bennett found his eyes drawn to it, wondering what the skin there would taste like. All at once, he was not quite as frozen as he had been. Part of him immediately began to warm at the thought.

In an effort to distract himself, Bennett spent several minutes pointing out every constellation he knew and, to his complete delight, she apparently knew every myth that had earned them their names and was able to find the ridiculous in all of them. Far from making him feel as if he were lecturing her on something dull, she appeared genuinely engaged in the topic. In silent agreement, they both began to stroll slowly back through the shadowy garden towards the house as he continued to point out the things that he hoped she still found interesting.

'You are very well read, Miss Mansfield.'

'I used to work at a circulating library and made good use of the stock.' The smile on her face faltered as soon as she said this, then returned, a little forced, as she gazed purposefully back up at the sky. 'If it was not the middle of winter and the ground was not so cold, I would be lying on the grass now to look at it all properly.'

'Like you did in my hallway? I fail to understand why you would need to do that when you can see just as well simply by moving your head back.'

She rolled her eyes and sighed in mock exasperation. 'Yes—but you only ever get to see a fraction that way. Your perspective is distorted. You miss things because the picture is disjointed.' She stared deeply into his eyes and Bennett found that he was unable to look away. 'Only when you can see the whole thing in its entirety do you fully appreciate it. Your wonderful ceiling mural is an excellent case in point. It is beautiful when you turn in a circle to look at it, but it is quite breathtaking when viewed from the floor.'

Breath-taking. Two words that perfectly summed up Miss Mansfield in such close quarters. She was breathtaking. Had he ever thought that about a woman before? Pretty, certainly. Even beautiful, occasionally, but to see a face that made your words catch in your throat and your heart race at the mere sight of it? That had never happened to him. Bennett found himself staring at her lips as she spoke and wondering how they tasted too. What would that trim womanly body feel like pressed close to his? Even better, what would her bare skin feel like next to his? Would it be so terrible if he succumbed, just this once, to temptation so that he could find out?

She was staring at him with such intensity, her lips ever so slightly parted, and he was sorely tempted to just give in and kiss her. When the tip of her tongue nervously traced the top of those lush lips he almost did...until the sounds of the ballroom began to drift towards him, reminding him that they were not really alone and he panicked.

'Well, I shan't be lying on any floors soon.' The words came out as an admonishment because her presence unsettled him. Bennett instantly regretted his harsh tone. Unfortunately, his brain and vocal cords did not appear to be aligned because more of the same nonsense came from them. 'I have a perfectly good perspective of the world without having to sprawl on the floor like a commoner.' Now he had offended her. Her feline eyes narrowed and her lovely mouth flattened. He tried to save the situation, but his wayward mouth had gained too much momentum. 'And it has not escaped my notice, Miss Mansfield, that despite my previous admonishment you were once again out in the dark. Alone.'

Even with her father lurking within a stone's throw, and despite the fact that he was also a member of the aristocracy, Amelia had been enjoying the Duke's company.

Had.

When he wasn't being the Duke, Bennett Montague was actually a very knowledgeable man with a dry, clever sense of humour. His grasp of the universe was quite impressive and he managed to explain it all without sounding patronising or haughty or pompous.

For once.

And that had been the problem. At some point while they were strolling back through the garden, the cosy intimacy and easy conversation had made her forget that he was a pompous duke and Amelia had enjoyed being with the man. Seeing him as a pompous duke, it did not matter that his silvery blue eyes sparkled in the moonlight or that his quiet, deep chuckle made her insides melt like butter. Seeing him as a man, Amelia was keenly aware of those things. Repeatedly, she'd found herself staring at his profile as he gazed at the sky. The mist in the air had tousled his hair so that it fell over his forehead, and each time they'd paused to look at another constellation she had been sorely tempted to brush it away from his eyes. And then the air around them hung heavy with the weight of promise and she had the distinct feeling that he was going to kiss her. At that moment, to her complete surprise, she would not have minded in the slightest.

However, the closer they'd got to the house, the more duke-like he'd become. Now the Duke of Aveley was back with a vengeance. His posture was as stiff as a plank and his arms were clasped imperiously behind his back. It had been the most sudden, and unwelcome, transformation. Almost calculated. It was obvious that he had no intention of even pretending to be amiable when he was anywhere near his peers and would be mortified if anybody saw them together, even though there were already several people taking the air on the terrace a few feet away, so their presence out here could be easily explained. Yet he had called her a commoner—maybe not directly, but the implication was clear—and the spell he had cast around her was broken.

Thank heavens.

The very last man she would ever want to kiss would be a man with a title. Just like her father, Bennett Montague could change from reasonable man to self-righteous aristocrat with a click of his fingers. Underneath all of that amiability he was just as mercenary and she would do well to remember that.

'I hardly think that walking in a garden in Mayfair counts as a clandestine outing. And, even if it did, I am employed by your aunt. My free time is mine to do with as I choose.' Gathering her blanket tightly around her, Amelia turned and marched around the side of the house towards the French windows she had left open. She heard him start after her.

'Wait. I am sorry. My tone was unnecessarily harsh and I apologise. It's just that…'

Amelia whipped her head around angrily and cut him off. 'Save your apologies; I have no need of them. We both know that your aristocratic stodginess returned the very moment you realised that you might be seen talking to someone as lowly as me!'

'Stodgy!' That word, out of all that she had used, clearly offended him the most and he thrust out his square jaw in protest. Well, Amelia had a jawbone too and could not stop herself from using it.

'Yes. Stodgy. You have no need to fear for your aristocratic reputation, Your Grace; I would rather not be seen with you either. Commoners can be quite particular about who we talk to.' Her feet tore up the ground and the elusive French windows came into sight. Unfortunately, her short legs were no match for his much longer strides.

'I did not mean that either, Miss Mansfield.' He was in front of her now and intent on blocking her path. He ran his hand through his thick hair in agitation and then stood a little awkwardly. It was apparent that he did not know what to do with his arms until he clasped them firmly behind his back again. 'I just…'

'It does not matter.' Amelia was in no mood for hollow explanations or meaningless apologies. She was well aware of her place in society—and of his. Experience had taught her a great deal about the titled male's mind; any doubts she had about the mind of this man in front of her had been amply filled with the drivel in his silly book. She had been foolish to allow her head to be turned, even for a few minutes, by a man who lived according to such a strict and ancient code of conduct.

But she had promised Lady Worsted that she would be on her best behaviour whilst she was a guest in his house; no matter how galling she found it, her position in the household meant that she had to keep the peace and swallow her pride. 'You are a duke. I am a servant. You have been very charitable to have honoured me with your conversation this evening and I thank you for it. However, the vast chasm between our stations makes it impossible for you to continue in that vein in the company of others. I understand that. Let us not make more of it than it is, Your Grace.'

'Stop interrupting me!'

The next thing that she knew, he'd hauled her against him and covered her mouth with his.

Chapter Eleven

*Marriage to a politician has to be viewed as a
treaty. The nation will expect you to ally yourself with one of the great families of England to
maintain the high standards of the government...*

There really was nothing stodgy or reserved about
his kiss. The moment his lips fused with hers, it lit a
fire within her that burned too hot to extinguish. Not
that she gave that much thought at the beginning. All
thought was suspended while Amelia gave herself over
to the wonderful sensations he created.

Amelia had been kissed before. There had been a
couple of chaste kisses from intellectual young men
who fervently believed in the same causes that she did.
In each case, those romances had fizzled out because
neither party felt the same fire for the relationship that
they did for the plight that united them. Then there had
been the other kisses which had been an unwelcome
intrusion. A violation even. There had been quite a
few of those too. Things were earthier in the slums and
those who did not try to take what they wanted were

invariably left with nothing. And she had been a young woman all alone and there were a great many who had sought to take advantage of that fact. Fortunately, in every circumstance, she had been able to fend off the male who tried to take from her.

This kiss fell into neither category. He was passionate—yet tender. The kiss firm yet achingly gentle. And his strong arms felt so very right wrapped around her that she gave in to the flash of desire and allowed her own arms to coil around his neck so that she could cling to him for dear life. It was only when she felt the blanket slither from her shoulders when his arms searched for, and found, her waist, then drew her hips to rest intimately against his that she realised that she was in trouble.

Serious trouble.

This intoxicating man was a duke. A duke who was hell-bent on finding his perfect duchess—a woman who would be well-bred, compliant and aristocratic. He had already reminded her that she was a commoner and therefore unworthy. That meant there was only one thing that he could possibly want from Amelia—and that was the same thing that every chancer and bounder had tried, and failed, to achieve.

Decisively, she dragged her hands to his chest and pushed him away with all of her might. She might well be a commoner now, in fact she was proud to be one, but she would not be her mother and be seduced by his wealth or his power. Or, heaven forbid, his ghastly title. The measure of a man was what he was inside and not who he was born to be. Whilst the Duke might have a bit more substance than some of his aristocratic peers, his arrogant superiority was still ingrained into his soul.

Commoner!

How typically…aristocratic. As if being common was an infectious disease that he needed to be protected from! Well, he needn't worry on that score. He was too much like her father to even consider him. Not that he would ever offer her marriage, thank goodness. And she was not prepared to be a passing fancy for him either, no matter how much her body enjoyed his touch. Even if he were the very last man on earth, it would be a cold day in hell before Amelia would ever consider any form of dalliance with one in possession of a title.

However, that brought another problem immediately to the forefront. In her experience, the more powerful the man, the less understanding they were about being rejected. Amelia might well want to slap him stoutly on his perfect cheek, but she needed to keep her job. Humour and diplomacy would serve her much better than anger right now.

Bennett fought to catch his breath while he watched the alarming play of emotions on her lovely face. Kissing her had been a mistake. And a revelation. What had he been thinking? Perhaps, for once, he had not been thinking, which was somehow even worse. He never lost his head. Ever. He was always fully in control of every single situation and his emotions. There could be no volcanic eruption in front of Miss Mansfield.

Yet here he was, completely aroused and totally blindsided by a simple kiss with a wholly unsuitable woman. A woman who was now regarding him cautiously, her feline eyes wary and her body poised to either run away or attack. Without thinking, he took a step towards her, but she stayed him with her small hand.

'Before we continue, Your Grace, I just wanted to be sure that I am right to believe that I am now on your Potential list?'

Bennett had not been expecting that and confusion got the better of him. 'Um… I…' How exactly did one politely say that, although one found a woman attractive, alluring and completely maddening, she was wholly unsuitable to be his duchess? She did not meet any one of the criteria his father had deemed essential for high office—no, which Bennett knew was essential for high office. He needed a wife who would be a political asset. A wife with impeccable breeding and an innate understanding of social etiquette, neither of which this conundrum of a female possessed, more was the pity.

'I see.' She took his silence as an answer, then bent down and retrieved the blanket before slowly wrapping it around her shoulders and facing him proudly. 'That is most unfortunate, Your Grace. I am sure your aunt would be very disappointed to know that you had made improper advances to her companion.'

She was right. He had no place kissing her if he was not able to offer for her. Her polite censure made the muscles around Bennett's ribs constrict with the fierce wave of shame he experienced at his shoddy behaviour. Unfortunately, that shame did nothing to dampen his overwhelming need to kiss her again.

'I apologise unreservedly. You have my word that it will not happen again.' Saying that made his throat tighten until swallowing and speaking became difficult. After an uncomfortable moment of silence, he inclined his head stiffly and strode back towards the terrace and the safety of the crowded ballroom.

It was a tactical retreat.

If he had stayed a moment longer, he knew he would have been tempted to throw propriety to the wind and tell her that, frankly, he really did not give a damn about the circumstances of her birth. But he had to. He would never become Prime Minister if he scandalously married a woman so far beneath him yet, bizarrely, the vast chasm in their stations made him very sad. If she had not come from Cheapside, if her parentage had not been so lowly and her connections non-existent, if she was not so outspoken, or so impertinent, or his aunt's servant, and if his choice of bride had not been so very important in order to continue his father's legacy, then he had a suspicion that Miss Mansfield might well have been perfect for him.

Bennett had experienced an intellectual connection with her that was sadly missing in his life. For a few minutes he had not been the Duke of Aveley, he had been just Bennett. Free and unburdened from the constraints that his position and his career put upon him. And he had enjoyed that. If she had met just one of the criteria that his father had set down, he would have gone after her because he could be himself with her. The simple fact that he could not was devastating.

He waited several minutes before he entered the ballroom again, for propriety's sake, although he needn't have worried. Miss Mansfield was gone.

Amelia deftly avoided him for the next few days— or he was deftly avoiding her—which made life much easier. Her reaction to him had confused her. Not just the kiss, but the simple pleasure of being with *him*. She had not expected to feel that kind of connection with him, of all people, nor did she want to continue to be disappointed in his reaction when she had called him on it. She might well have intended her words to be a warning which she had wanted His Pomposity to heed, but a tiny, hopelessly romantic part of her had hoped that he might have surprised her. If he had said that he did not care that she was his aunt's companion and a commoner, or if he had miraculously agreed that she was, indeed, on his Potential list, then she was not entirely sure that she would have had the strength to have resisted him.

Saying that she had no interest in kissing the Duke of Aveley and actually meaning it was, apparently, quite another matter altogether. She had dreamed about the stupid kiss every night since and her traitorous pulse sped up whenever she caught a fleeting glimpse of him. Clearly, a small, errant part of her personality was greatly influenced by her mother's weakness for the wrong sort of man. Stupidly, she had developed a bit of a *tendre* for a man with a title—although it was definitely not his title that made him so attractive. It was everything else, inside and out. Even his stiffness was a little endearing.

Amelia sighed and pinned on her old straw bonnet. There was no point in getting upset about it. In a few more weeks she would go back to Bath and be spared the odd feeling that he ignited within her. For now, she could head back to Seven Dials. The factory workers' meeting and a few hours in the soup kitchen would purge her thoughts of the irritatingly handsome and priggish duke and his intoxicating kisses. She needed to hear some passionate speeches to remind her of the fact that men like the Duke of Aveley were not quite as important or special as they would like to believe themselves to be. They perpetuated poverty and silenced the masses to feather their own nests. So what if he claimed to want to clean up the slums? He would never agree to the more important changes that the so-called Radicals proposed. Fair wages, fair taxation or, heaven forbid, universal suffrage. And he would treat his future wife with the same dispassion that he had shown in his writing. She would do well to remember that next time her mind wandered back to that starlit walk and unforgettable moonlit kiss.

Fortunately, there was nothing to stop her going to Seven Dials today. The house was empty. The only fly in the ointment was Lovett. The butler had made it quite plain that if he knew she was heading out alone again, then he was duty-bound to send a footman, on His Grace's explicit instruction. If he had not shown her the servants' stairs that first time, those instructions would have seriously curtailed her outings, but he had and she had become quite adept at using them. Especially the dark back staircase that took her to a door that led directly to the gardens. Once outside, it proved to be surprisingly easy to skirt around the back of the house, behind the stables and down an alleyway that took her into the mews and freedom.

Bennett's speech had had to be postponed yet again, which had put him in a foul mood. The morning debate had descended into a shambles almost as soon as it had started and no amount of the Speaker calling order managed to stop the lords from braying like wild donkeys across the floor. After an hour Bennett left in disgust, intent on heading to the tranquillity of his own study in order to get some proper work done, but once again Piccadilly had been horrendously busy— thus making his foul mood fouler.

'Will you be returning to Parliament this afternoon, Your Grace?' The groom took the reins while Bennett dismounted.

'I am not sure yet.' He should go back for the afternoon session even though the idea of it made him frown involuntarily. 'I will send word if I need to.'

Bennett was sorely tempted to stay at home. The current behaviour of his fellow politicians was not conducive to getting bills passed and the less said about Piccadilly the better. For some reason, the peace of the gardens drew him and, instead of heading into the house, he found himself wandering towards the empty flower beds. Perhaps he should ignore the guilty knot in his belly and retire to Aveley Castle for a week or two? He had certainly earned a rest. Some time away from all of his mounting responsibilities might get his life back into perspective and help to shift the odd mood that had plagued him since the Renshaw ball— or, more specifically, since he had kissed his aunt's companion.

Who knew that such an impulsive decision would leave him so out of sorts? He had not felt fully himself in days and he certainly could not focus. He had lost count of how many minutes he had wasted reliving that brief experience and wishing that he could do it all again just to be certain that he had not imagined it.

He had barely seen her since, which was just as well, but he did need to stop thinking about her. With a groan, he sank down onto a convenient bench. This had to stop. He had also diverted far too much of his attention on thinking about *not* thinking about her, which was a ridiculous way for a grown man to behave. He was thirty years old, for goodness' sake, so he really should not be mooning about as a result of one silly kiss with a woman he had no reason to be kissing. Fortunately, their paths had rarely crossed these last few days and that was exactly how he liked it.

Unfortunately, at that moment Miss Mansfield scurried across the path in front of him, completely oblivious of his presence. If he had not memorised the exact shape of her beguiling figure, he might have mistaken her for a beggar or a gypsy, so scruffily was she dressed. The dull grey frock was clearly very old and had been patched in places with mismatched fabric. The heavy black shawl had definitely seen better days and the straw bonnet was an abomination. Its only adornment was one wilted, sorry-looking orange flower that dangled listlessly to one side. If her outfit was odd, her behaviour was odder. There was a furtiveness about her movements that made Bennett suspicious. She kept glancing back at the house and then towards the stable as if she was up to no good.

He pressed himself back against the bench and out of her eyeline so that he could watch her. Only when she practically sprinted past the stables did he realise that she was heading out towards the mews, which meant that she was once again ignoring his express instruction that she should not leave his house unaccompanied.

Did the woman have no regard for her own safety? The London streets were no place for a young lady, especially such a diminutive one. He might well want to avoid her, but he could hardly allow her to come to harm just because looking at her gave his body unwelcome ideas. Not to mention the fact that he was suddenly curious about exactly where she was heading, dressed like a vagabond. Wherever it was, she *clearly* wanted to keep it a secret.

Or perhaps it was not where she was going that she wanted to keep quiet, but who she was off to meet? She had told him that she had grown up in Cheapside—and she was an uncommonly pretty thing—it was not out of the realms of possibility that she was having a clandestine assignation with some unworthy young buck who did not have to behave like a gentleman. She had certainly not appeared to be a novice at kissing. No wonder she did not want to be constrained by a footman if she was off to meet another man! And no wonder she had not been interested in his clumsy attempt at a kiss! The surge of jealousy galvanised him and, before he could think better of it, he was trailing hopelessly after her, making sure that he kept far enough back that she would not be alerted to his presence.

It would have been impossible to keep track of her on the crowded streets had it not been for the abominable bonnet. The orange flower was like a beacon which he followed relentlessly like a hound after a fox, irrationally jealous and angry at his irrationality. In no time they were out of Mayfair and heading east on Piccadilly and then onto Shaftesbury Avenue. The further up that road they went, the shoddier the surroundings became and the less Bennett recognised until he was hopelessly lost. Genteel society gave way to the slums and his irrational anger was replaced by a growing sense of unease. These were not streets that any sane person would venture into without the protection of a carriage. He could think of no earthly reason why an educated young woman would willingly bring herself here, yet ahead of him Miss Mansfield was still marching with some purpose into it all undaunted, her ultimate destination still a complete mystery.

Of course, in her ragged clothes nobody gave her a passing look. She blended in perfectly. He, on the other hand, stuck out like a sore thumb. The inhabitants regarded him warily as they stepped out of his way and he became increasingly grateful that it was broad daylight. He doubted he would have been given such clear passage through these narrow, filthy streets in the dark. What had started out as morbid curiosity was now no longer funny, and Bennett decided that enough was enough. He quickened his pace to catch up with his quarry. He would fetch Miss Mansfield smartly and drag her, if necessary, out of this dreadful place where who knew what was waiting for her. Or him.

'Oi! You ain't paid me!'

Two dishevelled street urchins barged past him. Hot on their heels a shopkeeper gave chase and Bennett's attention momentarily shifted to the spectacle. By the time he flicked his gaze back towards Miss Mansfield, she had disappeared.

Chapter Twelve

When making social calls, a young lady must be selective in who she visits. The wrong sort of acquaintance will reflect badly on you...

To save some time Amelia cut through an alleyway that would bring her out just shy of the soup kitchen, and instantly regretted her decision when she realised that she had been followed. She knew better than to trust deserted streets like this one. Even in the middle of the day there could be danger lurking around any corner.

'Ain't you a pretty thing?' The first man was stocky and his toothless grin was not the least bit friendly.

'Them look like a nice pair of boots,' his younger accomplice drawled, eyeing her feet and then slowly trailing his eyes back up her body. 'I think you should give them to me.'

Amelia whipped around to run, but another larger man was now lounging against the wall behind her, effectively blocking her escape while he innocently cleaned his fingernails with the small blade of a penknife. Experience had taught her that screaming would be pointless. No one would come to her aid here. She also knew that they would want more than her boots if they heard her true accent.

'And I think you can get lost,' she replied brazenly, parroting their cockney. 'Go rob some toff and leave me be.'

The older man laughed and shook his greasy head slowly. 'Mayhap we will just have to take them, then, and perhaps we might just take you too. Pretty young girls are always worth something in Drury Lane.'

Amelia tried not to look terrified. Drury Lane was the home of the worst of the bawdy houses and it was well-known that some of those girls had been sold into prostitution rather than going willingly. Her only hope was bravado. And speed. 'Oh, get out of my way, you fools.'

The large man behind her scowled as Amelia smartly darted past him. Unfortunately, he was far quicker than his size suggested and he caught her roughly by the arm. 'Not so fast, darling. We ain't done with you yet.'

'Yes, you are.'

The Duke's deep voice brooked no argument, making Amelia momentarily slump with relief. She had absolutely no idea what he was doing here, but she had never been so glad to see another person in her life. The big man dropped her arm as her three would-be assailants immediately stalked towards him, and her relief turned to fear again instantly. He was just one pompous duke who was clearly out of his depth, and they were three ruffians used to violence. At least one of them had a knife. He did not stand a chance.

'Look what we have here, *gentlemen*,' the older man said sarcastically. 'This must be her knight in shining armour. Come to rescue the damsel, have you, *sir*?' The three men laughed, circling him and forgetting Amelia existed now that there were richer pickings to be had. And the Duke certainly looked rich. Even in the grey daylight his diamond stickpin shimmered on his pristine white cravat. Nothing stayed white very long in the slums.

To his credit, he did not look even slightly frightened and his voice exuded aristocratic confidence. 'As a matter of fact, I *am* here to rescue her, so I would ask you all to stand aside and let us be on our way.'

The men acknowledged this with amusement. 'And what will you do if we don't stand aside, *sir*?' The older criminal offered a goading toothless smile. 'After all, we are three against one and we are not in Mayfair now.'

Amelia elbowed her way into the circle and stood in front of the Duke. 'Your business was with me, not him. Leave him be.'

No sooner had the words escaped her lips than the Duke grabbed her and pushed her behind him. 'Go, Miss Mansfield! Let me deal with this.' He pointed to the exit with his finger, but his eyes never left the men.

'Ooh—it's Miss Mansfield, is it?' The older man doffed his cap to her, to much sniggering from his friends. 'I suggest you heed this fine gentleman's advice and go, missy. Our business is no longer with you.'

Although the most sensible course of action was probably to run and fetch help, Amelia could hardly leave him. These men were not the sort to just rob a member of the aristocracy. They would know that the full weight of the law would come raining down on their heads if they did. They would have to make sure that there was no possible chance that he could identify them in the future. For his own good she had to intervene.

Amelia stepped in front of him again. If she made more noise and a complete nuisance of herself, then it might attract enough attention to scare off the attackers. 'Help!' she screeched at the top of her voice. 'Murder! Murder!' At least that was one word that was guaranteed to rouse some interest from the local inhabitants. They might tolerate all manner of evildoings in Seven Dials, but they drew the line at that.

The older man lunged forward in an attempt to silence her and Amelia heard something whistle past her face. It was only when she heard the ominous crack of bone followed by an alarming spray of fresh blood that she realised that the sound had come from the Duke's closed fist as it had connected with the criminal's nose.

The man stumbled backwards and fell onto his bottom in agony while his two accomplices stared slack-jawed. After a beat of silence, they both launched themselves at exactly the same time. She watched in horror as the Duke was pushed to the ground and the smaller man punched him in the face. Fortunately, the fist glanced off his jaw, but the blow must have hurt nevertheless. Despite the threat of the small knife that was still clasped in his raised hand, Amelia did her best to block the largest man from joining in, knowing full well that the Duke would be well and truly done for if both men went for him together.

'Leave him alone!' Throwing her full weight at him, she looped her arms about the brute's neck, pulling him backwards until he stumbled. Her teeth sank into the flesh of his wrist and the penknife fell to the floor. Scrambling after it, Amelia kicked it into the safety of the muck-filled gutter and watched with relief as it sank beneath the muddy water. Her relief was short-lived when the big man turned back towards the Duke on the ground with murder in his eyes.

The larger man's boot was poised to kick Bennett in the head, so he braced himself for the impact. Miss Mansfield suddenly flew at him like a banshee and jumped onto his back screaming, her hands clawing at him. Her small fists made little impact as she pummelled them against the man's ribs. In one swift motion, he lifted her off her feet and threw her unceremoniously to the ground. She yelped as he bent down and dragged her back to her feet, holding her by the hair while she continued her assault against him. The distraction was all Bennett needed to bring his left knee swiftly up into his own attacker's groin. Instantly, the man howled and rolled sideways, clutching his jewels for all he was worth, allowing Bennett to jump to his feet. For good measure he kicked the fellow in the stomach and winded him, then he stalked towards the final assailant, ignoring the blood that had begun to pour from his own nose.

The last man standing still had Miss Mansfield by the hair, but even so she refused to be cowed. For a little thing she was much tougher than he had given her credit for, but she was no match for the blackguard who held her. Bennett could not remember a time when he had ever been so angry.

'Let go of her now or I swear I will kill you!'

When the brute ignored him, Bennett took great

pleasure in smashing his closed fist into the man's face until he complied. The three injured men gathered together and quickly regrouped. As one, they glared murderously towards him and Bennett feared that the situation had spiralled dangerously out of his control. Like a tiny warrior, Miss Mansfield was still glued to his side, glaring at the men with a menacing gleam in her eye. As much as he appreciated her loyalty, her safety was paramount. 'Go and fetch help,' he muttered. 'I can keep them here while you run.'

'No.'

She did not even do him the courtesy of looking at him and made no further attempt to explain her preposterous decision to ignore a reasonable order.

'Miss Mansfield—I must insist.'

Her eyes narrowed defiantly; however, further discussion was impossible. Their attackers were once again edging slowly towards them, each looking more furious than the next. Beside him, she stiffened, her small hands closed into angry fists, ready to strike whoever dared to come near them, so Bennett did the same. For several tense moments they all stared at each other, ready to do battle, until they heard a blood-curdling war cry from behind.

'I'm coming, Your Grace!'

A familiar face shot past them, holding a large piece of wood aloft in his meaty hands. It was Terence, his burliest footman, and at that moment he did look utterly terrifying. The ruffians' eyes widened in alarm before they hastily turned and ran in the opposite direction, disappearing down another alleyway and out of sight.

Once he was certain the threat had gone, the footman rushed back to them, breathing heavily. 'I am so sorry, Your Grace!' Terence took in the scene, including Bennett's bloody nose, and the colour drained out of his face. 'Mr Lovett assigned me to follow Miss Mansfield, but I lost her in the crowd a few streets back. This is all my fault.'

'You are quite mistaken, Terence. There is only *one* person who I hold accountable for this sorry episode, and I can assure you that it is most definitely not you.'

Bennett grabbed Miss Mansfield by the elbow and unceremoniously dragged her out of the alleyway into the street. He wanted to shake her until her teeth rattled and demand that she explain what she was about, but such behaviour in public—even in the slums—would be unseemly. As soon as they were safely back home, he was going to tear her off a strip. And, hopefully, by then he would have wrested control of his boiling temper.

Chapter Thirteen

When selecting a bride, choose a biddable woman who defers to your superior opinion in all matters of importance...

The silence in the hastily procured hackney was deafening. Judging from his stony expression, tight jaw and white knuckles, the Duke was furious. Amelia supposed he had every right to be. His perfect nose was bleeding profusely and there was an angry red swelling just under his cheekbone that would probably turn into a nasty bruise before the day was out. His once pristine shirt was completely ruined and she doubted that there was much hope for his expensively tailored coat either.

But he had surprised her. Not only had he stood up to the gang without any sign of fear, he had held his own admirably and proved himself not to be the soft, pampered aristocrat that she had previously thought him. Although it was also plainly evident he had no idea how to deal with the bloody nose.

'Tilt your head backwards,' she offered helpfully as he swiped at it ineffectually with his ruined handkerchief, 'and pinch the bridge like so.' Amelia demonstrated the technique on her own face. His serious silver-blue eyes briefly locked on hers and the disgust in them was obvious, but he did as she suggested. Badly.

'Not like that. You need to try to stop the bleeding.' She moved over to the opposite bench to sit next to him and applied the necessary pressure. He stared stonily at the ceiling, clearly determined not to speak to her.

'Thank you for saving me.' It felt like such a lame expression of gratitude in view of the pasting he had just received on her behalf. 'Where did you learn to fight like that?'

'Surely a more pertinent question is what the hell were you doing in that awful place to begin with? Alone. Again.' The blue eyes were icy-cold and his tone was not much better. Under the circumstances there appeared to be little point in attempting to lie. If Terence had been following her since her arrival, Lovett would have no qualms about appraising his master of all of her comings and goings, and there had been quite a few.

'I was going to a public meeting.' Somehow she felt he might find this more palatable than telling him about her regular attendance at the soup kitchen.

'Do not expect me to believe that rubbish. What sort of a public meeting takes place in that hotbed of criminality? The Rookery is notorious. Every thief, pickpocket and ne'er-do-well in London lives there!'

How typical that he would jump to such a conclusion. 'The Rookery forms only a small part of Seven Dials. Good people live there too. Poverty does not make them all criminals. Saying such a thing is like blaming all of the French for the behaviour of Napoleon. Most of the residents have no choice but to live there. They cannot afford anything better.'

'If you are so well informed about the capital's vilest slum, Miss Mansfield, then why did you not have the good sense to stay out of that deserted alleyway? Or do you think that those ruffians were simply the unfortunate victims of *poverty* and did not actually *mean* to threaten you?' He batted her hand away from his nose and glared at her, his breathing far too laboured for a man in full control of his anger. 'Have you any idea how much danger you just put yourself in? You were about to be sold into a life of prostitution!'

Now he was simply being dramatic. She would have thought of something to get herself out of the predicament, just as she always had in the past. 'Usually I am more careful—but today I was a little distracted.' Amelia had been thinking about him, not that she would openly admit that, and more specifically she had been pondering her extreme reaction to his kiss.

'Usually?' His face was a mask of molten fury. 'You make a habit of coming here?'

'I admit that I made a grave mistake today but, in my defence, Seven Dials in an area I know well and I have never encountered such a problem before.' That part was a lie. There had been numerous occasions when she had been in exactly that sort of danger, and worse, but not for a couple of years. It just proved that she had been foolish to become so complacent about her surroundings and she would not be so lax going forward.

'How, pray tell, do you come to know Seven Dials well?' He sounded horrified.

For the briefest of moments she actually considered

telling him. It would be interesting to see how he absorbed that sorry tale. 'You already know that I take an interest in the plight of the poor, but to do that effectively it is imperative that I go where they are living in order to help. When I can, I help out at a soup kitchen that is run by the church. They feed some of the most unfortunate souls one hot meal a day. Often it is the only food those people get. Sometimes I attend meetings and lectures run by sympathetic organisations that continue to lobby Parliament for change. That is where I was going today.'

He regarded her with incredulity. 'You are talking about *Radicals*, Miss Mansfield! Organised groups of agitators, hell-bent on starting a revolution.'

'In my opinion, they are unfairly labelled as Radicals. They are good people whose only crime is to seek reasonable political reform.'

'*Reasonable* political reform occurs in Parliament, not in shady taverns and back rooms. If you wish to make your opinions known, you would be better advised to write a stern letter to your Member of Parliament so that he can raise your concerns in the House properly.'

Amelia was momentarily astounded at his ignorance. 'What utter nonsense! Do you seriously believe any one of those idiots would listen to a letter from a woman? Those fools do not listen to anybody who is not in a position to vote for them. In case you have failed to notice, that means that the majority of the population are of no consequence to them. They do not care about the poor. Nobody in Parliament does.'

This raised his ire further and when he answered it

was practically a growl. 'There is no justification for consorting with *Radicals*!'

'What you, in your fine clothes and gilded life, might dismiss as Radical others see as simply good people demanding basic fairness. What is wrong with asking for reasonable wages for an honest day's labour? Then the poor could at least feed themselves and pay for a roof over their heads. The tragic souls in the soup kitchen all work as hard as they can—yet their masters pay them such a pittance that they are forced to live on charity.'

'My *gilded* life!' He had a habit of only hearing the few words that were particular to him, a trait common to his ilk.

'Yes, your *gilded* life. What do you know about being poor? Have you ever been truly hungry? Or not had a comfortable bed for the night or the money to buy what you need? You claim to want to do what is right for all of this nation's loyal subjects, yet you have no concept of how difficult life is for the poor.'

'I do not need to have experienced those things to know that they exist. I am a politician. A servant of the people. I make it my business to find out about such things and push for reforms that will alleviate their suffering.'

'A servant of the people? How very self-sacrificing and noble.' Amelia found her pointed finger poking him in his chest. The patriarchal arrogance of the man was astounding. 'You cannot learn about the effects of poverty from reading.'

He grabbed her finger and pushed it away. 'I have visited the places you speak of. I have been to factories and slums and workhouses.'

Amelia rolled her eyes at that. They were all the same, well-meaning aristocrats who believed themselves to be enlightened and benevolent. 'Did you go there like this?' She gestured to his fine clothes sarcastically. 'I am sure that all of those establishments were very eager to put on a good show for the *illustrious* Duke of Aveley. I am sure when you visit everything appears splendid. Tell me, what does your world smell like? Fresh paint?'

'Are you suggesting that I am purposefully misinformed?'

'I am suggesting that your *perspective* of poverty is very different from the perspective of those *actually* suffering from it. I have experienced those problems first-hand and believe me when I tell you that there is nothing enjoyable about being one of the voiceless poor.'

'Well, you certainly will not be experiencing any such problems in the future. From this point forward, you are expressly forbidden to ever go to Seven Dials or to meet with your revolutionary associates again!' At her outraged expression he held up his hand imperiously, just as her father always had when he had issued a decree. 'And you are *also* forbidden from leaving Aveley House without my aunt or a footman under any circumstances, and if you do I am to be informed beforehand.'

Amelia felt her own temper rise at his dictatorial tone. She was not a child or a chattel. She had been an independent woman since the day her mother had died almost four years ago. That independence might have been foisted upon her, but she was damned if she would surrender it to another titled man just because he said so. 'You cannot order me around. I answer to no one.'

His big hands curled into fists in his lap and his deep voice was more clipped and aristocratic than she had ever heard it. 'Might I remind you, Miss Mansfield, that *you* are employed by my family? Although I am becoming increasingly convinced of the fact that you are wholly unsuitable for the position in which my aunt has entrusted you. If you wish to remain in my aunt's employ, you *will* do as I say or, the moment we arrive at Berkeley Square, you *will* pack your bags and you *will* leave!'

And there it was. The stark choice that she had been dreading but expecting nevertheless. Could she leave the safety and security of Lady Worsted's employment and embark on yet another awful journey of toil, hardship and misery? Morality was all well and good, but it did not put food on the table. But a tiny part of her refused to be subservient to another powerful man and his unreasonable demands, no matter what the personal cost. Could she give up trying to change the world for the better and watch others do it from the wings? Probably not. Her quest for a better deal for the poor had given her a reason to carry on at a time when she had been convinced her life was over. It had shaped her. Changed her. Made her stronger. At least on her own she would still have her self-respect.

'Then I shall leave tonight, Your Grace.' The rebellious part of her executed a mock bow before she removed herself to the opposite seat again. 'And gladly so.' The pompous Duke, his fine house and his fine kisses could all go to hell.

* * *

The rest of the journey seemed interminable as they both sat in outraged brittle silence. To make matters worse, their arrival at Aveley House caused quite a stir. Bennett would not have been surprised if every servant had stood in wide-eyed shock at the sight of him caked in blood and Miss Mansfield's hair resembling a giant bird's nest, while the rest of her was bedecked in rags.

His mother immediately rushed towards him, ready to fuss. 'Oh, good gracious! Bennett! You are injured.' She began directing maids to fetch witch hazel and salve. Uncle George wisely stepped back. At least one person knew that he was in no mood to be trifled with.

Aunt Augusta regarded both of them very carefully before speaking to Miss Mansfield. 'Amelia, dear, you look an absolute fright. Let us get you upstairs to repair the damage. Lovett—send up a tray of tea, if you please, and perhaps a tot of brandy would not go amiss.'

As they left, Bennett had the distinct impression that his aunt was not quite as surprised by the state of his companion as everyone else was. There were clearly words that needed to be said there, but not yet. His first port of call was not tea, nor salve. It was Lovett.

'My study. Now!' Bennett strode away without a backwards glance, forcing the butler to scurry after him.

'But, Bennett,' his mother wailed to his retreating back. 'You are injured!'

'Not that injured, my dear.' Uncle George stepped into the breach. 'Aside from the blood, he appears to be very hale and hearty. And angry. Give him a little time to calm down and then I am sure he will happily allow you to attend him.'

Too furious to be contained by a chair, Bennett began to pace the floor of his study while his butler entered calmly and closed the door. Only then did he allow the tirade to begin.

'Apparently, you have been complicit in allowing Miss Mansfield to visit Seven Dials unattended.'

'Not unattended, Your Grace. The first time she went, I followed her myself. After that she was always accompanied by Terence.'

'But you still allowed her the freedom to go! She *thought* she was alone and her visits to that place went unchallenged.'

Lovett stood ramrod-straight and sighed. 'I was not aware that Miss Mansfield was a prisoner, Your Grace. Had I known, I would have chained her to a banister.'

Sometimes the man's impertinence was grating. 'You know full well what I mean, Lovett. If you knew that she was off to such an unsavoury and insalubrious place, you should have informed me.'

'I do not make a general rule to follow all of the staff during their time off, nor do I ever recall a time when I was required to appraise you of their whereabouts. And, unless Miss Mansfield's position in this house has changed of late, I had no reason to treat her as anything other than your aunt's companion. I *did*, however, ensure that she was always accompanied. Terence was relieved of all other duties and expressly instructed to keep a close eye on her because I had warned her that you would not be impressed by her choice of destination. But I knew full well that those visits were likely to become a regular occurrence the moment I saw her working in the soup kitchen. She did seem very at home there. Fortunately, after I introduced her to the servants' back staircase, she was surprisingly consistent in her choice of escape route. Terence has become quite familiar with the area now. Up until today, there has been nothing untoward to worry Your Grace about. I also knew that she would become very difficult if she had any hint of the fact that she was being followed. Miss Mansfield gets *that* glint in her eye.' Lovett shuddered as he said these final words.

'*That* glint?'

'Indeed, Your Grace. Miss Mansfield reminds me a great deal of my wife. Mrs Lovett, God bless her, has a similar glint from time to time. Fourteen years of marriage have taught me to be very wary of it, as its arrival usually does not bode well.'

Chapter Fourteen

The roles and responsibilities of a husband and
wife are vastly different, and necessarily so...

Bennett was rapidly losing patience. 'Spit it out, man!
I have no blasted idea what you are talking about.'

'That does not surprise me, Your Grace. As a bachelor, you have been spared the awful trials of attempting to understand a woman's mind. Believe me, there
is no arguing with them when they believe that they
are in the right, or that the path they have chosen is
the only route to travel. That is when they get *that*
glint. I have learned, through bitter experience, when
that glint arrives, no matter how wrong the woman
might be, reason will not sway her. Nor will lordly
commands. The best course of action is to take a step
back and allow them to do what they are set on doing—
but to be prepared to step in and salvage the situation
should the need arise. Hence, when Miss Mansfield
forcefully informed me that she had no intention of
heeding my warnings, I found another way to keep
her safe. A compromise, of sorts, although it was one

she was not aware of. The very worst thing you could do to a young woman like Miss Mansfield is to forbid her from doing something.'

'Nonsense.' Bennett had heard enough of this idiocy. 'That is just cowardice, Lovett. I told Miss Mansfield that she was forbidden to visit Seven Dials again or she could pack her bags and leave.'

'And how did she take that, Your Grace?'

'Despite her claims to the contrary, I fully expect her to see the logic of that decision once she has calmed down. You will see, Lovett. Sometimes all that is needed with a woman is a firm hand.'

His aunt chose that moment to barge through the door without knocking, wearing a face like thunder. 'What on earth have you done to poor Miss Mansfield, Bennett? She has stated her intention to leave this house immediately.'

Bennett stifled a groan. 'I merely informed her of the fact that she is not to visit Seven Dials again.' Out of the corner of his eye he saw Lovett smirking. 'I am sure that she is just being a little rebellious.'

Aunt Augusta glared at him as if he were mad. 'She is already packing her bags, Bennett.' Then she marched towards him and began to jab her finger into his chest. Clearly it was a day for females to jab him in the ribs. 'You will fix this, Bennett. Have you any idea how many years it has taken me to find a half-decent companion who does not bore me to tears? I am immensely fond of the gal. She told me about your heavy-handed behaviour towards her in the carriage. How dare you threaten to dismiss a member of *my* staff? I have my *own* household, Bennett, which I pay for with my *own* money. You do not support me and you never

have. It is not *your* place to decide who is and who is
not a suitable companion for me. You only have to suffer my company for one month every year; surely you
can tolerate Amelia for such a short period of time?'

'Heavy-handed!' Could his aunt not see the state of
his nose? 'I will have you know that, had it not been
for my intervention, your *dear* Miss Mansfield would
likely have come out much worse at the hands of those
ruffians. And are you aware that *poor* Miss Mansfield
is consorting with Radicals?'

His aunt flapped her hand at him dismissively. 'The
gal has a great sense of civic responsibility, that is all,
and a heart of gold. I think that it is admirable that she
feeds all those poor wretches soup.'

'You would not say that if you had seen Seven Dials.
That place is a den of iniquity. Filled with thieves and
layabouts. It is no place for a young lady.'

Again, Aunt Augusta appeared nonplussed. 'Most
normal young ladies, yes. But Amelia is made of much
sterner stuff than most.'

'Have you not seen her? She is barely five feet tall
and looks as though a gust of wind would blow her
over.' But she had bravely stood in front of him, ready
to fight beside him. And she had jumped on that bruis-
er's back and, in doing so, stopped him from receiving a sound beating from two men simultaneously. 'It
is ridiculous that she thinks that she would be safe in
a place like that alone.'

'For pity's sake, Bennett, stop being so high and
mighty. Amelia lived in Seven Dials for *three years*
all alone and managed well enough.'

'What?' That did not bear thinking about. Petite,
lovely Miss Mansfield came from *that* slum? 'She told

me that she lived in Cheapside.' And *that* place was bad enough.

'She did. For a while. Amelia has lived in many different parts of London.' His aunt's face suddenly became closed and Bennett realised that the wily old bird knew a great deal more than she was prepared to let on. 'Make it right, Bennett. I shall never forgive you if Miss Mansfield leaves. Try to see things from her perspective.' Then she sailed out of his study imperiously.

Perspective.

What was it with women and that blasted word? First Miss Mansfield, now Aunt Augusta. As if his own perspective on the world was somehow incorrect. As if he were the one in the wrong because his own view of the world was skewed. Well, he wasn't going to apologise.

'Shall I send for Miss Mansfield, Your Grace?' Lovett was still standing staring at him, his face completely devoid of any emotion, but his eyes were blatantly laughing.

'No,' he replied petulantly and then huffed in defeat. 'Kindly send word to Miss Mansfield that I should like to *talk* to her after dinner.' Perhaps his tone had been a little dictatorial. And judgemental. It was not as if he had known that she had lived there. Had he known, he might not have been so forceful. 'Tell her that I would like to...' Wring her lovely neck. Kiss that smart mouth of hers to silence her until she saw things his way. Talk to her about the stars and forget that he was a duke for a little while. 'Tell her that I would like to discuss a compromise.'

The butler scurried off, leaving Bennett alone with his thoughts. If he was brutally honest with himself, his anger was born more out of fear for what might have happened than at her blatant disregard for his wishes. Those three men had meant her harm—of that he was sure—and the thought of her being at the mercy of such men made him feel sick. When that man had grabbed her, Bennett had wanted to cause the blighter pain. Hell, he had wanted to kill the bounder who had thrown her to the floor. He still did. And now he knew that she might well have had to deal with such things repeatedly, and all alone, did not even bear thinking about. It was inconceivable to think that she had survived such a trial. And how had she come to live in Seven Dials in the first place? Was there no family left to have taken her in?

His peace was quickly interrupted by his mother, who was hanging on the arm of Uncle George. His uncle gave him a look that spoke volumes. *Your mother is worried. Let her fuss.* So Bennett subjected himself to being dabbed with witch hazel and endured his mother's flapping with gritted teeth while he recounted a toned-down version of the events that had led to his injuries. Only then could he escape the confines of his study to change his clothes and organise his thoughts.

He did not want her to leave.

Why that was, Bennett was not prepared to consider, but as his anger subsided he acknowledged that he had not handled the aftermath of the incident as effectively as he could have. He had not allowed her to state her case and he hadn't listened. He would try to see things from her perspective—even though he was perfectly certain that he had a very good perspective of things to begin with. He was a forward-thinking politician who was known for his sympathetic stance towards the

poor. Hell, he had become known for being more forward-thinking than his own father, who had not cared
one whit about the poor, so he deserved some credit.
Once she had her say, Miss Mansfield would then have
to listen to his side of things, when hopefully he could
reassure her that she did not need to continue to serve
soup in that hellhole because he, and other fine men
in Parliament, had things well in hand.

As he approached the staircase, his eyes wandered
up to the big mural on the ceiling, the very one that
had been there for every single day of the thirty years
of his life, and he paused. Perspective? As if he could
not see something that was right before his eyes. Bennett scanned the hallway to see if anyone else was
there. Only when he was absolutely certain there was
nobody around to see him did he place himself in the
very centre of the atrium and lie down on the floor.

It took less than ten seconds to learn that Miss
Mansfield, damn her, might well be the one in the
right after all.

Lady Worsted insisted that she come down to dinner, citing her nephew's desire to make amends as
the reason. Amelia wasn't so sure. Whilst she felt ex-
tremely grateful and guilty in equal measure for the
fact that the Duke had come to her rescue, she was still
smarting at his tyrannical tone and his insistence that
she had to abide by his rules or leave. She had been
forced to leave one grand house in Mayfair because
of Viscount Venomous's unreasonable demands and
being issued with an unreasonable ultimatum by the
Duke had hurt—but it was not wholly unexpected. It
was inconceivable that she would abandon her work

at the soup kitchen; there had been far too many ulti-
matums in her life already, and none of them had led
to a positive outcome for her.

Now, apparently, he was prepared to discuss a compromise and she was certain that his idea of a compromise and hers were very different things. No doubt, in
his mind, it meant her capitulating entirely to his unreasonable demands in return for her being allowed to
walk in the park once a week without asking his permission first. If she had wanted that sort of control in
her life, she would be already married.

Unfortunately, Lady Worsted was also right. She
had to endure Bennett Montague only until the end
of December. Was it really worth throwing away the
best job she had ever had just for a few more weeks of
curtailed independence? At least back in Bath, even if
the political societies were disorganised and provincial
and the poor did not need her quite so desperately, she
could come and go as much as she pleased. But it was
not London and it never would be. In London Amelia made a small difference. In Bath she would be old
and wrinkled before anything drastic was achieved.

Yet here she was, sitting at the grand table in the
family dining room, doing her best to appear polite and
acquiescent to her hosts. His Royal Pomposity had yet
to make an appearance and the atmosphere was awkward, to say the least, while they all waited until the
clock chimed seven and he would miraculously appear.
Amelia would not put it past him to be loitering outside
in the hallway, pocket watch in his hand, waiting for
the precise moment to stride in. He was such a stickler for correct form that to deviate from exactly seven
o'clock might cause him to have some kind of seizure.

As the first chimes tinkled the hour, it seemed that they collectively held their breath and made a concerted effort not to look at the door. True to form, he strode in, issued a formal 'Good evening' to one and all and took his place at the head of the table. The well-trained servants immediately began busying themselves with tureens, while Amelia looked at her hands.

Once the soup was served, they ate in silence until Sir George was brave enough to break the tension. 'Well, if nobody else is going to speak, I might as well start. First of all, let me say how relieved we all are that you came to no serious harm today, Amelia. Bennett has told us that you were accosted by three scoundrels and I am very pleased that he was there to assist you. We all now know that you regularly help the poor, which is admirable, and that you were unfortunate enough to have had to experience life there first-hand. But, if I may be so bold, I should like to ask the question that we are all aching to know the answer to. How did you come to be living alone in Seven Dials in the first place?'

The soup in her mouth suddenly turned to dust and she glanced up at Lady Worsted to see if she could find any guidance on how much to tell. Finding nothing in her employer's face that would help, Amelia put down her spoon. Lying would be pointless. It would not take a great deal of investigation for the powerful Duke or his wealthy family to uncover the truth.

'My mother became very ill and I had to care for her. When our money ran out we could no longer afford to stay in our house in Cheapside. The only place that we could afford was Seven Dials. When my mother died I stayed there until I could better myself.'

Fortunately, nobody probed further because they were all horrified by her sanitised version of events. In truth, Viscount Venomous had refused to continue his meagre financial support the moment he had secured an annulment from her mother. After that, it was as if they had ceased to exist in his mind. With no income, they had been turfed out of their tiny apartment in Cheapside and Amelia had been forced, at the tender age of seventeen, to take employment wherever she could.

With her mother's failing health, permanent employment had been impossible. She'd never known when she would be needed to nurse her, so Amelia had taken casual work to help pay for their awful room in a boarding house. When the consumption got so bad that Amelia could scarcely leave her mother's bedside, even that awful room had been callously removed. It had been Amelia's idea to go to the workhouse. At least there, her mother would have a bed and proper medical attention. It made no difference that Amelia was made to do all manner of demeaning jobs inside that institution as a punishment for the terrible crime of being poor. At least her mother had a roof over her head. When she had been informed of her mother's death, she had left that day, preferring to beg on the streets if need be than to suffer further humiliation at the hands of that inhuman institution. What would these fine people make of that? Even if she told them, she seriously doubted that they would understand.

'How on earth did you manage on your own?' The Dowager looked distraught on her behalf.

'I took jobs and saved my money until I could afford something better.' And her paltry savings had been stolen on two separate occasions. 'I managed well enough.' She'd come out alive. In Seven Dials, that was all you could hope for.

'It does sound dreadful, Amelia.' Sir George appeared sympathetic, then he winked at her when nobody was looking. 'I am surprised that you would willingly want to go back there. What is it that draws you to that place every day?'

Bless him. He had given her an opportunity to explain calmly. The silent, pompous Duke was too well mannered to cause a scene at dinner. That would be bad for digestion.

'My own experiences taught me that poverty is a terrible affliction that the sufferers have not chosen. Nobody decides to be poor or chooses to live in a slum. They are there because that is the only choice available to them. Fortunately, I am well educated. That opened doors to me that would normally remain firmly closed to the majority of those people, and through no fault of their own. I suppose, once you have lived through something like that, it changes you. Now that I am in the fortunate position of being able to do something to help them, I feel that I must.'

'But surely you could do just as much good without putting yourself at risk. You could knit stockings or gloves, for example, like many charitable ladies of my acquaintance do.'

Amelia liked the Dowager and did not want to offend her, so she chose her next words carefully. 'Whilst the poor are grateful for those things, I know that they would prefer food in their bellies. It is easier to work when you are properly fed, and then perhaps they would be able to make enough to buy the other things that they need. A roof over their heads, for example, trumps woollen stockings.'

'Are you telling me that many of them do not even have homes?' Now the Dowager was incredulous, as if such a thing was so far out of the realm of her understanding that she could not even conceive of it.

'A great majority live from day to day. They work to earn enough to eat and to buy a bed for the night. Seven Dials, like all of the slums, is made up of lodging houses. The poor call them doss houses. For a few coins, they can pay to sleep on the floor of large communal rooms. While the unscrupulous landlords make a good living out of this, it makes it more difficult to be able to afford a proper room somewhere. There is more money to be made by offering nightly board. Oftentimes, many people have to resort to sleeping on the streets because they cannot afford even that. The poor become locked in a cycle that is near impossible to break.'

'Did you have to sleep in one of those lodging houses?'

It was the first time that His Holiness had spoken and Amelia was forced to turn towards him. To her surprise, anger shimmered in his silver-blue eyes, but for once it was not directed at her. 'On occasion,' she admitted and saw that anger burn brighter. 'But not for long.' Desperation, she had discovered, made her quite resourceful.

The first course finished, they all sat quietly while the servants cleared and laid the table with the next. Perhaps sensing that the conversation was not really something that the staff should hear, Lovett then promptly dismissed them and instructed the Dowager to ring when they were finished. As soon as he pulled closed the large double doors, Sir George spoke again.

'The picture that you paint is very dire indeed, Amelia. However, what I struggle to understand is why those poor wretches continue to have children when they do not have enough money to put food in their own stomachs. I am patron of a foundling hospital, and I can assure you that it is full to bursting. Every week another child is left on the doorstep.'

Amelia tried hard not to be annoyed by his ignorance, but it was difficult. How could he hope to understand when he had been shielded from the truth? 'No mother willingly gives up her child, sir. Their circumstances must be very dire indeed for them to have resorted to such a thing. For many, they hand over their children in the hope that those children will have food and shelter. If it is a choice between seemingly abandoning their baby or consigning their child to death, that choice is easier to make. It is also worth stating, although it pains me to do so, that you are assuming that those women had those children willingly. Many do not have a choice in that either. There are many unscrupulous men who take advantage of poor women.'

An uncomfortable hush settled over the table as the full meaning of her words sank in. Sir George actually blushed. Both the Dowager and Lady Worsted covered their mouths in shock. The Duke's voice was clipped as he stared pointedly at Amelia. 'This conversation is hardly appropriate for the dinner table.'

Chapter Fifteen

*Once damaged, a woman's reputation can never
be restored. If there is even the slightest whiff
of anything unsavoury, she is definitely not the
wife for you...*

'Mother, I wonder if we should all visit Aveley Castle at the weekend.'

His mother grasped those words with both hands, as he had known she would, and soon all attention was drawn away from Miss Mansfield's unfortunate past and to excited preparations for a few days in the country. Bennett had changed the subject not because he had felt it unseemly, but because the images her descriptions put into his mind were making him so angry he wanted to smash something. To think of her, so young and so alone, sleeping on straw with a bunch of stinking strangers or, worse, taken advantage of by 'unscrupulous' men made his blood boil.

'You will love Aveley Castle, Amelia,' his mother gushed. 'It is surrounded by the most beautiful parkland and, although it is not the largest of castles, it is delightfully cosy and so very peaceful. Although it might be the perfect opportunity to do some entertaining. It has been an age since we have had people visit the Castle. Do not panic, Bennett; I have no intention of subjecting you to a house party, but I would enjoy inviting a few acquaintances for afternoon tea as we are so close to town, and perhaps some horse riding.'

'Do you ride, Amelia?' This came from Uncle George.

His aunt answered for her. 'It has been years since Amelia has been on a horse, hasn't it, dear? Perhaps you could take her out, George, to refresh her memory and remind her of the skill? George taught Bennett to ride, so you will be in very safe hands.'

Bennett let the chatter wash over him. Frankly, he had too many things to think about and none of them were pleasant. Like the fact that he had been unaware that the poor might be trapped in a cycle of poverty which they were helpless to change. What good were cleaner streets if people did not even have homes? Or food? And had Miss Mansfield suffered unduly during that dreadful time? If he found out that anyone had done anything even slightly untoward, he would personally enjoy tearing them limb from limb. And how was it that absolutely everyone now called her Amelia, but he still had to call her Miss Mansfield? Or did she think him so 'stodgy' that he would prefer to maintain that stiff formality, even though he *had* kissed her and she *had* kissed him back?

When the interminable meal finally came to an end, Bennett stood. 'Miss Mansfield, if we might have that word now? I shall direct Lovett to send some tea to my study.' Even that came out like a clipped order, making him inwardly cringe as he marched out of the dining room, expecting her to follow him. He was beginning to think he was incapable of sounding anything other than like an army general in her presence and wished fervently that he didn't.

To make him feel even worse, when he sat in one of the comfortable chairs closest to the fire, expecting her to sit in the other, she stood primly in front of him like a soldier waiting to be inspected. It was up to him to put her at her ease.

'Did any of those unscrupulous men take advantage of you?' He barked the words. Clearly he was doomed to be incapable of acting anywhere near normal around her. His nerves kept getting the better of him, making him sound like an old curmudgeon. No wonder she stood to attention.

'That depends on your definition of *advantage*, I suppose.' She knew damn well that was not the sort of answer he wanted, but he forced himself to wait. If he spoke, he would bark again and probably send her running to pack her bags before they had a chance to talk. Eventually, she sighed and perched on the edge of the chair. 'Many tried to take advantage, but fortunately none succeeded.'

Bennett felt himself physically sag with relief. He would not have to commit murder just yet on her behalf. 'I am greatly relieved to hear that, Miss Mansfield.'

She nodded her dark head in acknowledgement and then sat quietly, waiting for him to continue. It was obvious she had no intention of making this encounter any easier, so Bennett took a deep breath and tried not to sound irritated.

'Under the circumstances, now that I am better informed about your situation, I am prepared to concede that my tone this afternoon was…'

'Boorish? Dictatorial? Impossibly rude?'

'Perhaps…' He risked a small smile at her continued impertinence and saw her hard expression soften slightly. It spurred him to be honest. 'You must understand that you gave me the fright of my life. When I saw those men and heard what they had planned for you, my fear might have made it appear as if my anger was directed at you. It really wasn't. I was angry that you had put yourself in danger; I still am. It makes no difference to me how well you may know that area or how independent you have been in the past; as far as I am concerned, I still believe that it is foolhardy for you to venture there alone. But I will not try to prevent you from going. I can now see how much helping those people means to you. I overreacted and for that I am sorry. In my defence, I had just been punched. Repeatedly.'

She glanced down at her clasped hands in her lap, but he could see that there was a hint of a smile on her lips. 'Under the circumstances, I suppose I can forgive your overbearing tone. And I am sorry that you were hurt because of me.'

'It was my pleasure.'

Her eyes flicked up then and she grinned when she saw that he was being ironic. 'How is your nose?'

Fortunately, it was not broken. 'A bit sore, but I shall endure it manfully.'

His sarcasm made her giggle and her dark eyes sparkle. All at once the world was a better place. 'You did surprise me. I thought that they would beat you to a pulp. Yet you gave as good as you got. How come an illustrious duke punches like a barroom brawler?'

'I am a politician, Miss Mansfield. As a rule, politicians are not very popular and some people are inclined towards violence when they come into contact with one. After the Prime Minister was assassinated a few years ago, I thought it might be prudent to learn how to properly defend myself should the occasion ever arise.'

'Well, I am grateful for your interference today and, in the spirit of compromise, I shall take Terence with me next time I venture out. Those ruffians gave me quite a fright as well and I do not wish Lady Worsted to worry unduly about me.'

'I am very glad to hear that too.' Suddenly self-conscious, Bennett glanced at the pile of paperwork on his desk rather than let her see the blatant emotion in his eyes. She took this to mean that he had much better things to do than waste more time with her and stood, looking a little bit flustered and embarrassed.

'I should probably go and tell Lady Worsted that peace has returned between us.'

'Indeed.' What was the matter with him? He was all stiff and formal again and she was almost at the door because he did not know how to stop her from leaving. 'I took your advice and lay down in the hallway.' Bennett could feel the beginnings of a blush as she turned around, but he ploughed on, feeling inordinately stupid at the admission. 'I did not realise that those cherubs were throwing flowers about like confetti to rain down on my head.' He was cringing so much that his toes began to curl inside his boots. Her dark eyebrows were raised in question and he realised that he was not really making himself clear. 'What I meant to say is that perhaps you are right about perspective. Perhaps it is important to see things from different angles.'

She stared at him thoughtfully and he found himself hoping that she might be re-evaluating her opinion of him. 'I am glad to hear you say that,' she finally said before closing the door behind her.

Amelia did not see him the following day until he made a late appearance at his mother's reading salon. He tried to slip in unnoticed while Lady Cecily was reading a sugary poem and stood leaning against the wall in the furthest and most unobtrusive corner of the room. However, his arrival caused a stir regardless. The Potentials were out in force and were falling over each other to impress him with their suitability to be the next duchess. Lady Cecily began to aim her recital directly at him with limpid eyes and trembling lips, to the consternation of Lady Priscilla and Lady Eugenie. As the ethereal Cecily continued to spout rhyming adoration at the Duke, all they could do was primp and preen and hope that he noticed them; Amelia was very pleased to note that he didn't. It said something about his character that he was not impressed by their obvious public displays, but it was hugely entertaining to watch, especially as she was sitting next to Sir George, who kept making humorous insults which made her giggle.

Unconsciously, her eyes kept darting back to where he stood, seemingly engaged in the readings. Since yesterday, the Duke of Aveley had occupied the majority of her thoughts, leaving Amelia feeling decidedly off-kilter. The man's physical appeal was undeniable. She had known that since the very first moment she had clapped eyes on him. But Amelia was not so shallow to allow that sort of superficial attraction to affect her judgement of a person, especially a person in possession of a title. She was far too intelligent to be won over by a pair of striking blue eyes and a broad pair of shoulders. Her pulse might well ratchet up several notches whenever she was near him, and she might well have an overwhelming desire to pat her hair and smooth down her dress out of vanity in his presence, but as she was neither blind nor dead she supposed such feelings were only human. Fortunately, his pomposity at their first meeting had allowed her to put her understandable reaction to his golden beauty to one side. He had been an arrogant, self-righteous aristocrat, just like her awful father, and therefore intellectually unappealing.

Yet now he was not quite so easy to pigeonhole. She now knew that he had many character traits that were, surprisingly, most admirable and served to bring her harsh opinion of him into question. Yesterday he had selflessly come to her rescue and then had the good grace to apologise for his bullish behaviour afterwards. And he had lain on the floor to look at his painting in order to see for himself if there was more than one perspective. She wished she had seen that. And he had been kind when he had caught her walking home alone in the dark, shared his horse with her and changed his route, when most men of his calibre would have simply ridden on without giving her any thought at all.

When one got past the formality and starchiness of his ducal exterior, he could be quite charming really. Like him, that charm was understated and contained, but he understood irony and had the capacity to be self-effacing. If he carried on being charming, then she might have to stop thinking of him as pomp-

ous—and then where would she be? Already she sus-
pected that his brusque manner might have something
to do with his own discomfort rather than his inflated
opinion of his own importance. He had admitted that
he found large social gatherings awkward when she
had found him hiding in the Renshaws' garden. Was
there the chance that he might also find personal in-
teractions difficult as well? It must be quite difficult
being a duke and a member of the cabinet. Especially
if you were a bit shy.

Now she also knew that he could be eminently reasonable too. He had apologised, after all. When did
titles ever apologise? And, gracious, the man could
kiss! Not a day had gone by since the eventful night
when she had not allowed her mind to wander back to
that unexpected, but not unwelcome, encounter under
the stars. If Bennett Montague had not been a dyed-
in-the-wool aristocrat, Amelia would be very tempted
by him indeed.

'Thank goodness—' Sir George's exasperated whisper brought her back from her wool-gathering '—I was
beginning to believe Lady Cecily might go on all night.
That was one of the worst poems I have ever heard.'

Amelia turned to him, grinning. 'I am beginning to
think that you disapprove of Lady Cecily. Do you not
think that she would make a good duchess?'

He looked about him carefully and then dropped
his voice further. 'Can I entrust you with a secret, my
dear?' When she nodded, intrigued, he bent close to
her ear. 'If you want the honest truth, I heartily disapprove of all of the Potentials.'

Those words surprised her. 'Whilst I agree that
Lady Cecily is a little too calculated for my liking,

surely they are not all like that? They would not have made the list in the first place unless they had the requisite attributes for the position.'

He waved away her comment, his grey eyebrows drawn together in consternation. 'I am sure that they are nice enough girls in their own way. But you misunderstand me. It is not so much the ladies themselves that I disapprove of, it is the manner in which Bennett is seeking a wife. Holding these women up against a set of criteria laid down by my brother is not the way to make such an important decision. Now every girl is trying too hard to behave in the manner they all think he expects, it has become virtually impossible to distinguish between them. They have camouflaged and suppressed all of the character traits that might have made them interesting in the first place. It is no surprise to me that he is struggling to choose one. I am not altogether convinced he is particularly enamoured of any of them, despite his insistence that he wants the sort of wife that his father would have chosen for him. But Bennett is not really like his father at all, if you want my opinion, although he might think that he is. I grew up with my brother and I have been there for every step of Bennett's life and, in personality, they are quite different. My nephew has inherited his father's talent as a politician but there is more to him than that. With my brother, his political ambitions superseded everything else. Bennett does not have that selfish single-mindedness. He cares about people too much. That is why he campaigns for causes that his father would never have touched. My brother never would have championed reform and risked upsetting the House. But Bennett does so if he intrinsically believes that it is the right thing to do. Therefore, it stands to reason that the sort of woman he should marry would be very different to the sort my brother conditioned him to believe that he should.'

Without thinking, Amelia's eyes flicked back to the man in question and she was surprised to find him staring right back at her. Then a slow smile turned up the corners of his perfect mouth just a little and she found herself drowning in that heady blue gaze, smiling back at him like a doe-eyed fool while her heartbeat quickened and her lips tingled of their own accord.

Irritated at her own silly reaction, Amelia resolutely refocused all of her attention on his uncle again. 'At least we have been spared another reading from *The Discerning Gentleman's Guide* tonight. That should give you some comfort.'

'Now you have jinxed it.' Sir George groaned and then rolled his eyes. 'Lady Eugenie is still to read and she is *so* very eager to please.'

'Am I interrupting?'

Chapter Sixteen

*It stands to reason that your wife will understand
that your first mistress is your duty...*

Amelia's insides did a funny flip-flop at the familiar deep voice and she braced herself inwardly to be
dazzled by the Duke's smile before she turned and
faced him.

'Not at all, dear boy,' Sir George replied cheerfully.
'In fact, I insist you take my chair while I go and find
something better to drink than this dreadful sherry
your mother insists on serving.' The traitor had made
no complaint before this moment, which led Amelia to
believe that he was leaving her alone with his nephew
on purpose. As his uncle stood up, the Duke quickly
sat in the seat that he had vacated. Amelia tried, and
failed, to ignore the wonderful aroma of bay rum and
golden duke that emanated from his well-fitting coat.

'Have I missed anything interesting?' He was leaning ever so slightly towards her so that he could speak
quietly. This had two, very unwelcome, effects. Firstly,
it made Amelia intensely aware of her own skin. Every

inch of it seemed to have come alive at the sultry sound
of this man's melted butter voice. Whilst her nerve endings danced in anticipation of something they had no
place to be anticipating, almost all eyes in the room
were suddenly turned in her direction. Wondering why
the Duke had singled her out for particular attention,
the Potentials, as one, all shot daggers at her.

'Not yet. So far, none of your admirers have enter-
tained us with a reading from your book.'

Amelia was quite pleased that her voice sounded
normal because enormous butterflies had arrived in
her stomach and were flapping around ferociously as
a result of his close proximity and the unexpected intimacy of their whispered conversation.

'Thank Heaven for small mercies. Try to hide your
disappointment at that, Miss Mansfield, or my feelings
might be hurt. I know you disapprove of my book.'

When he was like this, affable, playful and unas-
suming, it was easy to forget he was a duke. 'It's not so
much that I disapprove of it—although I do, of course,
because it is drivel—just the more I learn about your
character, the less likely it seems that you would have
written it in the first place.'

'Is it not stodgy enough?'

Without thinking, she nudged him playfully and
that earned more evil glares from his admirers, which
she decided to ignore. 'Oh, it is stodgy to the point
that it has atrophied—which I suppose is the problem.
Underneath all of that stodginess, there appears to be
a reasonable, enlightened man struggling to get out.'

He grinned triumphantly at her compliment. 'Reasonable *and* enlightened. That sounds positively gush-

ing. Are you feeling unwell, Miss Mansfield? All of this unexpected flattery might go to my head.'

'Why did you write that book?' Because it really did not sound like him.

The Duke sighed and then looked sheepish. 'In my defence, it was never meant to be widely published. I simply jotted down all of the advice my father had given me. I wanted to honour his memory with something solid to pass on to the next generation.' They were not really his words; that was something. 'I never got to see him in action in the House, but he took a great deal of time to educate me about the legacy that I have inherited and the importance of doing things properly. It was only appropriate that I share that.'

'But you must agree with your father's advice or you would never have taken the time to write it down.'

'Being a politician is a vocation and a great responsibility. Therefore, to do the job justice, you have to live by example. The difference between a good politician and a great one lies in their trustworthiness. How can the public have respect for their leaders if the leaders do not hold themselves up to a higher standard and, by default, their wives as well?'

Amelia could not help wondering if those words too had first come from his father's mouth. 'I should like to believe that most people have the good sense to judge our leaders by their deeds rather than their choice of wife. And who decided that your father's high standards were the right ones to judge a great politician by, aside from himself?'

The Duke went to reply and then stopped himself. His sandy brows drew together in thought and he wore an expression of confusion as if he was contemplating a concept that was completely new but, whatever his answer was going to be, Amelia was denied hearing it.

'Lady Eugenie, have you brought something to read to us?' The Dowager brought the gathering back to order and smiled at the last Potential benevolently. Amelia could already see *The Discerning Gentleman's Guide* clutched in the girl's hand like an amulet.

'I should like to hear Miss Mansfield read us something,' Lady Cecily interrupted pointedly while her eyes shimmered with spite in Amelia's direction. 'This is the second time she has attended the reading salon and we are yet to hear *anything* chosen by her.'

Amelia smiled sweetly back at the girl, trying not to be intimidated. Stupidly, she had not brought anything even vaguely suitable to read because she had not thought that anyone would call on her to do so. Companions were usually ignored, so it was easy to blend into the background in situations like this. But now she had inadvertently incurred the wrath of the Potentials, who were all staring maliciously at her in the hope that she would disgrace herself, so she had become fair game. To make her discomfort worse, the political pamphlet she had brought to pass the time was a little too large to slot in between the pages of her book of poetry, so Amelia had chosen a substantial tome from the Aveley library, purely on the basis that it was large enough to hide the pamphlet. She glanced down at the book on her lap at exactly the same moment as the Duke. *The Cultivation of Potatoes and Other Root Vegetables* glared mournfully back.

'Do you have an interest in horticulture?' She could tell by his hushed tone that he was vastly amused.

'Not particularly.' Everyone in the room was watching her expectantly. Lady Cecily was smiling from ear to ear. It was blatantly obvious that the girl had also seen the potato book and was hoping to humiliate Amelia with it. It was inconceivable that she would read about root vegetables. Her pride would simply not allow that to happen, even if the alternative meant offending her hosts and all of their guests.

'I have been studying the writings of Edward Poole.' Boldly, Amelia slipped the controversial pamphlet from its hiding place between the pages. 'I should be honoured to read you a small passage.'

The group stiffened at the mention of Poole; they would all be aware of him as a staunch Radical and supporter of the American Revolution. Undeterred, Amelia stood and began to read.

The rich have little concept of how their fortunes are made. They blindly make their investments without knowing how the profits come from the sweat and toil of honest working men.

Mining, for instance, is one industry that the aristocratic sensibility is happily ignorant of.

They do not see the deep, dangerous tunnels or the men that are forced to squat in the darkness and chisel away at the walls.

They do not see the bleakness in the eyes of the women and children who are forced to drag the black gold out of the ground.

They are happily ignorant of the noxious fumes that can rise unexpectedly from the mineshaft, poisoning the lungs of these people.

Nor do they hear their tortured cries when the walls of the mine collapse, killing all still inside. All the rich see is their profits. It matters not the human cost of such bounty.

A stony silence prevailed for what seemed like an eternity after she had sat down and slotted the offending pamphlet back into the folds of the book. Next to her, the Duke was the first to break it.

'Have you ever been to a coal mine, Miss Mansfield?'

Expecting a public set-down for daring to read the work of a Revolutionary when he had expressly requested that she avoid all Radicals, she shook her head and waited for the onslaught.

'I have. I visited the Felling mine a few years ago and I have never seen a more wretched place in all of my life. At the time, I was concerned for the safety of the workers but was assured that everything was perfectly safe. A year later, there was a horrific explosion deep under the ground. Over ninety perished, many of them children. I have petitioned Parliament many times since to make laws to force the mine owners to improve safety. Unfortunately, so far, my pleas have fallen on deaf ears.'

She really had not been expecting that to come out of his mouth. He had compassion. He did care. A small part of the wall she had built around her heart crumbled at the realisation.

'I think it is time for some refreshments.' The Dowager hastily rang the bell for tea, thus sparing her privileged guests from witnessing a discussion about the depressing and harrowing topic Amelia had inadver-

Your Grace. Try not to scratch it. You will get used to the discomfort soon enough.' Lovett made no attempt to hide his delight at the spectacle of his employer dressed like a labourer and stepped back so that he could take a thorough survey of his creation. 'You almost pass muster, Your Grace.'

'Almost? What is wrong?'

At that, Lovett stepped forward and held up his palms. 'If you will permit me to make some minor adjustments, Your Grace?'

The Duke nodded and the butler plunged his fingers into his master's hair and ruffled it mercilessly. At the top of the stairs, the valet whimpered at the destruction of his only piece of work this morning and then scurried away with his hand covering his mouth in mortification. Satisfied, Lovett grinned. 'Perfection, Your Grace. Now you look as common as muck.'

No, he didn't, thought Amelia with mounting alarm, he looked delightfully dishevelled and completely accessible. The mussed hair, stubble and bare throat made him appear as she imagined he would had he just got out of bed. A part of her was disappointed that he was wearing clothes. A larger part was horrified that she would even think such a thing.

'The carriage is outside, Your Grace, and I have instructed the driver to drop you in Piccadilly.'

'Very good, Lovett. Shall we, Miss Mansfield?' Solicitously, he held out his arm and smiled at her boyishly, the last vestiges of the pompous Duke gone.

Amelia nodded curtly. It was the only response she could muster at that precise moment. It was all so surreal, and so utterly charming, that it was overwhelming. He was charming. And handsome. Even in hobnails.

And an aristocrat.

She had to remember that. The clothes did not make the man. Underneath the coarse coat he was still a duke and she should never lose sight of that fact.

Chapter Seventeen

The perfect young lady is very industrious. She sews and paints, plays the piano, sings or composes poetry. Such pursuits are wholly suitable for the delicate female temperament...

Miss Mansfield was unusually quiet in the carriage and wore an expression of uncomfortable bewilderment. Whether that was because she was stunned that he had actually come with her today or she was horrified to be stuck with him for the duration he could not rightly say, but the effect was unnerving. Nobody was as surprised as Bennett himself at what he was about to do. A week ago, if somebody had said that he should dress as a pauper and work in a soup kitchen, he would have told them in no uncertain terms that he had much better things to do with his time. Like helping to run the country. He was more knowledgeable about the poor than anybody else he knew. Hadn't he read extensively on the topic? Hadn't he visited the mines, factories and workhouses on numerous occasions? Hadn't he lobbied for change on their behalf?

However, since he had lain in his own hallway to look at his own painting in wonderment, he could not shake the feeling that there were other things that he had once been quite certain of which he was now convinced he might have got wrong. From that moment, it had been imperative that he find out for himself what was actually going on in the slums as an ordinary working man rather than as a duke who lived, as Miss Mansfield had scathingly called it, a gilded life. There were so many things that now needed urgent clarification that he did not know quite where to start. What sort of people went to a soup kitchen? Surely they were only the most wretched? What were the doss houses like? He needed to know how Miss Mansfield had suffered to reassure himself that it was not as bad as his imagination warned him it had been.

And what did those people really think of the government? Because if the government was as out of touch with reality as he was beginning to think, then perhaps there *was* a very real possibility of a revolution in England whereby all of the old would be ruthlessly swept away, much like it had in France and America, and everything that Bennett stood for would be gone. Somebody needed to do something to prevent that from happening and that somebody might as well be him. He had a duty to all of the people of Britain to do right by them, not just the noble few. He just wished that Miss Mansfield was as confident in his abilities as he was himself. And why was it that her good opinion of him was suddenly paramount?

'I shan't let you down,' he blurted as the carriage lurched to a stop at the end of Piccadilly. 'Nobody will know that I am a member of the aristocracy, if that is what you are worried about, and you will still be able to continue your good works unaffected after today.'

She gave him a lacklustre smile. 'I am sure that you will do your best, although your accent might well betray you.'

'I can change that,' he offered reassuringly in his best impression of a cockney. 'I knows how the common man speaks.'

Her answering smile was genuine. 'Where would you like to go first? We have an hour or two before I need to be at the kitchen.'

Bennett shrugged as he helped her out of the carriage. 'You are my guide today. I want to know the truth, Miss Mansfield, no matter how awful that might be. Show me all of the things that you think I should see.'

'All right. But I am curious to know what you intend to do with the knowledge.'

That was easy to answer. Bennett had always known what his role in the government was. 'I shall use the knowledge to try to change things. I am well aware of the need for reform; however, I am prepared to concede that the reforms I believe are the most pressing might not be so for the poor.'

'That is all well and good; however, Parliament is notoriously slow at bringing about change. You have said yourself that it has tantrums that prevent any meaningful work from being done. What makes you think they will be open to listening to you?'

Bennett pondered this for a moment. She did make a valid point. 'Change is always slow. That way it can occur without alarming anyone.' Or so his father had always said.

'By "anyone" you mean the aristocracy. Yet they are the people least affected by reform.'

Another valid point that completely contradicted his father's wisdom. The more time he spent with this vexing woman, the more uncertain about his unshakeable beliefs he became. 'Perhaps. However, there are a great many politicians and aristocrats who realise that reform is inevitable. The last thing we all want is a revolution here on our own doorstep. Which is precisely why a slower pace of change is preferable. Reforms should come via compromise rather than forcibly. It is better for everyone that way. In a few years, things will be very different.'

Her lovely face screwed up in consternation. 'And in those few years, thousands will have died as a result of the poverty they are trapped in. I doubt they would agree that the introduction of slow reform is preferable—but, as they do not have any say in what is done to them, either in Parliament or outside of it, I suppose it is easier to ignore their pleas. England's laws are made without their consultation.'

'We do not want to alienate the aristocracy either.' All at once Bennett felt defensive of the system of government he had always believed in, a system that had taken hundreds of years to create. 'We need them to agree to pay more in taxes to help fund the improvements we must make for the poor.'

'Heaven forbid that they should be lighter in the pocket. Why, once a week they might have to eat fish instead of beef. Or a lady might have to suffer the indignity of one fewer gown each season. Meanwhile, innocent children are dying.'

When she put it like that, it was difficult to defend

his father's argument— No! His own argument. Or was it their argument? 'Once I take on a cause, I do not abandon it. Show me how things really are in Seven Dials and I give you my word that I will do all that I can to help, Miss Mansfield.'

For a moment he thought that she would continue to argue, but then she shrugged. 'That is a start, I suppose.' She set off at her customary brisk pace and Bennett did his best to march beside her in his unwieldy hobnailed boots. They had walked less than ten paces when she stopped and glared at him. 'If you are going to blend in, it might be better if you unclasped your hands from behind your back. Your posture is far too noble.'

Feeling decidedly odd with his arms dangling loose, Bennett offered one of them to her and she laughed as she took it. 'Put your other hand in your pocket. That is what pockets are for.'

She led him nimbly through Covent Garden and along Shaftesbury Avenue to the edge of the infamous area known as Seven Dials. A place where seven rancid streets all converged around a sundial, as if the sun could blaze through all of the squalor in the overcrowded narrow streets to show anyone the time.

The first thing that struck him was the smell. Even on this crisp winter's morning, it was a pungent combination of rotting vegetables, raw sewage and human sweat, so powerful that it began to make his eyes water. Before, when he had visited the poor, he had taken a perfumed vinaigrette to sniff in order to minimise the foul air, but only the rich did that. The poor had no choice but to be offended by the stench until they were used to it, so he soldiered on. Miss Mansfield sensed his discomfort and squeezed his arm reassuringly. 'You won't notice it in an hour. Your nose becomes quite immune to it all after a while.'

But it strengthened his resolve to clean up the streets. Nobody should have to live in filth like this. Yet they did. Huddled in every doorway and alleyway were people, bundled up in rags to ward off the cold, their sunken eyes and drawn expressions stark evidence of their desperation. A man and a woman stood shielding two scrawny, shoeless children from the worst of the frigid breeze. 'Why are those people just standing around?'

'They have nowhere else to go. The streets are their home.' She said this kindly, almost as if he was a child and she was trying to soften the blow. 'I am sure that when they can they take refuge in a lodging house. Later, we will probably see them at the kitchen, unless they find work in between.' Bennett was not reassured. The children were clearly half-starved and it did not take a genius to know that their time on God's earth was likely to be limited.

'What sort of work is available here for those people?'

'Mostly casual labour. The flower market might pay them to fetch and carry. Many factories will decide on the day how many workers they need and recruit accordingly. Usually, the normal practice is for the workers to wait outside the factory gates early in the morning in the hope of getting something—but many will leave empty-handed if there is no work to be had. Those that can afford a roof over their heads can earn a living from piecework, although that is equally as hard. To pay for the room, several people all club together, sometimes I have known as many as ten or twelve souls all squashed in one tiny room. The majority of the inhabitants survive day by day.'

She painted a very grim picture that was at odds with what Bennett had always been told about the slums. He had believed that the poor were divided into three distinct categories. Those who wanted to work and did so cheerfully; those who did not want to work and preferred to make a living out of foul means; and those who could no longer work because of illness or age. But the sight of that tragic young family had bothered him. They had been trying to protect their children from the cold with their own bodies. The father probably desperately wanted to earn enough to keep them all safe, but the circumstances in Seven Dials made that impossible. If he were in that position, he might well resort to stealing if it meant that he could get those children out of the cold.

They walked on further and turned into Norfolk Street, a street dominated by one huge municipal brown brick building surrounded by a high wall. 'That is the workhouse,' Miss Mansfield said matter-of-factly, although something about her expression did not quite ring true as she scurried past it without breaking her stride. 'It is run by the parish and provides board and shelter for the most desperate.'

'Surely board and shelter is better than living on the street?' The image of the young family still haunted him. Here they would be fed. Be warm. The children would be shod. 'Is it full?'

'There are always plenty of inmates, but nobody enters those gates willingly.' Those gates, he noticed, she hurried past with more speed than she had anything else.

'Why?' Bennett tugged on her arm and forced her to stop.

She faced him reluctantly before she answered. 'It is like a prison. The work is hard and monotonous and the inmates are constantly reminded of the fact that they are a burden to society. You might well be given basic amenities and food, but the cost of that is dreadful. Families are separated.' At that she pointed to different parts of the building a little too dispassionately. 'The men are housed to the left, and the women on the right. The children have a separate wing at the rear of the building, near the infirmary. It is forbidden for them to mix with each other.' She shivered as she looked back at the heavy wrought-iron gates, her expression bleak. 'Many desperate people go in, but few come out. It is a place to die. A place of no hope.'

Bennett could have sworn he saw tears shimmer in her dark eyes before she turned away and continued along the street as if her life depended on it. All at once, he was filled with an enormous sense of foreboding. Miss Mansfield was not passing on second-hand information, he suddenly realised with a jolt. She had experienced it.

'You lived here.' It was a statement rather than a question and she nodded without slowing her pace. Bennett felt anger curdle in his gut and his instantly clenched fists ached to punch something. All of that sudden fury resonated in his voice. 'How did that happen?'

She shrugged in an attempt to make him believe that it did not matter and forced lightness into her reply.

'You already know that I came to Seven Dials when my mother fell ill. When her condition worsened I needed to look after her, which made it difficult to earn money. Doctors are expensive. They do not work for free. At least in the workhouse she received medical attention and medicine.' As the walls of the workhouse gave way to a small cemetery, she finally came to a halt, staring wistfully at the unkempt plot of land. 'She is buried here somewhere. I am not sure exactly where because I was only told of her passing after the funeral had taken place, but at least I have somewhere to visit.'

His heart ached for her. She stood so proudly and so still. That she had had to cope with all of that alone, and had not only survived it but emerged so determined to change things for others, humbled him. What a truly remarkable young woman she was. Suddenly, knowing the correct way to seat guests at dinner paled into insignificance when compared to Miss Mansfield's achievements. She had sunk as low as any human could, climbed out of the pit, dusted herself off and then rolled up her sleeves to fix things. He seriously doubted that any of the Potentials had that much gumption. Yet this tiny woman still managed to blithely carry on without complaining.

But now she was sad because she was remembering it all. He wanted to chase away the ghosts in her sorrowful eyes, so it felt like the most natural thing in the world to pull her into his arms and hold her close. She did not protest and went into his embrace willingly, her dark head resting below his chin as they both stared at her mother's pathetic excuse for a grave. 'Did you have no one else who could help you? Family, perhaps?'

'Nobody who was willing to help. My mother's family were long dead and my father was indifferent.'

Up until that point Bennett had assumed her father to be dead and he stiffened. 'He was alive at the time?'

'He is still alive, although he has long been dead to me. He washed his hands of us when I was only twelve. I haven't seen him in years.'

Chapter Eighteen

*A young lady's outward appearance gives you
many clues as to her character. One who wears
gowns that are too bold or too plain should be
avoided...*

Amelia had no idea why she felt compelled to be
truthful, aside from the fact that she was enjoying the
sensation of being held by him and of feeling protected
for once. Years of being on her own had made her forget how heady that feeling was. That and the painful
location where they currently stood. Norfolk Street
always elicited a powerful yearning for all she had
lost, reminding her of how awful things had been and
forcing her to recall images of her poor mother at her
absolute worst—weak, deathly pale, completely broken, inside and out.

Under normal circumstances Amelia would have
avoided the street like the plague, and had done for a
full year after her mother's death even though she had
lived only a few yards away. Usually she came here
only on the anniversary of the day she'd died—or, as

she had this year, on the closest day that she could get to that fateful date.

But these were far from normal circumstances. He had asked her to show him the things that she thought he should see, and there was no way of doing that properly without showing him the workhouse. She had intended to march past quickly; it had been his fault that they had dithered. He was not here on sufferance or out of a sense of duty. He had come willingly in order to learn, so it seemed wrong to pretend that she did not have personal experience of the utter desperation and complete degradation wrought by poverty. And now she was wrapped in his comforting embrace and wondering exactly how she might bring herself to willingly extricate herself from it.

'What sort of a father allows his wife and daughter to sink into poverty?' She could feel the anger in his body as his arms tightened around her possessively. 'Did he not know where you were?'

'I told him.' More truth. 'He did not care.'

'He let your mother die in the workhouse and left you to fend for yourself? A young girl in this terrible place?'

His incredulity at her situation made her defensive, although not towards him. Her outraged sense of injustice would always be directed at her hateful father. 'At the time, my options were the streets or the workhouse. I had hoped that I would be allowed to spend my mother's final days with her, but the wardens would hear none of it. Burdens to society do not deserve basic human kindness. And then it was too late. If I could do it all over again, I would choose the streets. At least then I could have been with her when she died. I am certain that my father will have to atone for his sins one day. That is a small comfort.' When that time came she sincerely hoped that he suffered for all eternity in the fiery bowels of Hell.

He held her at arm's length then and stared deeply into her eyes. 'Tell me his name and I will see that he atones for them now!'

The fierce determination in his eyes thrilled her. It was so very tempting that Amelia had to break eye contact to avoid answering. Lady Worsted had explicitly told her to keep that part of her identity a secret while she was in London, to avoid embarrassing her nephew with the scandal. It had been an easy bargain to stick to because Amelia had ceased thinking of the Viscount as her father a long time ago.

'He is dead to me,' she said instead without meeting his gaze. 'I would prefer to leave it that way.'

The Duke did not look convinced. Before he could press the matter further she set off down the road at a brisk pace. 'We should head to the soup kitchen now. There will be plenty to do before lunchtime and I am heartily sick of all this melancholy.'

The walk took less than ten minutes, during which time neither of them spoke. Her companion was deep in thought and clearly still fuming and Amelia regretted her loose tongue. He was here to see what life was really like for the poor, not to fight her battles for her, and she was feeling increasingly uncomfortable about talking about her past so openly. The Duke now knew more about her than any other living soul—even Lady Worsted had no idea about her stay at the workhouse and the hopelessness of her situation then—although she was beginning to trust him, which was a peculiar state of affairs in itself. He had a title, yet she trusted him? Enough to have told him about the workhouse—but Amelia hated feeling vulnerable and exposed, preferring to keep those uncomfortable emotions well hidden from anyone who might construe them as weakness. Which meant that she had kept them well hidden for four long years.

But now he knew that she had suffered at the hands of another, had been left with nothing and destitute, and she resented his pity almost as much as she resented her need to seek more of his comfort. Of all the men she should choose to confess her sorry tale to, she had to go and choose a duke. His sympathy would only extend so far, no matter how much her heart was becoming attached. At some point he would become a duke again, so she needed to remain resolutely detached.

As they walked closer to the Rookery, the character of the streets became darker. Drunkenness and squalor lived hand in hand here and from time to time Amelia saw the Duke's eyes widen at something he had glimpsed. She felt a pang of sympathy for him; she remembered her own horror when she'd first set eyes on this place, not quite believing that human beings actually lived like this. However, Seven Dials was also awash with the milk of human kindness. Those with nothing were often the most generous because they knew what it was to suffer. And the heart of that kindness was where they were heading. The Church of St Giles was the only building that did not look ready to fall down at any given moment. Its tall white spire stood proudly in stark contrast to all of the filth and depravity, like a beacon of hope in this place of despair. The place of her reinvention and salvation. Home.

Amelia directed the Duke around the back to the wooden hall where they distributed the poor relief but paused just outside the door. 'These people have known me for many years. I shall tell them that you are a friend of mine who wants to help out. They trust me and are wary of newcomers. Lots of people, including politicians, are highly critical of the good work that they do here, believing that providing food for the poor encourages them to become dependent on handouts rather than working. Try not to ask too many questions that might give away your identity.'

Bennett nodded and waited for her to go before him. The sight that met his eyes was as unexpected as it was humbling. There were perhaps ten people working side by side amongst the sacks of vegetables. None were dressed any better than he was now, which suggested that they were all fundamentally poor despite the fact that they were providing charity for the less fortunate, yet there was laughter and a bonhomie that made one want to be a part of it as they cheerfully peeled and chopped. A large, jolly-looking woman with a halo of frizzy grey hair held court but fell silent the moment she laid eyes on them.

Immediately, she dropped what she was doing, wiped her plump hands on the front of her apron and waddled over to Miss Mansfield before engulfing her in a big hug. 'I was beginning to think you weren't coming, Ames.' She released her and then turned to Bennett, her knowing eyes slowly raking down the length of his body and then back again. 'And I see you've brought a fella.' At that she burst out laughing and nudged her with such force that she sent poor Miss Mansfield sideways. 'Well, ain't you the dark horse, gal! He's a right proper sight for sore eyes! What's his name?'

Before he could speak for himself, Miss Mansfield did. 'This is Ben. He's a friend.'

Ben?

Oddly, he liked the informal shortening of his name. He especially liked the way Miss Mansfield said it, although she was having difficulty meeting his eye.

'A friend, is he?' The older woman chortled her disbelief. 'If that's all he is, girl, you'd best pull your finger out and stake a claim on him before somebody else does.' To his complete surprise, Bennett suddenly found his jaw clamped in that plump hand and turned one way and then the other. 'He's gorgeous, Ames! If I was ten years younger, I would steal him off you.'

Having never been treated like a piece of meat before, Bennett was at a loss as to what to say. He didn't want to offend the woman, but ten years was a poor estimate of the vast difference in their ages. This woman looked as if she had long been fully grown whilst he was still toddling around on leading strings.

Miss Mansfield looked thoroughly mortified at her friend's blatant appraisal. 'Oh, leave him be, Dolly, else you'll scare the poor man off and we could do with the help.' It was the first time that he had ever seen her blush and it made her look quite delightful. 'Ben, the woman manhandling you is Dolly. She means well.'

As his blushing guide was casually dropping her *T*'s and flattening her vowels, he did the same but felt so silly that he found himself staring at the floor. 'Nice to meet you.'

'Ooh, and he's a shy one too! I do love the strong, silent type. Especially if he's got all his teeth.' At that

Dolly grinned at him, displaying a set of gums devoid of them. 'But if you've come to help, you might as well start over there. Help Charlie bring all them sacks over.' She gestured towards the huge stack of vegetables in one corner and a pasty, unshaven man with a stooped back.

Bennett's eyes briefly flicked to Miss Mansfield's and she smiled encouragingly, even though she was still horribly embarrassed. 'Is that all right, Ben?'

He definitely liked the way she said that. It was a great improvement on 'Your Grace'. And he liked seeing her all flummoxed and pink too. 'Of course it is…Amelia.'

Of its own volition, his left eye winked at her saucily. He had never winked at anyone or anything in his life, but it had the most wonderful effect on her. Her dark eyes widened, her lush mouth opened slightly in shock and the soft pink blush turned instantly into the most vivid shade of cerise. He was off to haul potatoes, another thing he had never done in his life, yet suddenly all he wanted to do was grin. He was flirting! Him! Now he understood why Uncle George was so keen on it. It was strangely empowering.

He lifted the first sack and nearly dropped it. He had not expected potatoes to be quite that heavy, but *Amelia* was watching him, so he hoisted it with all of his might in the vain hope that he made it look effortless. Then he winked at her again and watched her scurry off, completely flustered. Her lovely hips swayed as she walked and Dolly caught him watching them.

'Just friends, are you, lad? And I'm the Duchess of Devonshire!' Then she winked at him and Bennett found himself blushing too.

The next few hours whipped by in a blur of activity. Bennett fetched and carried, was taught to peel vegetables by Dolly and was then put in charge of stirring the bubbling soup in three of the largest cauldrons he had ever seen. As it was hot work, Dolly insisted that he remove his coat, although he was almost certain that it was as much for her own benefit as for his. The old lady was blatantly ogling him as she stacked bowls with Amelia and shamelessly pumped her for information, not caring that he could hear or that her words were embarrassing her friend.

'Where did you meet your Adonis, then?'

'Um, at a meeting a few weeks ago.'

'You always did have a weakness for do-gooders. What is he, then? A Revolutionary?'

Amelia's pretty face was outraged at the suggestion and her eyes darted towards him briefly before she lowered her voice. 'I don't consort with Revolutionaries, Dolly. You know that. If you must know, it was a meeting about factory conditions. Do you know, at least one child a week is being killed by those machines?'

Dolly appeared unmoved. 'You're trying to change the subject. I want to talk about you and your fancy man.'

'He's not my fancy man!'

Dolly rolled her eyes and then grinned at Bennett. Despite his attempt to appear as though he was not listening, he found himself smiling back at the woman. It was nice to watch somebody else feel uncomfortable for a change, and his aunt's companion was certainly that. Every time he caught her staring at him she blushed like a beetroot and then pretended she had not been looking at him at all. His ego told him that she was casting him admiring glances. The truth was probably nothing quite so exciting.

He could hardly blame her for checking up on him. Her friends would judge her on the strength of his work. Thanks to Charlie, he now knew that the intrepid Miss Mansfield had first come here half-starved and penniless. Dolly had taken her under her wing and helped her find work, and since then she had continued to work here at the soup kitchen whenever she was able. To look at her now, the way she moved around with such purpose and the way everyone else clearly respected her, it would be easy to presume that she belonged here. Such respect would have been hard-won, he knew. He caught Dolly watching him and turned back to his boiling soup and could have sworn that she deliberately spoke louder so that he did not miss her next words of wisdom.

'There is no shame in wanting a bit of comfort from a strong, handsome man in the night, Ames, and he's a strong, very handsome man.'

Amelia did not know where to look, although she was certain it would not be in the Duke's direction. Heaven knew what he must be thinking. Later she would apologise for Dolly's crassness. Right now, if she protested too much, Dolly would become unrelenting. 'We share some of the same ideals,' she finally managed, knowing that perhaps that statement was true. 'But there is nothing else between us, I can assure you.'

'That's just a crying shame, then.' Dolly unceremoniously dumped the last pile of bowls on the long wooden table. 'It's about time you got yourself a nice fella. I hate seeing you all on your own. If you ask me, you're too independent for your own good. Not all men are rotters. I had some lovely ones in my time.' She sighed wistfully and clutched her hands to her generous bosom. 'My second husband, William, he was a lovely man to have around at night. So…vigorous.'

Amelia saw the Duke stifle a smile but decided to say nothing as any further discussion was likely to be a bit ripe. Dolly had no boundaries when it came to talking about her husbands. Fortunately, time was on her side.

'Shall I open the doors, Dolly?' shouted another volunteer from the other side of the room.

After that, it was all hands on deck. Amelia kept a close eye on her guest, fearing that he might find the reality of nigh on a hundred people swarming into the hall in search of a hot meal quite daunting; however, her concerns were unfounded. He coped brilliantly, spooning the nourishing soup into the municipal wooden bowls as if he had done such a menial task every single day of his life. As time went on, she saw him talking to people, a look of intense interest on his face sometimes and humour at others.

He spent a long time with the young family they had seen earlier, huddled in the doorway, listening intently and sympathising with their particular tale of woe. He ruffled their young son's hair, seemingly oblivious to the crawling nasties that undoubtedly lived within it, and crouched down to eye level with their pale and emaciated daughter, telling her some tale that nudged a reluctant smile out of the girl. All the while, Amelia watched for his superior stiffness to return to his body. At no point did he turn back into the pompous Duke, which bothered her immensely, although she could not quite put her finger on why.

When she saw him rush to help an old man who stumbled, watched him guide him to a bench and fetch him a bowl of soup personally, she realised why. As the Duke, he was easier to resist. Her heart was hardened against all men with titles and power. But here, in those ordinary clothes, he was just Ben. And she had no ready-made defences prepared to repel the torrent of tender feelings that were rapidly growing for this complicated and surprising man. One minute so stiff and formal, the next thoughtful and kind. A stickler for timekeeping and correctness who would risk his own safety to save her, who shared his horse and his home, but wrote a silly book about the perfect wife. He knew about coal mines and came to slums to see things from another point of view, a man who hid in gardens because he felt awkward and knew about the stars. A lethal conundrum of a man who looked like sin and kissed like it too.

When he shared a joke with the old man, then sat next to him to listen to his stories, her heart melted. As if he felt her staring at him, he looked her way. The ghost of a smile touched his lips and those intense silver-blue eyes told her that he finally understood what it was about this place that drew her.

Understood and approved.

In shock, she ladled hot soup over her hand and then hissed in pain. Dolly instantly doused the stinging flesh with cold water from her jug and then tutted. 'Just a friend, is he? You were looking at him as if the sun rises and sets with him.'

'I was simply distracted,' she said defensively although her heart was pounding in panic. Amelia felt a lump of pure emotion form in her chest, part wonder, part longing, and realised that she might have done something wholly unexpected and terrifying.

She might have just fallen head over heels for an aristocrat.

Chapter Nineteen

Whilst it is acceptable for a lady to drink ratafia occasionally, stay away from women who partake of other spirits. They cannot be trusted...

Bennett galloped on ahead of the carriages bound for Aveley Castle as soon as they left London, largely because they constricted him and because he did not want to keep trying to catch glimpses of her. Right now, he needed to be alone. Up until recently, he had taken fresh air for granted, but after a day in the slums he vowed that he never would again. Clean air, open roads, trees, albeit bare because of winter, suddenly all felt like such a tremendous luxury that he was very privileged to be able to enjoy.

Such luxuries were non-existent in the slums. He had struggled to sleep since his trip to Seven Dials. It had been an eye-opening experience and one that, if he was brutally honest with himself, had brought him up short. In many ways it was almost too much to take in. Squalor. Hunger. Homelessness. Indignity and injustice. And all just a few miles from Parliament, the only institution with the power to change it. For two nights he had tossed and turned, trying to understand it all and put it into perspective and deciding exactly what he could do to fix things; however, the more he thought about it all the angrier he became on behalf of the people there.

The soup kitchen had provided him with his best window on that world, and what he had learned there had been revelatory. It was not filled with the sick, lame and lazy. Many were undoubtedly sick and lame, but they still worked for a living. That had come as quite a shock. Day by day they toiled in jobs, working longer hours than he did, and yet they still could not afford basic food and shelter. As one old man had put it, a day's wages would pay for one but not the other, so you had to make a choice.

The very fact that the wages were so paltry was shameful. Not a single person he'd met could afford to rent a room. Their beds were the cold, hard floors of interchangeable lodging houses or they slept out in the elements on the street. But, through that, he had also seen humour and humanity. These people helped each other, made the best of things, found things to laugh about and celebrate. The bland vegetable broth and the hard, indigestible bread was the only food many of the poor ate all day, yet it was the people of that parish who continued to raise the money to provide that food. St Giles had no wealthy donors. It relied solely on the generosity of the poor. He'd seen children so malnourished that their young eyes had sunk into their heads. Shoeless. Older than their years. Hopeless. Amelia's description of the struggle had been an accurate one.

But it was mostly Amelia that was keeping him

awake at night. That she had lived through all that through no fault of her own and come out the other side of it determined to help all of the other unfortunates made him, alternatingly, proud at her achievement and furious at her suffering. He was coming to understand her lack of respect for his title. What had the aristocracy ever done for the people of Seven Dials except ignore them?

Yet there was something about her that called to his heart; it was certainly not pity and it was more than attraction. When he had eventually fallen asleep these past two nights, he had dreamed incessantly about her. Fevered dreams that left his body hot and aching when he woke up. He felt both desire for her and a desire to simply see her. Talk to her. In all of his thirty years, he had never experienced anything quite like that, so he could not put a name to it all. Whatever it was, it confused the hell out of him.

Those feelings were made worse by her sudden reluctance to have anything whatsoever to do with him. Bennett had no idea what he had done to deserve that. At the soup kitchen, they had shared a moment. Their eyes had met and, as much as he hated to sound poetic, he had felt that their souls had met as well. But when they had left that place she seemed unable to even look him in the eye. She had scurried back to Mayfair at such a pace that he had been forced to trail behind her. Conversation had been impossible and he got the distinct impression that she had done that on purpose.

Each time he had seen her since, she had been virtually mute and was stuck to his aunt like glue. Surely she was not put out by his one attempt at flirting and winking? The way Dolly was talking, he'd assumed that she heard and saw far worse at the soup kitchen. If he had inadvertently offended, he would, of course, apologise and bring his short-lived winking career to an abrupt end. Or had he done something else to suddenly make her wary of him? Or even hate him?

The thought of the latter made his throat constrict painfully. Just thinking about the woman was sending him mad. He wanted her to like him. But then what? What difference would that make to who he was and what he had to do? He had to marry well, and there were no useful political alliances in the offing with his aunt's companion, but now that prospect made him feel nothing but miserable. But he had promised his father that he would continue his legacy, which left him feeling torn.

Bennett craved the tranquillity of his little castle. Perhaps all he needed was a few days of relaxation in the country in order to get his head back to rights. A few days when he could be by himself and do exactly as he pleased. Or almost as he pleased. His mother had, of course, invited a few people to take afternoon tea with them on Sunday. The Potentials would be there and perhaps he could redouble his efforts to single one out, and maybe stop feeling so lonely and so obsessed with Miss Mansfield.

That aside, he was determined to make the most of his little break. Bennett could only stay the weekend. He was finally due to give his long-awaited speech on Monday afternoon, so he would leave the Castle at first light that morning. Amelia would stay with his family at the Castle for the rest of the week and he found himself both dreading and needing the separation. He was becoming far too obsessed with his aunt's companion.

Tempted by her. A week apart would hopefully allow him to focus on what he *had* to do, rather than what he selfishly *wanted* to do. He would use the two days to sort out all of his tangled thoughts and then plan what he was going to do about everything that confused him. Or specifically about the woman who confused him.

Miss Mansfield.

Amelia.

With a huff of pure frustration, Bennett realised that he had no idea what he should call her any more. Or why he should be so bothered either way.

Lovett stretched out on the bench opposite her and kicked off his shoes. He wiggled his bony feet and grinned at her. 'It's nice to have some company, miss. Usually I have the carriage all to myself when I travel with His Grace; I know the journey out to Aveley Castle is only an hour or so, but I do get a bit bored on my own.'

Lady Worsted had demoted her to the coach carrying all of their luggage just before they had left. 'With my sister and George, there will be three of us already. If the weather turns or dear Bennett decides he no longer wishes to ride alongside, it will be easier all around if you are already *in situ*. We can hardly expect him to sit in the servants' carriage.'

Of course they couldn't.

Normally, something like that would not bother her; however, now that Amelia had realised that she was a little bit in love with her employer's nephew, being consigned to the lesser of the two grand carriages that left Mayfair this morning served to effectively put her back in her place. Duke. Servant. Impossible. Perhaps now she would stop obsessing about the man who apparently had taken over all her thoughts of late.

'Do you play cards?' Lovett magically produced a deck and began to shuffle them like a professional.

'As a matter of fact, Lovett, I do.' Forcing cheerfulness into her voice, Amelia picked up her reticule and gave it a shake. The coins within jingled. 'If it is worth my while.' A bit of friendly gambling might just be exactly what she needed to stop thinking about *him*. It was not as if anything could ever come of it and she refused to lower herself to moping or, heaven forbid, pining.

'Marvellous!' The butler pulled his own purse out of one pocket and dropped it on the bench beside him and then rifled under the seat, wiggling his eyebrows as he sat back up, holding a bottle and just one glass. 'Because I am a gentleman, you can have the glass. I'll just drink from the bottle.'

'What is it?' Amelia wrinkled her nose. She hated gin and nothing on this earth would possess her to drink it.

'His Grace's finest port.'

'You stole his port?' she asked, part incredulous, part reluctantly impressed at the butler's nerve. 'You could be sacked for that.'

Lovett pulled out the cork with his teeth and poured the dark ruby liquid up to the very rim of the glass before handing it to her. 'Nonsense. His Grace is well aware that I take his port. I have been doing it for years and the worst I ever get is a stern look. My skills are far too valuable. Besides, it truly is excellent stuff. Taste.'

Amelia took a dubious sniff and then a small sip. Having never tasted port before, she was pleasantly surprised to find it rich and sweet. It did not burn her throat like brandy, or make her eyes water like gin, so she took a larger sip as Lovett tipped the bottle and poured some into his own mouth. 'I told you it was good,' he said smugly. 'He gets it brought over by the barrel directly from some fancy estate in Portugal where it's made and he hardly makes a dent in it himself. And port goes off if it is not drunk quickly, and I do hate to see good port wasted.'

'Are you sure that we won't get into trouble Lovett?'

'Of course I am sure. He will blame me, shake his head and look put upon—but I am too useful a servant to him for anything else to come of it.'

Amelia suddenly remembered the note Lovett had written to get his master out of the reading salon. 'I suppose you do have a knack for pulling him out of uncomfortable social situations in the nick of time with your little notes.'

Lovett eyed her thoughtfully. 'How do you know that? Did His Grace confide in you? Even his own mother is unaware of that little ruse.'

'I have my ways,' she offered cryptically and took another sip of the delicious drink whilst the butler dealt the cards. 'I found him hiding in the garden at the Renshaw ball.' Clearly port made one's tongue loosen. 'I suspect that the Duke makes a habit of hiding.'

Lovett picked up his cards and fanned them. 'I blame the Potentials. Since they came along, he's been hiding a little too often for my liking, which is a ridiculous state of affairs for a man who claims he is going to marry one of them. It is their fault that I am being dragged to the Castle. The moment Her Grace informed His Grace that she had invited those girls, he insisted that I come too. Although, in fairness, every time they have guests at the Castle I am press-ganged into service. I have a great talent for saving him at just the right time, you see. Not that I mind really. I consider it a good trade. I save him and in return I get to drink his port.'

He grinned and took another swig. 'In the last year I have had to invent so many excuses to help him escape, he has started to call me his saviour! Surely, if he was that keen to be caught in the parson's trap, he would be falling over himself to woo one of them? But not His Grace. In fact, if you want my humble opinion, I don't think any one of them is even remotely suitable.'

'Really, Lovett? Do tell.'

So much for not thinking about *him* today.

They made good time, arriving at the Castle just after lunch. Bennett had already made up his mind to have it out with Miss Mansfield and see why she was being so stand-offish, and if he had to humiliate himself by apologising for winking, then so be it. It would teach him a valuable lesson. He knew better than to behave in any way other than appropriately. He could only imagine what his father would have said. *Dukes do not wink, Bennett. It simply isn't done.*

Fortunately, her carriage arrived almost as soon as he dismounted, so he marched towards it with renewed purpose. Whatever he had done wrong, he had to make it right. Aside from his wholly inconvenient attraction to the woman, the insight that she'd given him into the lives of the ordinary people was invaluable. Bennett wanted to improve their lot in life. Of that he was now quite certain. In fact, he intended to make it his mission. Miss Mansfield might well be able to steer him in the correct direction. How exactly was he supposed to do his duty to the nation properly if things were strained between them? Therefore, burying whatever hatchet he had inadvertently wielded was the most sensible course of action, and that had absolutely nothing to do with the odd, tender, wholly inappropriate lustful feelings he had for her.

He saw his butler climb out first, closely followed by the woman who consumed his thoughts. She almost tripped on the last step but managed to right herself in time. It was only then that he realised that Lovett was, perhaps, not the sort of person she should have been left in a carriage with. The man tended to use the journey from Mayfair to Aveley as an opportunity to sample Bennett's port. And his brandy. Neither of them noticed him as he walked towards them because, for some inexplicable reason, Lovett appeared to be counting out coins and placing them in Miss Mansfield's outstretched palm. She appeared to be gloating. Lovett was definitely listing.

'Lovett!'

The butler snapped to attention. 'Your Grace. I trust you had a pleasant journey.'

'Not as pleasant as you, by the looks of things. Have you been at my port again?' Bennett already knew the answer. Lovett was definitely exhibiting the damning effects. Prematurely grey hair a trifle untidy. Cravat skew-whiff. A rosy glow to his complexion that only came from either rigorously polishing the silver or a healthy tot of spirits.

'Once again, Your Grace, you have caught me out. In my defence, I would state that it was a new barrel and I was only tasting it to see if it was up to standard. Your Grace will be pleased to hear that I can now confirm the new port to be most excellent. Would Your Grace like his tea brought to the drawing room or the study?'

Bennett made a mental note to have further words with his errant butler later when he had less pressing matters to attend to. If only he did not need him so very much. His mother had blithely invited a 'few' guests for afternoon tea tomorrow and only Lovett would know the precise moment to believably extricate him from that hideous gathering. And the wily butler knew it. 'The drawing room, if you please.' One day he would tell him off. His butler bowed and left, and his aunt's startled-looking companion went to follow.

'Miss Mansfield. Might I have a word?'

She blinked at him like a startled deer, her cheeks suspiciously rosy and her eyes a little bright. 'Of course.'

Correction, he was definitely going to kill Lovett later. It was one thing to steal a man's port, it was another thing altogether to ply young ladies with it. She blinked again and then, as an afterthought, added, 'Your Grace.'

Instantly, that felt very wrong. He did not want her using his silly title; he much preferred the way she said Ben. Just Ben. It had come out like a sigh and made his flesh warm just thinking about it. He should instruct her to call him Ben from now on, although how he was going to find the right words to explain that to her without panicking and barking at her like a subordinate he had no idea.

Already he could feel his posture stiffening, as if

his veins were suddenly filling with lead, and he had no idea what to do with his hands as he led her around the side of the house, where they would not be overheard. In desperation he clasped them behind his back, until he remembered that she had admonished him for that. Instead, he let his arms dangle, feeling a bit like a chimpanzee, and tried to formulate an apology in his suddenly dry mouth.

'I should like to apologise, Miss Mansfield.' Why was his voice clipped?

This was met with confusion. 'Whatever for?'

'For whatever I did to upset you during our visit to Seven Dials.' He shifted his weight awkwardly and then cleared his throat. There was no point in procrastinating, no matter how mortified he was by the subject matter. 'I had thought that we were getting on famously. Perhaps my behaviour towards you was briefly a little coarse…'

'Coarse?' Now she appeared genuinely baffled and was staring at him as if he had suddenly sprouted two heads, instead of merely looking like a stiff, awkward, lead-veined ape. Or perhaps she was merely just being polite and knew exactly what he was talking about after all.

'There is no need to spare my feelings by pretending you do not remember my shameful lack of manners. Dolly was making insinuations about our relationship and you were very embarrassed. At the time, winking at you like that seemed amusing.' Good heavens, he was actually starting to blush. Despite the cold, he could feel the heat of it burning his ears.

'Winking?'

'Yes.' His whole face was ablaze now and his hands

were desperate to cover it. Instead, he clasped them tightly behind his back and tried to brazen it out. 'I winked at you and you blushed.'

'I remember the winking.' Her lips began to twitch at his obvious discomfort and then bloomed into a smile. 'I found that quite charming.'

Now he was even more confused. If she found him charming then, he must have done something quite unforgivable afterwards. 'Then what did I do to offend you?'

'You really haven't offended me.' The amusement slid from her face and her expression became pained before she quickly turned and began to hurry away. 'Please do not give it a second thought.'

'Amelia.' Her footsteps slowed and he saw her shoulders slump as she exhaled. Waited.

'Why are you avoiding me?' Bennett lightly touched her arm and turned her to face him again. 'Whatever I have done to upset you, I sincerely apologise for it.'

She simply stared at him for a moment, her dark eyes troubled as she gazed deeply into his. 'You really are a silly man.'

Bennett couldn't disagree. He had never felt so silly and awkward in his whole life as he did at this precise moment. If only he knew what he had done! Before he could speak, she suddenly grabbed his lapels, stood on tiptoe and pressed her mouth to his. It all happened so quickly it left him off balance; he was so stunned that he stood stock-still like a statue, his upper lip so stiff that it could be used to slice strawberries.

But Amelia was kissing him and he was not a fool. Bennett's arms automatically curled around her waist and his lips responded hungrily. Whatever temporary madness she was suffering from, he was grateful for it. She tasted of port and temptation, her lovely warm body felt so right melded against his, so he deepened the kiss and then lost himself. Nothing else existed except her in his arms. Nothing else mattered.

When one of her hands slowly crept up his neck and she weaved her fingers through his hair, he groaned against her lips and pulled her hips closer to his body so that she could feel his desire. He felt her sigh his name in response.

'Ben.'

Just that one syllable that said everything he wanted to hear. He was just Ben. She was just Amelia. Soft. Compliant. All his. His body was on fire and his heart was so filled with joy that he felt sure that it might burst with the pressure.

Then, as abruptly as she had started the kiss, she ended it, tearing her mouth from his and pushing him away before her small hands came up to touch her mouth in shock. She stared at him wide-eyed.

'I'm sorry. I forgot myself.'

Well, he wasn't sorry and he was damned if he was going to let her be. Bennett took a step forward, desperate to reassure her that there really was nothing to apologise for, but she stayed him with her hand, appearing completely distraught.

'You make me forget who you are!'

What did that mean? What was it about him that had made her pull away? His kiss? His character? His title? Before he could stop her, she had dashed around the front of the house, and then it was too late to ask anything.

'Isn't Aveley Castle beautiful, Amelia?' Lady

Worsted gushed as she stepped out of the second carriage and threaded her arm through her companion's. 'We shall have tea and then you can unpack my trunk for me. I do not trust the maids and you know exactly how I like things to be.'

Amelia resisted looking back at him as they made their way inside.

Chapter Twenty

A marriage binds two good families together so that they can assist each other on matters of importance. And if those matters also assist in serving the nation, then only a fool would overlook such an opportunity...

Bennett tried not to become frustrated with his uncle's meandering reminiscences about growing up in the Castle.

'Do you remember the day that I taught you to fish, Bennett? What fun we had that day!'

'If that is the same day that you also decided to teach me to row, I recall we caught nothing because you capsized the boat and we ended up swimming in the moat.' Exactly how long did it take one old man to drink one tiny glass of port, anyway?

'It was a jolly good thing that I had taught you to swim the summer before, else your mother would have had my guts for garters.'

'As I remember it, she did.'

His uncle chuckled. 'That was hardly a telling-off,

Bennett. It was nothing like the tongue-lashing she gave me when I taught you how to slide down the banisters at Aveley House. It was hardly my fault that you lost your balance and fell off.'

'She thought I had broken my arm.' Bennett watched in frustration as his uncle slowly swirled the dregs of his port in his glass as if he had all the time in the world to drink it. Which he didn't. Bennett really needed to speak to Miss Mansfield before bedtime. When he could stand it no more he stood. 'I think it is long past time we rejoined the ladies.' For emphasis he pulled out his pocket watch and stared at the dial.

Uncle George gave him a slow, thoughtful perusal and then chuckled. 'You always were a dreadful liar, boy, but I shall play along.'

'I am not sure I know what you mean.' Bennett did his best impression of a bored aristocrat, which only served to make his uncle's shoulders bounce in time to his rumbling laughter.

'Do you not? Then I suppose your haste has nothing to do with the lovely dark-haired damsel that you have been staring wistfully at all evening? Have I misconstrued your heart-wrenching mooning at the delectable Miss Mansfield? Perhaps it was the tapestry behind her that held you so transfixed. And perhaps her pretty blushes and furtive glances in your direction were merely a trick of the light.'

Had she been furtively glancing in his direction? And, if she had, was that a good sign? His uncle would know. He had a talent for understanding the ladies. But Uncle George's advice was always so contrary to everything his father had drilled into him that Bennett felt disloyal to seek his counsel now, no matter how much he desperately wanted to. 'I have no idea what you are talking about. Where do you get such fanciful ideas, anyway?'

'Ha ha! The best form of defence is attack. What did you do to her, lad? Have you stolen a kiss yet or are the pair of you lamenting the fact that you haven't?'

'We are not having this conversation, uncle.' Bennett mimicked his father's disapproving glare before walking towards the door.

'On the contrary, dear boy, you might not be having this conversation, but I am.' For an older gentleman, Uncle George was surprisingly spritely and was at his elbow in a flash. 'I heartily recommend you lure her into some dark corner this weekend and get the job done smartly. You will both be the better for it.'

Bennett ignored him and strode into the drawing room, only to find Miss Mansfield not there. He sat and made small talk with his mother and aunt while he waited impatiently for her to return. After what seemed like an eternity, Uncle George put him out of his misery.

'Where has the lovely Amelia got to?'

'She was feeling unwell and retired for the evening.'

Bennett felt his spirits plummet at this unfortunate piece of news. She was avoiding him again. Now he would have to wait until the morning to speak to her, although heaven knew what he would say. Why had she kissed him? It was hard to remain indifferent to a woman who kissed with so much passion and made his heart ache when she avoided him. Was she as miserable and confused by her feelings as he was? Should they talk about what had happened or should he pretend that it hadn't happened at all? And why had his father never given him any instruction on how to deal with these powerful, insistent emotions when he had so much to say about everything else?

'I might turn in for the night myself. It has been a busy week and I am very tired.' And miserable and so blasted aroused every time he thought about that kiss that he feared his breeches might split. Or burst into flames.

Out in the hallway, he collided with Lovett. He should tear the man off a strip but did not have the energy. The best he could muster was a polite inclination of his head as he trudged towards the staircase.

'If I might be so bold as to offer an observation, Your Grace? But you appear a little out of sorts.'

Out of sorts? That was a very delicate way of saying it. 'I am just tired, Lovett. I am off to bed.'

'That appears to be a common affliction this evening, Your Grace. Miss Mansfield claimed much the same, but she has decided to take some air on the battlements before retiring for the evening.'

Amelia made a sacred vow never to drink port again. Whilst she had always had a tendency to be a bit impulsive, this afternoon she had surpassed herself. She had kissed him. Kissed. *Him!* And that had made everything excruciatingly awkward. Who knew what the man must be thinking? She had survived the interminable dinner and had escaped, pleading a headache, the moment the men had left to drink the same dreadful port that had caused her current predicament.

Instead of retiring to her room, she had found her way up to the battlements to breathe in the crisp winter air and unscramble her wits. Fortunately, if she could avoid him tomorrow, she would not have to see him for another week. By then, with any luck, she would have thought up a viable excuse for attaching her mouth to his quite so fervently and worked out why she had gone and done it in the first place. And what a kiss it had been! Her lips still tingled at the thought of it, but at least the other parts of her had stopped tingling. A few more seconds of that glorious onslaught and she might well have tugged him into the nearest bush and begged him to have his way with her.

Amelia stared up at the clear night sky and sighed. She really had made a dreadful mess of things and hiding up here wasn't helping. If she had not been feeling quite so cowardly, she would go back downstairs and apologise. She could blame the port, but she would be lying and it would get Lovett into trouble when it really wasn't his fault at all, or she could simply tell the Duke the truth. *I find you ridiculously attractive, I have developed a silly girlish crush on you and, even though I know that there could never be anything more between us other than passion, I couldn't help myself.* Given those two choices, these cold battlements were more appealing.

She sensed him before he spoke. 'So this is where you are hiding.'

His deep voice was a little breathless, almost as if he had been running, and when she turned towards him she saw him staring upwards while his hands were clasped, customarily, behind his back. Her heart clenched at the sight, but she had no idea what to say. Fortunately, he filled the gap.

'It upsets me to think that you are avoiding me.'

'Avoidance, under the circumstances, was the only

thing that I could think of to *avoid* dying of embarrassment. I am sorry about earlier. I am not sure what came over me.' A lie.

'I really didn't mind, you know. If you should feel the sudden urge to kiss me again, I will not make any attempt to stop you.' He was flirting now, a little awkwardly, which she found utterly charming. Once again, her silly heart lurched even though she had intended to harden it.

'Kissing you is dangerous. It makes me forget all reason.'

A completely male, totally arrogant smirk crept over his face. 'That is excellent news.' He began to prowl towards her, his intentions clear in his expression. Knowing that she would not have the wherewithal to stop him if he started to kiss her again, Amelia held up her hand before he got too close. 'But kissing you was a mistake and one I am not in a hurry to repeat. I think it is probably best avoided, going forward.'

'I see.' He sounded disappointed. And a little churlish. 'Why?'

'There are so many reasons that I do not quite know where to start. But the most important one is you are a duke and I am a servant and we both know that there can be nothing between us.'

'I hardly call what we have *nothing*. We have a mutual attraction for one another; we get on very well.'

If only that was all that mattered. 'You want to be Prime Minister one day.'

'That has nothing to do with this.'

'Of course it does! You have spent the past year looking for the perfect woman to be a Prime Minister's wife and, whilst I take a great deal of issue with your silly book, I do understand that a high-ranking politician must have a wife who is beyond reproach.'

'We could still be together. Somehow.' The 'somehow' highlighted the huge gulf between them.

'Are you suggesting clandestine meetings? Am I to be your dirty little secret? The skeleton in your cupboard?' She tried not to sound waspish and insulted, even though she was. It was better for them to face the harsh reality of any future relationship between them now, honestly, rather than pretend that they stood any chance.

'When you put it like that, it makes me feel awful.' He sat down on the bench next to her and stared into the darkness for several moments while the air around them hung heavy with things that neither knew quite how to say. Eventually, he took her hand and warmed it between his palms. 'I need to know if you feel it too, or if this overwhelming attraction that I feel is completely one-sided.'

'I feel it too.' Lying was pointless when she had already admitted to the deadly effect of his kisses. 'But I wish with all of my heart that I didn't.'

'Am I so terrible?'

It was difficult to keep a level head while the feel of his hands on hers was having such a profound effect on all of her nerve endings. It was so tempting to just give in to the sensations and consider the consequences later. 'Not at all, which I suppose is the problem. You are exceedingly likeable once you get past all of that stodginess you wear like a uniform. But you are a duke, for goodness' sake. A powerful and wealthy duke with a great deal of expectation resting on his shoulders.'

His brows came together as he tried to understand

why such a thing was a problem. She saw the exact moment that he gave up trying. 'I fail to understand what my being a duke has to do with anything. I have been led to believe that being a duke is considered quite a good thing amongst the ladies of the ton.'

'And there you have it. I am not part of the ton. I am a companion. A servant. We come from different worlds that are best kept separate, Your Grace.'

The sound of his honorific on her lips appeared to anger him. 'Please just call me Ben... I prefer that.'

'I cannot, Your Grace, because you will always be a duke.'

'A few weeks ago it was too much trouble for you to say *Your Grace*. Now you insist upon using it to *purposefully* create distance between us. And whilst I am prepared to concede that this attraction that we feel for each other is not ideal, I would still prefer to pursue it.'

He really was not getting it at all. Because he was a duke. 'It is not ideal for you, you mean.' And he had no idea how much he kept insulting her with his casual words. A familiar knot of anger began to form in the pit of her stomach, reminding her of her past experience with an aristocrat who had reluctantly compromised. Her father had done so for money and then had come to regret it bitterly and used his power to cast her mother aside. Would the Duke of Aveley lower himself just because of lust or would he slake that lust before he came to his ducal senses and severed their attachment? Amelia already knew the answer. She had lived it. 'Tell me, how much of a sacrifice are you *prepared* to make for us, Your Grace?'

Amelia watched his throat bob nervously as he

shifted in his seat. 'I suppose I could consider marriage...'

There was a definite wince as he said it. Amelia laughed bitterly and tugged her hand out of his so that she could stand. It would be easier to put him in his place if she was not being distracted by his touch. 'I *suppose* I *could*. Have you any idea how offensive those words just sounded?' Her hands came to rest on her hips as she glared at him in bold accusation. *How dare he?* 'I am sure that you think that I should be positively thrilled to receive such a *generous* offer from a man *so* socially superior to myself. What girl would *not* wish to marry a rich and powerful duke, after all? You are Bennett Montague. The perfect catch. Women fall over themselves to impress you. They grovel and simper and hang on your every word and read your stupid book out loud. You have five of them dangling on your hook as we speak, and they are grateful to be there. I suppose I should be eternally grateful that you have lowered yourself to make such a huge sacrifice on my behalf!'

She watched his silvery blue eyes narrow and harden into cold crystals. 'Would you prefer it if I lied to you? Do you want me to pretend that marrying you would not have any effect on my political career? My reputation has always been beyond reproach and I have worked very hard to keep it that way. How do you think my peers will take it if I marry a...' He stopped abruptly, the harsh words hanging ominously unsaid, so Amelia finished his sentence for him.

'A guttersnipe, Ben? At least have the decency to say it.'

'That is not what I meant at all.' He stood angrily and edged towards her. 'I did not intend to insult you.

I was merely thinking through the ramifications of such a decision. I was born into this life. From the moment I could talk I have been moulded and shaped to serve this country. If you think I take that responsibility lightly, then you are sorely mistaken. I want to change things. I want reform. I want to end the harsh reality that many loyal subjects have to deal with and I *cannot* do that from the back benches. If I am going to have the greatest influence and instigate real reform, the best way that I can serve the people of England is as their Prime Minister. Therefore, there is an expectation on me to marry well. There always has been. You know that. Marrying my aunt's companion would be a complication…but perhaps not an insurmountable one.'

He raked his hand through his thick hair in frustration and took several even, calming breaths. 'I have a great many supporters in Parliament that might be sympathetic to our particular circumstances. Of course, it will have to be carefully orchestrated to ensure that it is received properly…and perhaps we will have to be very careful what we tell people about your background…'

The pompous Duke had returned again and he had not even realised it. *'Ramifications! Complications!'* Amelia was sorely tempted to kick him. *'Our particular circumstances!* Be still my beating heart!' Amelia found herself prodding him in his magnificent and arrogant chest instead. 'I rather think that you are entirely missing the point. Whilst I am sure that most ladies would be prepared to grovel and beg for your ducal affections, and that they would be delighted to suppress every part of their natural character in order to fit in with what society expects them to be, I can assure you that I am not one of them. I *loathe* aristocrats!

It is the aristocrats of this country who continue to oppress the poor for their own gain. They toss away lives with the same lack of regard that other people throw away potato peelings! I suppose that I should happily accept that I am unworthy, lie about my background and pretend to be some vapid adornment who pours tea and embroiders. And, of course, it goes without saying that the future Duchess of Aveley would never be seen serving the poor in a soup kitchen, or setting foot in Seven Dials or marching towards Westminster demanding the vote for ordinary working men. Yet you, like all aristocrats, think that you have a divine right to be obeyed, although heaven knows why when you all gained those lofty titles by being either bullies or sycophants.'

'*Bullies or sycophants?* And which, pray tell, am I?' His voice dripped sarcasm.

Illogically, she was becoming more offended by the second, though not at the sarcasm but because of that telling wince. That wince that told her, in no uncertain terms, that he was going to deign to tolerate her past, just as her father had tolerated the dreadful stigma of being married to an American. He would tolerate it until he decided that his low-born wife simply wasn't worth all of the effort. She had practical experience of how disposable a wife could be. 'I suppose that depends on how your illustrious family chanced on their title.'

'We did not chance on it; the Montagues came over with William the Conqueror. I am the Sixteenth Duke of Aveley.' He was prowling after her on the darkened battlements and his temper was definitely hovering dangerously close to the surface. A sensible woman would end the conversation here and now. Amelia was not in the mood to be sensible.

'Would that be the same William the Conqueror who murdered all of the English nobles and replaced them with his cronies?' She tapped her lips with her index finger as if in thought. 'I would say that you fell in the bully category then, wouldn't you? Had you toadied around a king to get your title, then you would be a sycophant—but, then again, you are one of the Regent's most *trusted* advisers, are you not, Your Grace, so perhaps you now fall into both categories.'

He caught her angrily by the arm to face him. 'You are on the cusp of unacceptable impertinence. This is not how I expected you to react when I have stated that I might be able to offer you marriage.'

She had to crane her neck upwards to look him squarely in the eye and stare into those stormy, swirling depths. '*Might?* How romantic! Your arrogance is quite staggering! I do not want to marry a man who believes that I am *not ideal*, who has offered me the *possibility* of marriage as an act of charity on his *sufferance*. And as I would prefer to be completely impertinent rather than merely hovering on the *cusp* of it, *Your Grace*, I should add that the very last man that I would ever choose to marry is one in possession of a title!'

Chapter Twenty-One

It is the fashion nowadays for couples to marry for love. Whilst this may appeal to the romantic side of your character, it is not an advised course of action. Once you have chosen an eminently suitable woman, love will blossom in time...

His fingers closed possessively around her hand and pressed it against the hard wall of his chest to prevent her from prodding. 'I do not believe that you are prepared to throw away everything between us just like that, Amelia.' His other hand snaked around her waist, pulling her flush against him so that his mouth was a few scant inches from hers. 'You feel the pull between us, and it has nothing whatsoever to do with my title and everything to do with desire.'

She wanted to deny it, but her body was already calling her a liar. The hand that rested against his chest was splayed over his steady heartbeat, the other had already found its way to his lapel. His mouth descended onto hers savagely, but Amelia was powerless to resist kissing him back with equal force.

She wanted him. Pure and simple.

One last kiss goodbye was not too much to ask for, surely? And it would be goodbye. It had to be. Tears prickled her eyes, but she poured all of her tangled emotions into it. She greedily wound her arms around his neck when he imprisoned her against the battlements with his body. His lips gentled as he deepened the kiss and Amelia was powerless to do anything other than cling to him while her senses and every nerve ending came alive.

Each stroke of his tongue caused her womb to constrict, almost as if there was some secret hidden thread that linked the two halves of her body together that only he knew about, while her breasts felt suddenly heavy and ached for his touch. Unthinkingly, she arched against him and he responded by sliding his hands down to rest possessively on her bottom, drawing her hips intimately against his. She revelled in the insistent nudge of his hardness against her belly, pressed herself against it while her hands explored his chest beneath his snug waistcoat, felt the tension in the muscles of his abdomen and thrilled at how laboured his breathing was. The shallow, rapid rise and fall of his ribcage mirrored hers.

Amelia moaned when his warm palm closed over her breast, wishing that it was not encased in layers of clothing and laid bare to his fingers. Her wish was granted when he edged his hand gently beneath the neckline of her bodice and she groaned again when the pad of his thumb grazed her taut nipple, moaning against his lips in wanton encouragement. No matter what she had said, or how much she distrusted men like him, she still wanted him more than she ever had any man before. If only he was indeed just Ben... Then she would willingly succumb to him. Marry him. Whatever it took to just be with him.

'I want you in my bed, Amelia.' His voice came out strangled with desire. 'Let us not fight this attraction we feel.'

Temptation warred with common sense. If she went to his bed, what then? In one swift motion, she tore her mouth from his and darted out of the cage of his arms. 'This is just passion, Ben, and passion fades.'

'It is more than just passion and you know it!' He looked more handsome than she had ever seen him. His hair was delightfully tousled from her touch, all evidence of his formality and stuffiness gone; his eyes were burning with lust for her. The man. Who happened to be a duke.

'It makes no difference what we feel, Ben. The barriers that stand between us are too great.'

His broad shoulders slumped in defeat and he hastily turned and rested his hands on the impregnable castle walls, staring out at the stars. 'So it is hopeless, then?'

Amelia came behind him and rested her head on his shoulder, felt the strength in him, the warmth and the goodness one last time. 'Of course it is hopeless. It always was. You are a wealthy and powerful duke and I am your aunt's companion who has lived in a workhouse and begged for scraps in a soup kitchen.'

'I never had you pegged as a coward, Amelia. At least I am prepared to try to find a way for us to be together.'

'I am not a coward.' Perhaps she was? Her feelings for Bennett Montague terrified her. 'I am a realist. We come from two vastly different worlds. Soon

I shall head back to Bath with Lady Worsted and you shall head back to Parliament, and by the time we visit again next year, all of these odd emotions will have faded.' Another lie. Bennett Montague would always have a special place in her heart. She would not come next year, or any other. Lady Worsted would give her leave and she would spend those weeks in Seven Dials, where she belonged. It would be too painful to see him again, especially if he was married to one of his Potentials and happy.

'I don't need to be Prime Minister.'

Amelia sighed and stroked his back tenderly. 'Of course you do. Being a politician is who you are and the electorate are fickle. I understand that too. The very last woman you should choose is one who has lived the life I have. I am a scandal just waiting to happen. The moment the press or the opposition found out about me, which they would eventually, my past would be dredged up and you would be judged as a result. I will not be held responsible for that.'

Nor did she want to suffer the backlash of his inevitable reaction to that, but she did not say it. He would dismiss her fears as ridiculous, although Amelia knew that if it came to it he would have no choice but to use his power to curtail her activities and try to mould her into the type of wife that society expected her to be. She had seen her father chip away at everything unique and rebellious about her mother, leaving her an empty shell with no real identity of her own aside from being an aristocrat's wife. She did not want to resent Bennett for that. 'I cannot stop campaigning for change or consorting with so-called Radicals because that is who I am also. So we will always be at odds with each other.'

He glanced up at the sky and she felt him inhale slowly. Acceptance. 'It is apt that we should be here under the stars discussing this. If ever there were a pair of star-crossed lovers, it is surely us.'

'In the grand scheme of things, none of this matters. We both have things that we must do, causes that drive us and beliefs that we both hold too strong to simply ignore. Anything else would be too great a compromise. You might not see it now, but you would come to resent me for damaging your political career and I would resent you for having the power to control me. In time, we will both realise that things are as they should be and this is all for the best.' Even if that made them both miserable. A tiny piece of her heart died, the rest simply ached for all that could not be.

They stood in silence for several minutes, both staring out at the infinite blackness of the night sky, two small, insignificant specks in the universe. There really was nothing else to say. Eventually, she dropped her hand and stood back.

'Goodnight, Your Grace.'

The fact that he let her go without another word somehow said it all.

Bennett sat holding a cup of tea he did not want, surrounded by a growing sea of people he definitely did not want to be with, and glared across the room at his mother. Once again, her definition of a few people over for afternoon tea was vastly different from his. At least seven laden carriages had arrived so far and, by the looks of things, several more were expected and it was not yet noon. Like her definition of 'a few', his mother's idea of 'afternoon tea' was apparently also quite different to everyone else's. These people were here for luncheon first, then afternoon tea followed by whatever 'fun' activity she was going to rope them all into, and Bennett had been effectively held hostage for the duration.

He now knew, thanks to Uncle George, who had also conveniently been kept in the dark, that his mother was doing all this to further his political ambitions. Apparently, she was worried that he was neglecting his supporters because he was always too busy to entertain; therefore, whilst he was here resting, and thus not busy, it would be the perfect opportunity to extend some hospitality and strengthen some alliances. It was the very last thing he wanted right now. In reality, all he wanted to do was gallop across the frozen fields hereabouts and lick his wounds in private. Heaven only knew what irritating sycophants and social climbers he would now have to socialise with. His mother's grasp of who his most ardent supporters were, like her definitions of 'few' and 'afternoon tea', left a lot to be desired.

The Potentials were all there and, to his great irritation, so were their mothers and their powerful fathers. The five men all regarded him in accusation, no doubt all thoroughly fed up with the fact that he had still not made a decision and chosen their daughter to be his duchess. His head very well might sympathise, but his heart was aching at the thought. Not one of those young ladies held a candle to Amelia. They were not as intelligent, or as interesting, or as passionate or as irritating as the diminutive dark-haired temptress who sat quietly in the furthest corner of the room, doing her level best not to notice him.

He knew that she had been irritatingly right about

their unfortunate situation, but knowing she was right certainly did not make him feel any better about it. He was still in two minds as to whether he should have acquiesced quite so easily. Perhaps there was still hope for them?

'Stop mooning after the chit and talk to her,' Uncle George hissed from behind his own teacup. 'You know that you want to.'

Of course Bennett wanted to. He wanted to march over there, grab her hand and drag her outside. He wanted to kiss her until his head spun, make mad passionate love to her and force her to fight for them. He wanted to tell her that he did not care about the difference in their stations or that she consorted with potential Revolutionaries or that he might lose momentum in Parliament; none of that mattered because he only wanted to be with her. Which, of course, would mean political suicide. Decades of political manoeuvring, diplomacy and holding his tongue would have all been for naught. All his father's hopes would be dashed and his legacy would be lost. And she was definitely right about his not being able to help the poor from the back benches. His presence in the government was now more important than ever if he was going to be the one to champion their cause.

'I am not sure why you think that you have the right to give me romantic advice when you have never been married, Uncle.' Uncle George blinked rapidly and Bennett instantly regretted being so curt. It was hardly his uncle's fault that he was now imprisoned by towering, insurmountable, invisible brick walls. 'I am sorry, Uncle. That was uncalled for.'

Uncle George smiled kindly in that way he always

had when Bennett had made a hash of something and he had to rescue his nephew. 'I might never have married, Bennett, but I know the pain of being in love with someone when the circumstances make it seem worse than hopeless.'

Now that was an interesting snippet Bennett had never heard before. He had not realised that his uncle had once been in love. Perhaps hearing the plight of another star-crossed lover might make him feel better. 'Why was it hopeless?'

Uncle George's eyes dropped to his hands and his expression became guarded while he considered what he should say. 'The young lady in question was betrothed to another, better prospect than a second son. She had to do her duty for the sake of her family. But never mind that. It all turned out for the best.' Something about the older man's expression told Bennett that his uncle did not really believe that at all, which made him think about Amelia's same assertion last night. *In time, we will both realise that things are as they should be and this is all for the best.* Perhaps she was wrong too.

'You could have moved on and married someone else.' As he must.

'What? And make an innocent woman's life a misery because my heart would always belong to another. That would not have been fair. Love is very powerful, Bennett. It shouldn't be ignored.'

Why was he talking about love? Unless his uncle mistakenly thought that the lust and attraction Bennett felt for his aunt's companion was something more than it was. 'I am not in love with Miss Mansfield!' The very notion was ridiculous. He had scarcely known the girl for a few weeks. Love was something that blossomed slowly, perhaps taking years to develop. It was born out of mutual goals and beliefs, shared experiences, familiarity—much as it had for his own parents. Theirs had been a quiet, comfortable emotion. There was nothing comfortable and quiet about the feelings he had for Amelia.

'Do you think about her constantly?'

'Well...yes, but...'

'Does she drive you to the point of distraction?'

'She would drive anyone to distraction, uncle. I hardly think that can be used as an effective gauge to measure it by...'

Uncle George held up his hand and held his gaze intently. 'Would you do anything to keep her happy or safe, even if that meant sacrificing yourself to achieve it?'

'Well, of course I would! If you recall, I did get punched in the face.' And he had listened to her ramblings last night even though he had wanted to rail against her for being so pessimistic. 'But I would have done the same for anyone in a similar situation. I am fond of Miss Mansfield, I will grant you that, but it is not love. Her background is wholly unsuitable...'

'Oh, for goodness' sake, boy! That is your father speaking and a colder fish never walked on this earth. He was my brother and I loved him, but he was not an easy man to like. He made your poor mother miserable and I will not allow his petty prejudices to cloud your judgement and force you into a life of misery too!'

The force behind his uncle's words took him aback. In all of his thirty years, Bennett had never heard his uncle criticise his father once. *Cold fish?* His father

had been reserved, yes, but he had cared enough about
Bennett to ensure that he was prepared to take on the
life of great responsibility ahead of him. *Petty prejudices?* Was Uncle George referring to his father's advice about his future bride? He knew that his uncle
found the Potentials a little exasperating, but surely he
could understand why such a woman was necessary to
be the wife of a member of His Majesty's cabinet. And
as for his claim that his father had made his mother
miserable— Well, frankly that was preposterous! His
parents had had the perfect marriage. His father had
often said so. If there had not been so many people in
the room, Bennett would have shouted his outrage.

'He did not make my mother miserable!' His heated
whisper earned him a few curious stares from those
hovering closest to where they sat, so he forced himself to calm down. Now was definitely not the time
or the place for a volcanic eruption of all the warring,
turbulent jumble of emotions that had been troubling
him of late.

Uncle George set his jaw stubbornly. 'Of course he
did. All he cared about was his own blasted political
ambitions. He was always too busy for anything else.
Why do you think that it was me who taught you to
ride and to shoot? I stepped into the breach when he
abandoned you to follow his own path—a path, I has-
ten to add, that he has forced you down as well. I hate
the way he controls your life from the grave. Do you
remember your father's presence here for the duration of all of those summers and Christmases? Don't
you ever wonder why you are an only child, Bennett?
Your self-important father was far too interested in his

own position in the government that he neglected your mother for the entirety of their marriage.'

Mortally offended, Bennett stood and promptly took himself to another corner of the room without another word. If he stayed next to his uncle, he would only disgrace himself in public. As soon as the moment was right, he would speak to his mother in private so that he could satisfy himself that his uncle was lying. Except, now that he came to think upon it, there might well be some weight to Uncle George's impassioned assertions.

His father had rarely come to Aveley Castle. Nor had he taught him how to ride or shoot or swim. He had certainly never slid down a banister with his father—that would have given the man an apoplexy of epic proportions—or capsized a boat or waltzed around the ballroom with him because his big feet had such trouble with the steps. Had there ever been a momentous occasion in his life when his uncle George had not been present? His father, certainly, had missed a great deal, but Uncle George had been by his and his mother's side for the lot.

Another uncomfortable thought suddenly occurred to him as he watched his uncle march across the room to his mother. He saw her put her arm affectionately on his and smile in understanding as the old man undoubtedly vented his frustration about Bennett. Uncle George had always been there for her too. Every step of the way. In all but name, they were like a married couple who adored each other. Surely he had not been so preoccupied with his own career *not* to have seen something like that? They all lived under the same roof after all... Damn it all to hell, they all lived under the same roof. Like a family! Like his blasted ceiling mural, could he have been so determined to see things one way, when in fact there was an altogether different picture when viewed from another perspective? Was this yet another thing he had got entirely wrong?

Bennett wandered to the table and accepted another cup of tea from a servant and tried to get a better view of his mother and his uncle to see if his ridiculous, implausible new suspicion actually carried any weight. Was his uncle right? Was his father controlling him from the grave?

He had no time to ponder that. Lady Cecily was already edging towards him with a purposeful gleam in her eye, closely followed by both her mother and her father. A quick glance at the mantel clock told him that it was only just past noon and he had told Lovett to extricate him from his mother's tea party at two. Now he was stuck here for another couple of hours, in a foul temper and more confused than he had ever been in his life about almost everything.

'Your Grace! How wonderful it was to receive your invitation.' Lady Cecily was practically simpering and batting her eyelashes in a way that he could only assume she thought was beguiling. As if he wanted an obedient marionette who simply batted her eyelashes at him! Or parroted his book or followed every one of its edicts! She slid her arm through his and offered him a demure and adoring smile. Realising that he was completely doomed with no hope of redemption, Bennett was left with little choice other than to paste a polite smile on his face and suffer her unwanted attentions manfully.

Amelia sat with Lady Worsted and pretended that she was not boiling with jealousy at the sight of the

Duke chatting happily with Lady Cecily as though he did not have a care in the world. After all that had been said yesterday evening, she could not help self-ishly feeling put out by his rapid return to normal. He might have had the decency to take a little more time in getting over her. The conniving Cecily was grip-ping onto Ben's arm as if he were a trophy and cast-ing gloating glances at her rivals—including Amelia.

Sir George wandered over looking peeved and promptly folded his arms across his chest the moment he sat down next to them. 'I really have no idea what possessed Octavia to invite so many people when none of us are in the mood to have them here. Did she tell you what she had in mind?'

Lady Worsted shook her head mournfully. 'All I knew about were the Potentials. I believe it was her intention to help Bennett to choose one of them in a less formal setting. Surely there cannot be any more carriages? We must be up to twenty guests already.'

The three of them all turned to watch the Dowager greeting another couple at the door and Sir George rolled his eyes. 'And they keep on coming! At this rate, we will soon run out of chairs.'

The Dowager sailed towards them, smiling like the perfect hostess with the latest arrivals in tow. 'Augusta, George—you remember the Sandfords, don't you? I shall leave them in your capable hands while I go to greet the Viscount and Viscountess of Bray. Lovett has just informed me that their carriage is arriving.'

Amelia froze and then experienced a moment of sheer, unadulterated panic. One look told her Lady Worsted had also just realised that a catastrophe of huge proportions was pending.

'Did you know about this?' Amelia's throat began to tighten as she gripped Lady Worsted's hand in panic.

'Of course I didn't!'

Her employer was on the cusp of flapping, which would be no use to either of them, so Amelia stood sharply and tried not to shout. 'I cannot be seen here!' If she was fast, she could escape and avoid them. She would have to spend the entire afternoon locked inside her bedchamber, but at least she would avoid causing a scandal.

Amelia stumbled blindly to the door and in her haste to flee she collided with a footman carrying a loaded tray. Cups and cutlery clattered noisily to the floor, drawing everyone's attention. 'I am so sorry!' she said to the footman as she simultaneously picked up her skirts and hurried towards the door to freedom.

'Amelia—wait!'

Bennett's voice called from behind her, but still she did not stop. It was better to be horrifically rude to a duke in front of a room full of guests than to publicly embarrass him with the scandal that was poised to happen. Perhaps later she would explain. If she absolutely had to. Or she could just run towards the woodland and keep on running. That might be preferable.

'Wait!' His voice was insistent as he stayed her arm and turned her towards him, his cobalt eyes filled with concern. 'What has happened?'

Frustrated, angry tears gathered in the corners of her eyes, threatening to fall at any moment. She knew that he deserved the truth, but there was no time, so she lied. 'I am not feeling very well. I need to go and lie down.'

It was obvious that he did not believe her because he

refused to relinquish his hold on her arm. 'Something has upset you. Please tell me what is wrong.'

'Let me go, Ben, I beg you. I will explain everything later, but please let me go.' The bothersome tears would not be held back any longer and began to trickle down her cheeks. If that was not mortifying enough, the people nearest the door were watching them with barely disguised interest, which meant she had already caused a scene, despite her father's imminent arrival.

Ignoring the questioning stares, his hand slid down her arm and clasped her hand. With his other hand, he used his thumb to gently wipe the tears from her cheek tenderly. 'Not until I know what is wrong. I hate seeing you like this.'

His sympathy was almost her undoing except, behind those gathered at the door, Amelia could already see the Dowager looking for her son. Next to her was Viscount Venomous, smiling nauseatingly at his hostess and no doubt congratulating himself on gaining an invitation to visit such a powerful duke.

As the crowd parted to allow them to pass, Amelia snatched her hand away and considered her options. The grand, echoing hallway offered few hiding places. The odd ancient suit of armour or the impressive waist-high Grecian urns would not suffice for long. Her inadvertent charade was about to unravel like knitting and she had no earthly idea how to stop it. In desperation, she camouflaged herself behind the biggest thing in the room.

Bennett.

'Oh, there you are, Bennett!' His mother was striding purposefully towards him, completely oblivious to the fact that Amelia was upset and huddled behind him. Under the circumstances, he was glad that she was hidden. At least it would give her a few moments to compose herself before she had to make a reappearance. He already knew enough about her to understand that she would hate to be seen in such an exposed and weakened state by anyone. 'I believe that you must know Viscount Bray. He is one of your greatest supporters in the House.'

Reluctantly, Bennett held out his hand to shake the other man's, doing his best to maintain Amelia's privacy. He had met Bray before and had never particularly warmed to the man. 'Yes, of course. Bray, how are you?'

'Honoured to be favoured with an invitation, Your Grace. May I present my wife?'

Bennett had to turn slightly to take the lady's proffered hand and watched his mother's eyes dart curiously behind him. Automatically, she twisted to see who he was concealing and he fervently hoped that Amelia had rediscovered her composure.

'Oh, Amelia—I did not notice you there. Allow me to introduce you to our guests as well.'

He felt her step out from behind him, saw her stiffen her delicate spine and set her small shoulders proudly, then watched in fascination as the Viscount's face became florid at the sight of her.

'What the *hell* is *she* doing here?' The man was practically pulsating with rage.

Amelia appeared completely unmoved by Bray's peculiar reaction. She stared at him for several moments imperiously, then tilted her lovely head to one side before she spoke.

'Hello, Father. Abandoned any wives lately?'

Chapter Twenty-Two

Remember—when you marry, you do not simply gain a wife. You gain a family as well. Look carefully into their backgrounds before you align yourself with them...

Amelia felt a wave of unexpected calm settle over her as she faced her father for the first time in four years. She supposed all of her anger and hatred for the man would surge forward soon enough, but right now those emotions were absent and she was grateful for that. What she had to say was best done coldly and dispassionately. With dignity. The very last thing she wanted was to give her horrid father the impression that he still mattered.

People were already falling over themselves to pour into the grand hallway and witness the unfolding drama. As she scanned the faces, she saw Lady Worsted looking horrified, Sir George bewildered and Lady Cecily practically rubbing her hands together with glee. Amelia supposed the girl was well within her rights. There was an air of finality about what she was about to do that was too inevitable at this stage in the proceedings to be prevented.

Her father's head appeared about to explode. At his side she noticed his fists were clenched and she wondered if he would succumb to his temper and physically lash out, or if he would try to blag his way out of the situation because he was surrounded by his peers. He glared at her menacingly, the warning quite apparent, but she saw the raw panic in his eyes.

Next to him, the Dowager was wringing her hands together nervously while Bennett stood stock-still like a glorious Roman statue, his handsome face devoid of any expression that would let her know what his clever mind was thinking. At least, once this was done, he would give up any thought of continuing their association. That would spare her from ever having to see him again and wondering what it would have been like if things had been different. She did not want to live with that sort of hope. It would destroy her.

But for now she would draw strength from him as he stood loyally by her side. Amelia settled her eyes on her father and said the words she had waited to say, realising as she said them that she had needed to do this to lay the ghosts of her past to rest.

'You robbed my mother of her soul and her fortune and then you cast her out with nothing. Her blood is on your hands.'

Her father's eyes burned back, filled with hatred. Amelia saw his mouth begin to open, ready to rail against her charge with his customary vitriol and lies, but his words were halted by the sudden appearance of a large fist. It slammed into his face with such force that she heard the snap as his nose shattered. Blood sprayed in the air like a fountain and, as if in slow motion, her father flew backwards, his arms and legs flailing pathetically. Then everything seemed to suddenly speed up again and he landed flat on his back with a resounding thud on the unforgiving stone floor.

Everyone sucked in a collective gasp of shock before an ominous brittle silence settled over the room. All eyes darted between the Duke, Amelia and the Viscount, splayed on the marble. Sir George was the first to rush forward to kneel before the prostrate, static body.

'Is he dead?' The Duke's voice sounded flat and emotionless, but his fist was still raised.

Sir George felt for a pulse and looked relieved. 'No! He's just unconscious'

'That is a pity.' Bennett lowered his fist and turned to his butler calmly. 'Lovett, see that this mess is returned to its carriage, if you please.'

Then, without another word, he walked casually down the hallway away from the melee, his hands clasped behind his back and his posture erect, almost as if knocking out peers of the realm was something not at all extraordinary and something he did every day as a matter of course.

Amelia and the assembled guests stood gaping as Lovett clicked his fingers and two footmen appeared. She tried to stand proudly as she watched them manhandle her semi-conscious father off the floor and then carry him smartly away, grateful that she was flanked on either side by the Dowager and Sir George. Her knees were suddenly weak and there was a definite lightness in her head, so she tried to breathe deeply in case she swooned and joined her sire on the floor. Nobody spoke. Nobody quite knew the correct etiquette for such a bizarre turn of events. It was all Amelia could do just to blink.

'Well, I think you would all agree that was a splendid show. I hope you will all understand that this afternoon's entertainments are now concluded. Allow me to see you to your carriages.' Sir George took charge and managed to usher everyone towards the main entrance swiftly, ably assisted by Lady Worsted, leaving a stunned Amelia standing next to an equally stunned Dowager. Fragments of their casual conversation filtered back towards the spot where Amelia was currently frozen and she marvelled at how the pair of them could sound so nonchalant when she was still floored by what had happened.

Bennett had punched her father in the face.

Without a word of explanation.

For her.

Oh! How she loved him for that.

She was sure he had broken Venomous's nose and felt an overwhelming sense of guilt creep over her that she had caused such a distasteful scene.

'Please accept my apologies, Your Grace. I have ruined your afternoon.' To her own ears her apology was trite and she sounded emotionless, but really it had all been so wholly unexpected and surreal. How exactly did one correctly apologise for such an incident?

'No need.' Amelia turned her eyes towards the Dowager and saw that the woman's gaze was transfixed on the spot on the floor where her father had lain. There was a note of wonder in her tone. 'I have never seen Bennett ever do anything like that. He is usually such a reserved individual.'

The very fact that Amelia had witnessed that renowned ducal reserve crack on more than one occasion
made her feel both privileged and slightly ashamed.
She knew that such displays bothered him and there
was little doubt that she had been the root cause of all of
them. 'It is all my fault. I should have told you about my
background. If I had, this never would have happened.'

'Perhaps.'

The Dowager lapsed back into silence and remained
that way until the others returned.

They all gathered in the drawing room and Sir
George pressed brandy in her hand until, bit by bit,
Amelia told them all the truth. Even the parts that she
had kept conveniently hidden from Lady Worsted.
There seemed to be little point in lying. These people
had taken her into their home and now they had been
dragged into a scandal. The only omissions she made
to the dreadful tale were the parts that were personal
to her and Bennett; not only were they too private, but
Amelia had no desire to cause the Duke further embarrassment by suggesting that there might have been
something between them.

When the sorry tale was done, they all just stared at
her. Taking pity on them, she said what needed to be
said. 'I shall pack my things and leave today.'

Amelia went to stand when the Dowager unceremoniously pulled her back down onto the sofa. 'There will
be no packing or leaving, Amelia. Whilst your story
is shocking, it is not you who should be punished for
what happened. That responsibility lies solely with
your dreadful father. Now I understand why Bennett
hit him. If I were a man, I would be tempted to punch

the bounder myself. As far as we are all concerned, you now live under our protection and that is that.'

Amelia had no idea what Bennett would think, but she was more worried about where he was. Lovett had been sent to fetch him, only to return and tell them that His Grace had gone riding. Hell for leather, by all accounts, and with a face like thunder. As the afternoon ticked by and there was no sign of him, that worry only intensified.

He needed air.

And distance.

Or he would go back and kill that man for what he had done to her.

Bennett headed straight to the stables and saddled his horse swiftly, allowing the roiling, burning fury to consume him and enjoying the way it felt, hoping the rage would be cathartic. The horse was barely warmed up when he set them galloping across the parkland while his mind ran over every new piece of information it had been assaulted with.

Bray was Amelia's father.

He had no idea if she was his legitimate daughter or born on the wrong side of the blanket and he did not care. All that mattered was that the odious man had abandoned her to suffer poverty and destitution when she had barely left the schoolroom. He had blithely stood by while she had nursed her sick mother, had refused to give help and protection when she had gone to him and sought it. He had allowed her to suffer the indignity of the workhouse and the slums all alone, when he had the means and power to have protected her from all that. That one of his peers could do that disgusted him. That he had done it to Amelia made Bennett want to seek retribution.

Bray would pay. How? Bennett did not yet know. There were gaps in his knowledge that needed to be filled before he decided if he would murder the man with his own hands, tearing him limb from limb slowly to maximise the agony the monster would suffer, or use his own influence and fortune to simply ruin him and leave him destitute and pathetic in the gutters of Seven Dials, as he had his own daughter. Whichever fate he assigned to the man, one thing was for certain—Bennett would enjoy it.

The trees on the horizon signalled the furthest edge of his land and only then did Bennett slow his frenetic pace. Before he could deal with Bray, he needed to speak to Amelia. But, before he spoke to Amelia, he simply needed to hold her. When she had warned him that she was a scandal waiting to happen, he had assumed that she had been alluding to her years of slum dwelling and all of the depravity that entailed. Now he realised that there was a bigger scandal buried in her past. One so large that she had hidden it from everyone. How could she have been the daughter to a viscount and still live virtually destitute for so long? No wonder the girl had appeared upset at his mother's ill-conceived tea party. She had had to face that monster unexpectedly and probably felt dreadful for the scene she had inadvertently caused.

And no wonder she had been so vehemently opposed to marrying any man with a title. Her lack of respect for the aristocracy and her reluctance to submit herself to the bonds of matrimony all made perfect sense now. She probably assumed that all men in possession of a title were as selfish and heartless as her father. Bennett needed to reassure her that he put no blame at her door. It was hardly Amelia's fault that her father was so vile, nor had she requested that Bennett should react so violently on her behalf.

It was regrettable that he had done the deed in such a public forum, but he could not regret the act itself. It had been a pleasure to knock the man out. If the Viscount was stupid enough to still be there when he returned home, Bennett had every intention of punching him again. Only this time he would not stop until all that was left of the odious Viscount Bray was a sticky pile of unrecognisable entrails on the ancient castle floor.

Feeling the anger bubble again, and knowing that he was in no fit state to talk to anyone just yet, Bennett plunged onward. His emotions were running wildly out of control. Not just anger at Bray; that was merely the tip of the iceberg. Before that had happened Bennett had still felt on the very cusp of losing control. Aside from being blindsided by his uncle's charges about his father and his suspicions about the relationship he had with his mother, amongst all of that angst was the anger that had been created by his visit to Seven Dials.

Yet none of that came close to being the root cause of his current turmoil. The root cause was Amelia. His heart literally ached with the grief he felt at not being able to have her. And *grief* was the right word. It was like a death, but it was one that he was yet to accept. A tragedy.

A travesty.

He had lain awake all night, replaying all of their conversation, trying to convince himself that she had been right. Several times, he had been so infuriated by her sensible refusal that he had almost gone to her bedchamber to tell her why she was wrong. Once, he had even made it to her door before he had turned around and frustratedly paced his way back to his own room. He knew that he had been born to shape the future. He could not do that outside of the government, his father's voice cautioned, married to a nobody. But...

At the precise moment he had discovered that Bray was her father, Bennett had realised two things simultaneously. Firstly, the need to punch Bray had been visceral and inevitable because the man had caused Amelia pain. And secondly, and perhaps more importantly, he loved that woman with every fibre of his being and always would. She challenged him, excited him, irritated and amused him. Every time he laid eyes on her, his heart warmed and the sun came out. When he was not with her the world was a little greyer. As his uncle George had suggested, the idea of marrying another woman was now inconceivable when it was only her he wanted. Unfortunately, the obstinate woman was dead against it and that broke his heart.

All in all, his mind was in a mess. Every emotion he had tried for thirty years to ignore was demanding release. Anger, passion, pity, fear, indignation, blinding love and hopelessness all jostled violently for space in the vortex, on the verge of spilling out of him, and he was becoming powerless to stop them. Once those feelings found a breach in his defences, they were relentless and just kept on coming. Bennett felt like a rumbling volcano, like Vesuvius before it obliterated Pompeii. If he did not get a firm hold on his feelings soon, he was doomed to explode and that prospect terrified him more than anything.

Dukes did not explode. It simply wasn't done.

He could hear his father's voice inside his head, except this time it did not help to calm him. It fed the rage, mocking him for everything that he could not have. Bennett had to do something to shut all of these emotions out, so he tipped his head back and howled at the heavens in frustration, roaring like a savage going into battle in the hope that it might help. When it did not, he urged his horse forward towards the horizon and galloped like the wind.

Chapter Twenty-Three

Under certain circumstances a foreign wife is permissible. It is never appropriate, however, to entertain an American. Not only is their lineage sullied with impurities, they also harbour some worryingly Revolutionary tendencies...

He had failed to return home for dinner and Amelia was in no mood to sit with his family and pretend that nothing whatsoever was wrong. They had been understanding when she had excused herself and she had gratefully fled back up to the quiet battlements, where she could worry about him in private. A few minutes ago she had heard the unmistakable sounds of his horse returning but, like a coward, she had not gone downstairs to greet him because she was too frightened of what he would say.

'I thought I might find you up here.' He was smiling, a huge relief, considering, and was delightfully windswept still, and rumpled from his prolonged ride. Despite her better judgement, Amelia rushed towards him and wrapped her arms tightly around his waist, burying her face in his waistcoat.

'I have been worrying about you.' So much that she couldn't think straight. 'Why were you gone so long?' All the tears she had been holding back trickled over her cheeks afresh.

'Don't cry, love.' His arms came about her and he rested his chin on the top of her head. 'I was in no fit state to come home. So I rode.'

'I had no idea my father was coming here.'

'And I had no idea that your father was a peer, so I suppose we are equal. Why didn't you tell me that Bray was your father? I would have done something about it.'

The 'it' Amelia presumed he was referring to was her past. 'The damage was done a long time ago. I try to forget about him.'

'Well, I dare say questions will be asked now. Especially after my spectacular bout of public violence. I am still not sorry that I hit him, in case you were wondering. If I had a pistol, I would have shot him and been done with it. The man deserves nothing less. Lovett says that I thoroughly broke his nose, though, so that gives me some comfort.' His own nose was nuzzling into the sensitive space between her ear and her shoulder, reminding her of the intoxicating effect he had on her body. 'But I still want to kill him.'

'That is very noble of you. Please don't. I would hate to see you hang for someone so insignificant.' His lips had found the shell of her ear and he nipped the soft flesh with his teeth.

'Lie with me tonight, Amelia.'

'That is probably not a good idea.'

'Maybe.' He tilted her face to his, his eyes so intense

and so full of wanting that she found herself drowning in them. 'But I am so tired of feeling lonely. Tonight, let me be just Ben. Your Ben…please.'

She answered him with a kiss because she was incapable of saying no. Even though their situation was hopeless, she still wanted one night, still needed the comfort only he could bring. Amelia sighed against his mouth and allowed her fingers to weave a lingering trail through his hair. He was right. All of the obstacles between them would still be waiting for them in the morning, but tonight she did not care. 'Take me to bed, Ben.'

Wordlessly, he took her hand and led her back down the narrow spiral staircase, stopping halfway down to kiss her again, before leading her down a maze of dimly lit passageways and up another, even narrower, spiral staircase that went up and up. Eventually, they arrived at a heavy wooden door. Once he pushed it open, the room beyond was round.

'Are we in the turret?' The idea was so ridiculously romantic, yet so geographically impractical that it made her smile and he appeared delightfully sheepish as he nodded.

'When I was a boy, I had a wooden bow and arrow which I loved. I was convinced that I was one of the knights of old and that it was my solemn pledge to protect the imaginary queen who lived up here. I kept disappearing at all hours of the day and night, so one day my mother and Uncle George moved my bedchamber here, so that I could protect the castle at all times if we came under siege.'

'Very sensible.' Amelia tried not to let her nerves get

the better of her as he closed the solid oak door behind them and turned the heavy key in the lock.

'For privacy,' he said, looking suddenly worried that she might misconstrue his intention. 'You are not a prisoner.' For good measure, he clasped his hands behind his back and looked pained.

Amelia giggled then at the ridiculousness of it all. She had consented to be here and he had asked her to come yet, now they were here, the gravity of what they had come here to do made the atmosphere tense. It was all so ludicrous and awkward. Neither of them quite knew what to say to make it less so. Her laughter seemed to ease the tension and she was hugely relieved when he joined in. He unclasped his hands and brought them in front of him, staring at them in irritation.

'It is a nervous habit. I am trying very hard to be less stodgy.'

'I quite like the stodgy. It is endearing.'

He reached out and took both her hands, tugging her closer. 'You should probably know that you are the first woman that I have ever brought here. I usually visit…um…' He was beginning to blush and Amelia could not help teasing.

'When you visit what? Other ladies? Brothels? Your mistress?'

'No brothels.' He took a step towards her. 'And no mistress. Not any more.' He took another step to bring his hips flush with hers and she saw the light of passion begin to simmer in his gaze. 'In fact, my lovely Amelia, there has not been anyone in quite some time.'

Amelia enjoyed the sensation of smoothing her flattened palms over his broad chest until they came to rest on his shoulders. 'In the spirit of honesty, then, you should probably know that there has never been anyone. Ever.'

His Adam's apple bobbed nervously and he stared at her for several long seconds. 'Then you honour me, Amelia.'

His kiss was achingly gentle. His hands settled on her hips and did not move while he placed tender open-mouthed kisses along her jawbone and then slowly down her neck. Impatient, she pushed his coat off his shoulders and he watched in amusement as she undid the buttons of his waistcoat with slightly shaking fingers. Beneath her palms, she could feel the heat of his skin through the thin linen of his shirt, but when she attempted to untuck it from the waistband of his breeches so that she could plunge her hands beneath that unwanted barrier, he held her at arm's length.

'I will not let you hurry me. We have all night and I fully intend to thoroughly enjoy every single moment.'

With hooded eyes and painfully slow fingers, he carefully plucked each of the pins from her hair until it hung to her waist. To torture her further, he picked up a heavy lock and wound it around his hand before he kissed her again. 'I did not know until recently that I preferred brunettes.' He trailed his lips across her collarbone and then back up to her face. 'And beautiful brown eyes.'

Amelia felt his hands drift to the laces at the back of her dress, felt the bow at the base of her neck come undone, and then her tight bodice loosened as the laces slid effortlessly from their eyelets. Every part of her body began to tingle with awareness when he stood back again to watch as he bared her shoulders to his intense gaze. The fabric pooled at her waist, so it seemed appropriate to shimmy out of it; however, Amelia now felt self-consciously exposed, standing in nothing but her plain shift and half-corset.

Once again, he unlaced the small garment slowly and let it drop to the floor. His eyes drank her in, lingering at the swell of her breasts rising from the top of what was left of her clothing, before he stepped forward and scooped her up into his arms as if she weighed nothing at all. He kissed her deeply again, then strode to the bed. She managed to kick off her slippers before he lowered her onto the counterpane and slowly rolled off her stockings one by one and tossed them on the floor.

When his fingers went to the ties of her shift Amelia experienced a ripple of excitement, closely followed by a moment of fear. As the candles were all still glowing softly, he obviously intended to see her completely naked, and that was something that she had never been in front of anyone.

'Wait.' His fingers paused at her neckline and Amelia licked her lips awkwardly. If she was about to be naked, she certainly did not wish to be the only naked person in the room. 'Perhaps you should take off your shirt first?'

Without taking his eyes off her, he grabbed the bottom of the linen and pulled it up and off in one fluid motion. The sight of his bare skin, the shape of his intriguing male muscles and the unexpected dusting of golden hair across his abdomen and chest rendered her speechless. Without thinking, she reached out one trembling hand to touch him and experienced a moment of feminine triumph when she felt his heart begin to hammer beneath her palm. It was empowering.

Rising up onto her knees, Amelia began to explore his torso, first with her fingers and then with her lips. She heard his breathing become heavier, more erratic, but he did nothing to stop her. Only when her hand reached the waistband of his breeches did he take control again, but he allowed her to unbutton his falls while he undid her shift, before he pulled back again.

The bulge in his lap magically held his trousers up and held her transfixed. She was beyond curious to see what lay beneath that tented fabric and her open curiosity made him smile.

'You first,' he said, gesturing to her shift with a flick of his eyes, and then promptly crossed his magnificent arms over his magnificent chest and waited for her to comply. Feeling suddenly bold, she slowly slid the straps of her shift off her shoulders and allowed the fabric to fall far enough that it rested on the crest of her bosom. She gave him a knowing look beneath her lashes and heard him chuckle. 'Minx.'

One of his hands came forward and gave the soft muslin a tug, exposing her pert nipples to his eyes, and she watched them widen. The blue irises darkened further when she raised herself up onto her haunches and brazenly pushed the flimsy fabric over her hips, watching his gaze follow the journey intently until it rested on the dark curls at the apex of her thighs. She could tell that he liked what he saw. His eyes came back up to her breasts and then returned to her face and he licked his lips and swallowed.

'I believe that it is your turn now...Ben.'

Satisfyingly, a muscle twitched in his jaw as he fought to maintain his control, but then he grinned wolfishly. 'Help yourself.' He saw her hesitation and purposely folded his arms across his chest again. 'I dare you.'

Amelia had never been one to shy away from a challenge and she was almost squirming in her desperation to see him completely nude. She forced her hands to work slowly as she pushed the buckskin down over his hips, openly staring at the intriguing golden hair that appeared first, until his manhood sprang free, so hard and so much bigger than she had anticipated. Boldly, she traced the shape of it, marvelling at the heat and the smoothness until he growled, hauled her into his arms and sent her toppling backwards onto the bed.

From then on his onslaught was relentless. He kissed and nibbled every inch of her skin, avoiding her breasts and that intimate triangle of hair. The more he tortured her body, the more those parts cried out to be touched. Amelia pushed her breasts towards his mouth time and time again, and each time he found somewhere else to nip and tease until she was writhing on the mattress. 'Please!' She had no idea what she was asking for and she could tell that the wretch was openly enjoying the effect he was having. 'Ben—please! Touch me.'

'Where?' he asked with feigned innocence and then trailed his lips over the undersides of her breasts, then, inch by painful inch, he continued upwards until she did not think she could stand it any more. As his mouth finally closed over her taut nipple, she moaned and arched upwards, the pleasure was so intense. So perfect.

Once he had fully worshipped one breast, he turned all of his attention on the other while she raked her hands through his hair and made noises that she could not quite believe came from her. By the time his fingers wound a lazy path towards her most secret place, she welcomed them gratefully, allowing her legs to fall wantonly open. Amelia groaned as he gently explored the soft folds, and then almost screamed when his finger circled a part of her body that she had not known existed.

'Oh, Ben.' Her words came out on a sigh as she surrendered to his touch. Over and over again he teased that aching bud, staring down at her face as he did, so intently that it made her feel beautiful. When her body began to tense and her hips began to buck, he plunged his fingers inside her. Lights exploded behind her eyes and for a second or two she actually thought that she might die from the sheer bliss of it all. And then she experienced the most tremendous rush of pure, intense relief and floated back down to earth completely boneless.

'You look smug.' He did. Delightfully so and Amelia could not even muster the strength to cover her nakedness.

'I am smug. And you are perfect.' He shifted his body slightly so that the male part of him rested insistently against her stomach. Without thinking, Amelia moved to accommodate his hips and looped her arms languidly around his shoulders.

'Are you going to show me what happens next?'

'Only if you want me to. It might hurt, I'm afraid.'

'Will it feel as good as that just did?'

'I hope so. Eventually. Perhaps better.' His teeth had found the soft part of her ear again and already she could feel her body begin to reawaken. Unconsciously, she tilted her hips upwards and felt his hardness nudge at her entrance.

Amelia raked her nails gently down his spine and brought them to rest on his deliciously rounded, firm buttocks. 'Go on, then.'

So he did. With a look of intense concentration, he carefully pushed inside her. From the outset, she welcomed his intrusion, enjoying the sense of completeness at being so intimately fused with this wonderful man. The muscles of his abdomen were clenched so tightly, the tension in his big body so extreme that she knew that he was holding himself back for her. When he reached the barrier of her virginity he paused and rested his forehead against hers in apology. Instinct made her wrap her legs tightly about his hips. 'Please, Ben,' she whispered next to his ear. 'I want this.'

With a sigh of acceptance, he pushed through, screwing his eyes shut tightly so that he did not have to see her wince at the unexpectedly sharp, but brief, pain. Her own body tensed and she forced herself to relax. As soon as he began to move, she knew that everything would be all right. Because being joined with him, filled with him, was the most wonderful feeling in the world.

Bennett felt like a brute. She was so small and tight, yet so trusting and eager, and he was so big and clumsy. But then she opened her eyes and gazed up into his and he saw nothing but desire and pleasure in them. She wanted him and she wanted this. Emboldened, he began to move quicker and, to his complete delight, she moaned her encouragement loudly. When he thrust into her deeper, her hips came up to meet his enthusiastically and she clawed at his back, wrapping her lovely legs even tighter about his waist and writhed and cried out his name. There was nothing reserved or proper or awkward in what they were doing, only rightness. His body had been made to fit with hers perfectly, as if they were both created to be together like this. When he felt her body tighten and pulse around him, he gave up trying to be gentle and clamoured hungrily for his own release. All the while she urged him on, meeting him thrust for thrust until he lost the ability to think about anything except the way it felt to be buried deep inside her. Fused with her, almost as if he was a part of her. Meant to be. Perfect. His climax came out of nowhere and stunned him; on a guttural cry he spilled inside her. And then he collapsed into the warm comfort of her arms and buried his face in her neck.

Undone. Unravelled and changed irrevocably.

'Why did your father disown you?' She was curled against his chest contentedly, but Bennett had to know. They had been avoiding this conversation for most of the night and in the morning he had to travel back to London.

She shifted slightly so that she could prop her head on her elbow and absently trailed a finger down his stomach. 'My mother was American and an heiress. By the time she met my father, she was all alone in the world. He had gone to America to find himself a wealthy wife and she was the most obvious candidate. She was young, beautiful and impressionable and hopelessly impressed with his title, and he can be quite charming when he puts his mind to it. To begin with, he was happy with his choice but, after she had me, my mother found it difficult to carry another child. Like all of the aristocracy, my father needed a son and became more and more frustrated by her inability to provide him with one. After a while, he bitterly resented her. We were both shipped out of the house in May-fair and sent to live in Cheapside when I was twelve. My mother was convinced it was a temporary separa-tion, but my father had quite different ideas. He had her money, but he no longer wanted her, and I believe he even considered divorce. From then on I saw less and less of him. I didn't mind that. I had never really had that much to do with him anyway, but it destroyed my mother. She spent every hour of every day blam-ing herself for his disinterest. Then her physical health deteriorated too.'

Her hand stilled on his stomach and a faraway look came into her eyes. 'The War of 1812 gave my father the perfect opportunity to be rid of her. As soon as England went back to fighting with the Americans, my father applied for an annulment. By then, my mother's place in society was well and truly forgotten, so he was able to do it quietly. Fortunately for him, British hatred for America was at its peak, so the bishops were sympa-thetic to his plight and granted it. After that, he refused to continue to pay for the house on Cheapside and we were left to fend for ourselves. The law was completely on his side, of course, because once the marriage had been declared null and void he was legally absolved from any financial responsibility, despite the fact that a great deal of his money had originally come from my mother. Because the marriage had ceased to exist, I went from a viscount's daughter to being illegitimate overnight. I am not sure how much money he paid to keep the whole sordid affair out of the papers, but he managed it. In the end it all fizzled without much of a scandal and he was able to move on with his life and remarry. You already know the rest of the story.'

Something about the brief tale did not ring true. 'Annulments are difficult to obtain. Even if your mother *was* an American, that would not have given the bishops a valid enough reason to void the marriage, especially as your parents had a child.'

'Oh, Ben,' she said on a sigh. 'That is because I have not told you the worst of it. My father knew something quite damning about my mother's family that he was able to twist and use for his own benefit. My grandfather fought against the British in the Revolution, and not just as a soldier. He used his fortune to pay for an entire regiment of militia. A very bloodthirsty and successful regiment of militia. And his signature proudly sits on the Declaration of Independence. In the eyes of the British government, my grandfather was a traitor. And although my father knew about all of this before they married, he lied and told the bishops that she had concealed that pertinent information from him. As a loyal peer of the realm, he could not live with the shame of knowing that he had been duped into a marriage with the enemy. The bishops believed him and the annulment was granted with surprising haste.'

Bennett took a moment to let that all sink in. It was certainly much worse than he had anticipated. Not only was she illegitimate, but she was also the granddaughter of a known Revolutionary. Parliament might be accepting of the first, considering the circumstances by which it had come about, but it would never accept the second. Never in a million years would it accept the second. Unfortunately, she understood his silence. 'You cannot marry me, Ben. Your political career would be over.'

He pulled her close and held her tight. 'That doesn't matter, Amelia. So long as I have you I will be happy.' And perhaps he could be. He still had estates that needed managing, business affairs and investments that needed overseeing. His days could still be filled with purpose—a lesser purpose than he had been born for, granted, but he would make the best of it for her.

'Of course it matters. I will not be the cause of you abandoning all of your dreams. Besides, I am rather relying on you to change this world we live in for the better. You cannot achieve that from outside of the Cabinet and I am not prepared to allow you to make that sacrifice on my behalf.'

Bennett felt sick at the stark reality that she presented. 'What about us, Amelia?'

She was quiet for so long that he began to dread her answer. After tonight, surely she did not expect that he would be able to walk away? 'We will always have tonight.'

'I want you to be my wife!'

'We both know that is impossible, Ben. Please don't make this harder than it already is.' She rolled on top of him then and waylaid him with kisses that did not fool him. She was trying to distract him and because he did not know any of the answers he let her. His intense frustration at their seemingly hopeless situation combined with his building passion made further conversation on the subject impossible, and by the time he had finished making desperate love to her she claimed that she was too exhausted to continue to discuss it. So Bennett slept with her in his arms.

He wasn't the least bit surprised when he awoke in the morning to find that she was not there.

Chapter Twenty-Four

Emotional outbursts in public are unseemly...

Later that day, Bennett sat next to Lord Liverpool and waited for the end of the debate when he could deliver his long-anticipated, frequently postponed speech. It was no longer just about the need for cleaner slums. After his experiences in Seven Dials, there were a great many more issues that he needed Parliament to be aware of. After several attempts, he had abandoned trying to write down everything he wanted to say. If his speech was to be powerful enough it needed to be honest, not rehearsed. Bennett's words had to come from the heart, not the head.

He waited patiently at first, but when the half hour of shouting turned into an hour and it looked increasingly likely that it would have to be postponed yet again, his patience began to wane. A half hour after that, he had had quite enough. He was sacrificing his happiness for this institution; the least they could do was listen.

'People are dying!' He did not remember surging to

his feet or clenching his fists and shaking them or bellowing at the top of his voice, but the deathly silence that occurred after his outburst was something Bennett would remember with great clarity until his dying day. The stunned House stared back at him, clearly flabbergasted that Bennett Montague, Sixteenth Duke of Aveley, and normally a calm presence in their ranks, had sounded quite so impassioned. For a moment he felt as if the floor had been pulled from beneath his feet and then he decided that this momentary quiet might well be the only time that he had to state his case. 'I have been visiting the slums,' he began falteringly, 'and what I have found there is so grotesque, so unjust, that I can hardly believe that we are allowing it to happen.' Oddly, tears started to form in his eyes, something that had never, ever happened to him before, but he ploughed on. It was too important not to. 'I saw families starving. Children so emaciated that I doubt that they will survive the winter. If they are lucky, they get to sleep on straw in a filthy room but, more often than not, they sleep on the streets...'

'Spare us your bleeding-heart liberalism, Aveley!' someone shouted from the back, but Bennett continued undaunted.

'We have to do something to help these people. That we allow it to happen is not right...'

'Those lazy bastards need to find work and stop wasting their money on gin!'

'Hear, hear!'

'The slums are filled with criminals who do not want to earn an honest wage!'

Bennett shook his head, bewildered. Three sentences. That was all they would listen to. He was throwing away a life with Amelia for this? All around him, the lords began to shout their own bigoted, unfounded opinions of the poor across the floor like poisoned darts. Within seconds, they were back to braying at each other, the cacophony so loud that no voice or opinion or reasonable argument stood any chance of actually being heard. It occurred to him then that they sounded like a farmyard. A disorganised and disparate farmyard with no farmer to feed them. He turned towards the rest of the Cabinet for support, but they all looked every which way except at him. Only Liverpool glared at Bennett and he looked thoroughly appalled.

'Use your head, man! I am not sure what has brought on this sudden lapse in judgement, but this unseemly behaviour is not what I expect from a member of my Cabinet.'

Use his head? How many times had his father admonished him to do just the same? Perhaps that would always be the fundamental difference between him and his father. Bennett felt injustice in his heart first and wanted to right it using his head; his father had been pragmatic and always used only his head. He had had no time for emotional decisions. Or even emotions. How had his uncle described him?—a cold fish, incapable of basic human feelings. But Bennett was not his father.

Thank God.

The epiphany was both blinding and liberating. He was not his father! So why was he walking so carefully in his father's footsteps? He hated all of the chaos and compromise of Parliament. In which case, why shouldn't he let his heart guide his decisions? Slowly, he allowed his eyes to travel across the furore of the debating chamber, seeing it for the first time with objective eyes. The path here was blocked—but there were other paths. There *was* another perspective.

Who knew?

Now that he could finally see it, Bennett was amazed he had not considered it sooner.

'Aveley?' Lord Liverpool said sternly. 'What do you think you are doing?'

The huge weight of parental expectations that Bennett had always carried around with him melted from his shoulders as he looked around at the stunned faces of the Cabinet and then at the chaos on the floor. Any quiet here was only temporary, he realised in awe, because this was what they actually did. Bennett watched them all clamour to shout each other down, ears closed, minds closed. Wasting time. Throwing another tantrum. And, as always, any progress was so painfully slow that almost nothing meaningful would get done, even though there was so much that urgently needed doing.

He smiled at Lord Liverpool and shrugged because everything was suddenly clear. 'I do believe I am going to change the world, Prime Minister.' And, as there really wasn't another moment to lose, Bennett strode out of the chamber and out into the busy streets of Westminster.

Amelia wished that she were a hedgehog. Then perhaps she could roll herself in a ball and hide in a corner. As it was, she was sitting in full view, directly next to the Dowager and surrounded by a room full of intensely curious aristocrats, when by rights she should be safely hidden back at Aveley Castle for another few days. But the Dowager had galvanised them all into action early on Monday, insisting that the best way to deal with a scandal was to meet it head-on and dare anyone to be offended. Then she had promptly sent Lovett back to Mayfair with a stack of invitations for the usual Wednesday reading salon.

'They dare not cut us—my son is a duke!' she had announced imperiously the moment Amelia had questioned the logic of returning so soon. 'And dukes come much higher up the pecking order than venomous viscounts. Once they see that we are perfectly at ease with what transpired, and that we stand by you as the injured party, everything will return to normal. You will see.'

Sir George had been more circumspect. 'Fear not, Amelia, you will only be a circus sideshow for one evening, my dear. Sit proudly, it won't hurt to throw in the odd winsome sigh, and once they have all had a good look and a good gossip, they will move onto the next scandal.'

With her fate decided, she had been bundled into the same carriage as the Dowager, Lady Worsted and Sir George early this morning and now found herself sitting in the bosom of that family in their crowded London drawing room, listening to another dire poem read by one of the Potentials. The Dowager had been quite right—nobody had been brave enough to cut them and every chair was taken.

Amelia had yet to see Bennett. The last time she had, he had been gloriously naked and sound asleep in his charming turret while she had stumbled around in the dark, weeping and trying to find her clothes. She had no idea where he was, what he was thinking or even if he was going to make an appearance here this evening. All Lovett had said, rather cryptically, upon their return was that His Grace had been exceedingly busy and he had scarcely been home in days.

She hoped that he was all right, although she very definitely wasn't. Misery was not really a good enough description of what Amelia was currently feeling, as it was tinged with the twin pains of futility and longing. And those pains were relentless. She hadn't slept a wink since she had left the comfort of Bennett's arms. It was difficult to rest when one half of her desperately wanted to accept his offer of marriage while the other, better, half knew that she could not destroy all his hopes and dreams, because to do so would be utterly selfish.

In a week, Amelia was resolved to go back to Bath with Lady Worsted so that Bennett could forget her. It was ironic, when she acknowledged she had once been so dead set against him, that Amelia already knew it would be impossible to forget him. Clearly, a small part of her was exactly like her tragic mother. Once her heart was lost, it was doomed to be lost for ever. She loved Bennett Montague. Hopelessly and completely.

The door to the drawing room crashed open and her dashing duke strode in, closely followed by his loyal butler, and grinned at the assembled crowd. 'I am so glad that you could all make it tonight at such short notice.' He looked devilishly handsome with his hair windswept and still wearing his greatcoat. 'If I am not interrupting, I should be honoured to read something for once.'

'Please do!' shouted Sir George, even though the Potential was mid-poem. The poor girl simply closed her book and meekly sat down while Bennett produced a piece of crumpled paper and stood in the middle of the room. He had not even glanced at Amelia and the snub wounded.

'Ladies and gentlemen—a year ago I wrote a book. It was intended as advice to titled gentlemen like myself on selecting their perfect bride.'

Next to him, Lovett raised a copy of *The Discerning Gentleman's Guide* aloft so that everyone could see it and the Duke paused for effect. 'I should like to extend my humblest apologies to you all for having foisted such a load of patronising drivel on the world. They were not my words. If you bought a copy, I will gladly give you your money back, and if you have a copy this is what I want you to do with it.'

The Duke nodded to the butler and the crowd watched in fascination as Lovett ceremoniously placed it onto a silver tray and then carried it sedately to the fireplace. Almost as if it were something quite offensive, Lovett picked up the book with the tips of his fingers and tossed it onto the flames. Amelia heard an anguished whimper come from Lady Priscilla as those hallowed, sacred pages began to curl and blacken.

'You see, from my perspective, I was wrong about everything,' the Duke continued, smiling and slowly scanning the rapt faces in the room, 'It turns out that the perfect bride for me is not delicate or even-tempered. She does not only embroider or read poetry.' His eyes finally settled hotly on Amelia. The intense gaze made her pulse flutter as she remembered the last time he had looked at her so possessively, and she hoped that she would not blush. It was clear to everyone present that his next words were solely meant for her, and she felt her cheeks heat despite her best efforts to stop them. 'The perfect woman for any man is the one that his heart yearns for. In my case, she is fierce and impertinent, kind-hearted and loyal, obstinate and selfless, brave and beautiful.'

Amelia felt the weight of every pair of eyes in the room bore into her but could not seem to unlock her own gaze from Bennett's. Breathing was now apparently quite impossible. Was he truly about to talk about his feelings in public? That was such an un-Bennett-like thing to do.

'My darling Amelia, I am not sure if you are aware, but I am a rich and powerful duke. And, as a rich and powerful duke, I realised that Parliament was holding me back. Your soup kitchen did more good in one single day than Parliament had achieved in a whole year. Then it dawned on me. I am *so* rich and *so* powerful that I really do not have to wait for the cogs of government to slowly creak into action. I can change things myself. Instantly. As soon as I realised that, I resigned from the Cabinet.'

A collective gasp cut through the silence of the room. Amelia began to feel decidedly queasy—yet, underneath that, she experienced the first blossoming of something else. Hope. Bennett did not appear to have the slightest drop of remorse. In fact, he appeared more relaxed and comfortable in his own skin, in a public forum, than she had ever seen him. Almost as if a great weight had been lifted from his splendid shoulders. 'You resigned from the Cabinet? For me?'

'Not for you entirely, my love. For me. For us.' Then he shrugged those magnificent shoulders as if it was of little consequence. 'As soon as I left Westminster, I took all of my money to Seven Dials. It is amazing what you can achieve in such a small period of time, if money *really* is no object. I am quite disappointed in myself that I did not think of it sooner. I have had the streets cleaned! Imagine that. And already I am the proud owner of seven doss houses, five gin palaces and the soup kitchen. At the moment, they are offering free shelter to anyone who needs it, but I fully intend to knock them all down and build something new and purposeful in their place. I thought perhaps a school and a hospital, but I shall need your help to do it properly. And then I thought I might buy up the rest of the slum, because if Parliament is not going to do anything about it, then I thought we might tear it all down and build a better place from scratch. Revolutionise the place. And who better to do that with than the granddaughter of a Revolutionary who has lived in that slum?'

He walked slowly towards her and bent down on one knee. 'Amelia Mansfield, you are the woman I want to marry.' The Potentials began to mewl their distress, but Bennett appeared totally oblivious. His hypnotic gaze was fixed on Amelia. He actually wanted to marry her? Despite everything? When he took her hand gently and pressed a soft kiss into her palm, she melted. 'I know that you have every reason to distrust men with titles and I know that the idea of being controlled by one terrifies you. But you really mustn't worry. What makes you think that I could enforce my will on you, my darling, when I cannot even get my own butler to stop drinking my port?'

'He's right, miss,' Lovett said from his position by the fireplace. 'I drink gallons of the stuff. I have done for years and I fully intend to continue.'

Amelia tried to swallow past the enormous lump that suddenly manifested in her throat. Bennett made a valid point. Lovett was still Lovett. And Bennett was not her father. The remaining walls around her heart began to crumble until almost all of her reservations were gone.

Almost—but not quite.

Everyone was staring at them. In a tiny voice she tried to get him to see reason before all of her resolve collapsed. 'You cannot become Prime Minister if you marry me, Ben.'

A knowing smile spread over his features. 'Oh, I am not altogether sure that I want to be. That was my father's dream. Not mine. I was so busy trying to do what he wanted me to do that I never really considered if I wanted to do it. He had his chance. I am tired of walking his path because I am quite certain that it does not take me where I want to go. A wise woman once told me that she believed most people had the good sense to judge men by their deeds rather than their choice of wife. If Parliament has a problem with my marriage to a half-American, illegitimate former guttersnipe, then I do not give two figs. I am a duke, after all. I have no intention of sitting around and waiting for them to actually *do* something. Not when so much is left undone. Besides, as soon as we are married you will become a rich and powerful duchess. Together we will be unstoppable.'

Like a dolt, she started to sniffle and swiped the tears away. That he would do all this for her was overwhelming. It was a good job that she was seated because her legs had turned to jelly. Her heart was racing. Her pulse fluttered and, for want of a better word, she was gloriously *all aquiver* again. 'I just don't want you doing something that you will live to regret.'

'The only regret I have is that I never saw it sooner.' He stood then, pulled Amelia to her feet and looped his arms around her waist, oblivious to the shocked faces all around them. 'I could never regret choosing you, Amelia. I love you.'

'And I love you too, Ben, but...'

He hushed her by placing his finger over her lips. 'For thirty years I have listened to my father's voice in my head. I have tried to live my life as he wanted me to and it has made me miserable. And stodgy. The last few weeks have been the happiest of my life. A revelation. You drive me to distraction and challenge me, but with you I am a better man. I am not my father. And I am certainly nothing like your father. I am just Ben. So marry me, Amelia, and let's change the world together.'

Too overcome, she nodded and found herself dragged into his embrace and kissed until she was breathless, by a duke who was neither pompous nor stodgy. But he was hers, just as she was his, so nothing else really mattered. It was Lovett's polite cough that interrupted them.

'I am sorry to intrude, Your Grace, but an urgent message has just arrived.'

A magical note that must have blown down the chimney. But Bennett snatched it and scanned its lying contents with concerned gravitas.

'We are needed urgently in Seven Dials, my darling.' He winked at her saucily and then whispered close to her ear, 'I have an empty castle, just over an hour away. Would you like to run away with me?'

Bennett was not the only one who could act. Amelia clasped her hands together and frowned. 'Oh, Ben, that is a dire emergency indeed. We should probably leave right away.' And she couldn't wait. Not just to be alone with him again, but to start a new chapter in her life with this man who meant the world to her. He was right. He was not his father, or hers. And she was not her mother. All that was in the past.

Bennett grabbed her hand and dragged her with him to the door. Almost as an afterthought, he turned around. 'Uncle George, you were right. Love should never be ignored. I think it is high time you married my mother. Don't you?' His stunned uncle merely nodded and reached for the Dowager's hand. That task done, Bennett waved cheerfully at the crowd.

'If you will excuse us, ladies and gentlemen, we are off to change the world.'

And that, as it turned out, was exactly what they did.

* * * * *

If you enjoyed this story, you won't want to miss these other great reads from Virginia Heath:

THAT DESPICABLE ROGUE
HER ENEMY AT THE ALTAR